NEXUS

THE ALLIANCE SERIES: BOOK SIX

EMMA L. ADAMS

ADA

"Are you sure it's safe?" Nell tapped the edge of the doorway port with her finger, examining it from the side. The box-like contraption looked like something out of *Doctor Who*, plated in blue on both the inside and out. At the back were a set of metal doors, which at the moment, if you opened them, would have nothing but the wall of the boardroom on the other side.

"Of course," said Dr Helm, from behind a heavily-protected mask. Only his eyes were visible through a fortified glass shield as he manipulated dials on the machine, settling on a familiar symbol shaped like a cloud. The symbol meant Valeria. To be precise, Neo Greyle's Alliance branch, where my brother was going to join the team of scientists working on new warfare technologies.

"I've been through there before," I reminded Nell.

Alber, my younger brother, hovered behind us. Normally, he'd have begged to go through the port and see the Multi-verse. But that was before the war. Now the doorway port was a permanent fixture here at the Alliance's Central head-quarters on Earth. It worked as a shortcut between Alliance branches, but it would also let people come through to help us if we were attacked. And if the worst happened, and Central fell, it'd work as a last-resort evacuation point if we needed to evacuate all the Alliance personnel onto another world. Now the Alliance's biggest enemy was working with the most powerful magical empire in the Multiverse, the Passages between the worlds were easily as dangerous as the swampland.

Just thinking about it made my fists clench in helpless anger. My homeworld had declared war on the world I'd lived most of my life. The world that, for all its flaws, I'd come to love.

"Don't worry," said Jeth, my older brother. "I'll be fine. The lab's buried under a ton of adamantine."

So was Central. That was the only reason the building was still standing. Adamantine absorbed magic, even the full-on assault that had shook London only a few weeks ago. The fact that it was also my name pretty much summed up how messed-up my relationship with my homeworld was.

Nell awkwardly hugged Jeth. "Just be careful over there." Though she was our mother in every way except blood, she'd always kept a shield up, even around us. An aftereffect of being the Enzarian Empire's slave. Like I would have been, if I'd stayed on my homeworld. My family and I had helped countless people who'd lost everything, whose lives were shattered, and we'd always defined hope for them. Hope for a new life here on Earth. Now, that hope had gone, like a candle blown out in the wind.

"Honestly, I'm working in technology, not the intelligence division." Jeth returned Nell's hug, then moved to face Alber. "I'll bring you a souvenir."

"Hover boots!" said Alber, slapping him on the back. "Please."

Jeth grinned. "I'll do my best." He hugged me last, as the

doorway port opened into a blue-metal-plated corridor. At the far end, I glimpsed wide glass windows opening over the dizzying metropolis of Neo Greyle.

I stepped back and smiled, though it was hard. "You be careful over there, Jeth."

The way things were at the moment, every goodbye felt like the last.

"Hey, sis, it'll be all right." Jeth smiled. "I have to do this. It's what I'm good at."

I nodded. Of course I understood. My brother's ingenious ideas had changed the tech team already—and they would probably change the entire future of the Alliance.

If we survive the war.

"Call me as soon as you're at your new place," said Nell.

"Yeah, yeah." Jeth shook his head. He knew better than to make the usual arguments—he was twenty-three and this wasn't the first time one of us had gone for an extended stay in another world. Sure, there'd been a suspicious lack of hostilities since the battle on Central's doorstep, but it didn't mean the war was over. It just hadn't properly started yet. "I'll be back soon."

"If not, I'll have to claim your computers." Alber attempted a smile.

"You better not," said Jeth. "See you soon."

Dr Helm followed him over the threshold, into Valeria. The doorway port closed, and we were left on Earth, in the Alliance's boardroom. Ms Weston, my supervisor, had hastily set the doorway port up in here to call people in to help us defend Central during the last attack, and rather than removing it, this room had become the Alliance's official cross-world meeting point.

Behind us, Alexis Greene, one of Valeria's council members, cleared her throat. It meant, *step away from the door.* Though Valeria was more open-minded than most worlds, having an offworlder population of more than a quarter in their largest city of Neo Greyle, they didn't trust Enzarians like me. I couldn't protest, given the circumstances. But it made my chest ache all the same at the look she gave Alber. My seventeen-year-old foster brother was born mageblood, but like me, had been rescued from Enzar as a baby. While we wore contact lenses to cover our real eye colour—purple for Alber and Nell, diamond-white for me—and that was the only conspicuous sign of our homeworld, everyone in the Alliance knew my name.

Adamantine. Magic-wielder, Alliance guard turned Ambassador. Almost-destroyer of worlds. The girl who'd channelled a living magic source in an attempt to close a doorway. Not realising a bomb waited on the other side. Thanks to Lawrence Walker, everyone on Thairon was dead. And the magebloods were pissed at losing their army.

Rationally I knew I couldn't have stopped Walker from activating the bomb, but the guilt remained like a poison in my blood. A stain I could never wash away.

There was one person who understood, and I'd hardly seen him all week.

My family and I climbed the four flights of stairs down to the entrance hall. We could have taken the lifts, but Nell distrusted enclosed spaces. I knew the feeling. Sometimes I felt so trapped here, I wanted to scream. Sure, I couldn't go walking into Enzar and yell at my distant relatives to quit fighting one another, but the lack of a direct challenge was slowly driving me out of my mind.

Except for the messages. *We are coming, Adamantine. You are ours.*

They had to come from Enzar. The enemy knew I was alive. Even Nell, who'd lived on Enzar before it had fallen, couldn't explain how that was possible. The power used to be in the hands of the Royals, the nonmages. But when the magebloods had rebelled, war had broken out and the palace where I'd spent the first year of my life had been destroyed. I'd been on Earth by that point, under Nell's care, and even she didn't know how the magebloods knew my name.

"Ada." Ms Weston waylaid me on the stairs from the first-floor corridor, beckoning me into her office. The admin division was one of the few parts of Central that hadn't changed beyond recognition. Her desk was spotless, everything tucked away into cabinets and drawers. No, it was Ms Weston herself who had changed—she wore a guard uniform instead of one of her usual sharp suits. Like she expected to go to war along with the rest of us. She even carried weapons —Alliance-standard guns and stunners.

"I need to talk to you, Ada. About Enzar."

My heart dropped, and I closed the office door behind me. "Sure. What is it?"

"I looked further into the Alliance's files," said Ms Weston. "Of course, with Walker being present here, I was forced to hide anything he might use to infer the truth about your abilities and what happened to you on your home-world. It was a foolish decision, but based on the little I knew about Walker, I had no choice. For your sake, and for Kay's."

My throat was full of barbed wire. I just nodded, because there wasn't much else to do. My heart broke for Kay. His father had committed genocide. Everyone at the Alliance, and even offworlders, knew. Kay was no longer viewed as a hero, but the son of a murderer imprisoned here at Central.

Ms Weston kept speaking. "I found a file about Enzar I wasn't aware of before. It was shelved under Cethrax, which as I'm sure you can imagine, occupies a significant area of the archives."

I nodded again. Cethrax had been the bane of the Alliance as long as it had existed, and the whole reason the Alliance hired so many guards in the first place. But I'd never dreamed they'd team up with Enzar. Never in a million years.

"I found some… interesting information. I think it's best if you read it yourself, Ada."

She passed me a file over the desk. It was dated 1986, in sprawling black handwriting.

"It's a record of the last time Earth sent an Ambassadorial mission into Cethrax itself—apart from the most recent one, of course."

I struggled to decipher the handwriting as I flipped open the file. It was written in the dry, technical language preferred for Alliance reports, and I skimmed over several paragraphs dedicated to Alliance Ambassador regulations on entering hostile offworld territory before I got to the main account. Sounded like the Alliance had tried to bring the Vox in for questioning on the use of illegal doorways before realising the doorways were a natural occurrence. I already knew they were because I'd been dragged through a few of them in my time with the StoneKing. He'd been looking for Enzar.

I turned the page. A team had gone in and closed the doorways down, surprisingly without any fatalities or injuries. Cethrax must have been in a good mood that day. The text's dry tone carried a hint of the writer's surprise at the lack of retaliation and speculated on whether Cethrax had actually *wanted* the doorways closed.

I kept reading. *One of the doorways appeared to lead to a dead end, but when we activated our tracker to determine the magic level, the device was destroyed and we were forced to take swift action to close the doorway. Having brought the remains of the tracker back to Earth, we proceeded to make an agreement with a group of experimental scientists on Klathica to form a group known as KimaroTech…*"

My eyes bugged out, and I had to read the sentence again.

KimaroTech were the group who'd created the Stoneskins... and were also the biggest company on Klathica, responsible for most of their technology. But originally, they'd been a research group. And they'd been set up to research magic-based substances.

I knew how well *that* had turned out. It was weird beyond belief to read a vaguely optimistic-sounding account of the good this KimaroTech would do for the Alliance. Knowledge was power, said the writer. Reading between the lines, the person writing the account *had* power. They were looking for what *they* might gain from controlling auros—the substance the Passages and the doorway ports were made of, which could usually only link two worlds of the same magic level. That's why the random doorways appearing on Cethrax seemed to fascinate the writer. On their trip to Cethrax, they'd used world-keys to seek out every doorway possible, and logged all the worlds behind the doorways in a particular territory in a list.

Enzar was listed as one of several worlds postulated to be the world that had destroyed the tracker. At the time, Enzar had been in relative stability—which for Enzar, meant it was between wars. But the part that caught my attention came after. Earth's Alliance branch had apparently sponsored their investigation. Which meant...

I skipped to the end. The file was signed, *Robert Walker.*

Kay's grandfather had been involved in that mission? The only thing I knew about the guy was he'd been the one to announce the Alliance's existence to the people of Earth. He'd died four years before I was born, which was five years after the report had been written. I knew he'd started KimaroTech, but not that *Cethrax* had been the reason. So he'd been fascinated with doorways. The link with Enzar left me with little doubt that his experiment had had conse-quences.

I looked back at Ms Weston. "Have you told Kay?"

"No. If you feel he needs to know, it's up to your discretion, Ada."

"Okay," I said. "Only this feels... important. Really important. I didn't realise there was any record of the KimaroTech company on Earth. Kay said he didn't know anything about the link with Enzar..."

"It took some searching," said Ms Weston. "Unfortunately, the archives aren't equipped with a search bar, as my assistant put it."

Markos. It sounded like the centaur. "Where is he, anyway?"

"Searching more of the files from Cethrax, and Klathica, too."

"Uh, why not actually go to Klathica?"

"We do have people there, but they will not leave their secrets publicly displayed. We are, however, planning to send another covert operation there shortly."

"Can I go?" I realised too late that my plea sounded childish, but being stuck here at Central while my homeworld sent threatening messages was driving me out of my mind. "Klathica had links with Enzar, and... I know Izen, the council member, he told us Enzar's technology originally came from there, like Thairon. The magebloods are using KimaroTech's technology, and I know Klathica's Alliance *said* they'd had no contact with Enzar, but... I think they're hiding something." At least, Kay thought so. Izen had admitted that Klathica had sold weaponry to Enzar, to the magebloods, before the war.

"And you're ready for that?" Ms Weston's expression was surprisingly gentle. "Ada, I wouldn't push you—or Kay."

I heard the unspoken words. *We're not like Enzar.*

"I'm sure. I want to go."

Ms Weston must have seen something in my face, because

she nodded. "All right. I'll pass on your interest to the council. But Ada, I can't promise they'll say yes." She paused. "Also, while we cannot authorise any Ambassadors to enter Enzar itself, we did question anyone from the transition points on whether they knew if the enemy had information on our communications networks." She paused, with guilt in her expression, as another glass shard lodged itself in my throat. The transition point was the place Nell had taken me when she'd saved my life as a baby.

"Nobody has been back to any of the transition points since they were evacuated, so none of the people we questioned knew if the magebloods who attacked the Alliance might know they existed," Ms Weston continued, "but we're keeping an eye on certain areas of offworld territory on Valeria, and the other worlds involved in the operation."

"You think there might be spies from Enzar." My heart lurched.

"I personally do not," said Ms Weston. "But there are others who disagree."

I shook my head. No. The people who ran the operation had saved my life. Besides, nobody lucky enough to get away would ever want to bring the war here.

Wait a minute. The doorway port had reminded me of something. The transition points must work in the same way, as places between the worlds. Which meant... they must be made of auros.

Was that how the magebloods managed to send a message to me? Had they sneaked into a transition point after they'd been evacuated, weeks ago? I didn't even know which world they were based on, or if they were in between, like the Passages, but Ms Weston clearly suspected they had. It was a logical conclusion.

"The second floor of the Passages has been cut off," said Ms Weston. "The barriers are there long-term—perhaps permanently. The council came to the decision immediately following the attack. I didn't know if anyone had told you."

"I... no." The second-floor corridor was the place I'd spent half my life. Nobody had told me it'd been closed, possibly forever.

"Ada," said Ms Weston. "You must understand we didn't make the decision lightly. None of this is your fault."

"Tell that to the guards," I mumbled. Half the witnesses who'd seen the freakish magical lightning storm over London had thought I was responsible. Nobody outside the Alliance knew Enzar existed, aside from other offworlders. But even though Nell had never given out our address, two days after Thairon and Cethrax had attacked Earth on Enzar's orders, someone had thrown a brick through our window. That was the last straw for Nell. We'd packed up and moved to Central's underground shelters.

"Anyway," I said to Ms Weston. "None of that matters now. Can you let me know if you find anything else in the files about Enzar?"

"I think you've earned the right to know, but this file is all I've found so far. There isn't anything else you'd like to tell me, is there? For instance, from your time with the Stoneskins?"

Uh. No. Well, there was *one* thing, a rumour I'd only told Nell. But it was just a lie the StoneKing had wanted to tell the magebloods: that I was the nexus of all magic on Enzar. It couldn't be possible. No human could contain the magic of an entire world, let alone one I hadn't been to since I was a baby. Until the other week, that is.

"Not that I remember. I wish I'd tried to find out more."

"You did admirably, under the circumstances," said Ms Weston. "But the Stoneskins, and Thairon—" She cut herself off. "I don't like the implication that this happened not only under the Alliance's eyes, but within our own organisation."

Neither did I. Nobody had an answer. We were the last obstacle standing between Enzar and Earth.

"Nor me. But I want to fight on the Alliance's side. If I can."

"It's your choice." A new steeliness entered her expression. "I intend to join the war effort myself as soon as the time comes."

I blinked at her. "You do?"

"I always thought my skills would best be served in watching over others. After Stephen died, I was all Amanda had left. But she can make her own decision, and the same goes for my employees. If not for the council's change of leadership, I would already be out in the field."

She'd stayed here on Earth for *my* sake. And Kay's. Because the council didn't trust us. But now… well. It didn't take a genius to know why the offworld council wanted to keep a close watch on me. If they lost me to the enemy, the Alliance would fall.

"Anyway… you should go back to your family."

"Yeah." I turned the file over. A line of symbols were on the back. "What are these?"

"I don't know," said Ms Weston. "I'll pass the file onto Iriel. She's been scanning some of our other files using that… eye of hers."

I'd forgotten my fellow Ambassador's enhanced eye. "She can read other languages, right?"

"She's been working around the clock, assembling a list of all the mentions of Enzar, and of magic sources, in our files."

"Has she found anything yet?" I wasn't sure I wanted to know the answer.

"Ask her."

I found Iriel in Office Fifteen with Markos, behind a wall of paperwork stacked precariously on the desks.

"Don't open any doors or windows!" the centaur warned.

"I just stacked those," he added reproachfully, as I reached for a sheet of paper and brought a whole stack crashing down.

"Oops." I dropped under the table to collect them. "What's this, a record of every Alliance mission ever? Or just Earth's?"

"Every one," said Iriel. "Before fifteen years or so ago, anyway. After, we mostly have online records from places like Klathica and Valeria which no longer use hard copy."

"Seems like Earth should get on that." I stacked the papers back where they'd come from. "So—which are Enzar's?"

"Those." Markos pointed with his tail. I lifted down the stack, and groaned at the scrawling handwriting.

"The files only go back a few hundred years," said Iriel. "They're Earth-centric, and Earth wasn't actively involved in the Alliance for as long as some other worlds were. I think these files were originally kept somewhere else, before they built this flashy headquarters as the main base."

"I was hoping for some Enzarian history," I said. The Royals had rewritten history for their own purposes, and for all I knew, the magebloods had done the same, but maybe on a more neutral world like Earth, there might be answers.

"What exactly were you looking for?" asked Markos. "This doesn't seem the time for a history lesson."

"Connections," I said. "All I know is the Royals weren't native to Enzar. They moved in a thousand years ago." I thought back to Nell's stories. She hadn't minded talking about the *distant* past. But none of that would tell us who was really winning—or how they knew my name.

"You say you've taken everything out on ancient languages?" Markos asked Iriel. "That sounds like your area."

Iriel nodded. "The message Ada was sent wasn't in Enzarian script," she said. "It's not an Alliance world language, so the Alliance's translators wouldn't have been able to read it."

I couldn't read Enzarian script. I'd learned to write at a later age than most kids in my year, because Nell had been learning English from scratch. It hadn't done me any harm, anyway, but I wished I'd pushed harder to find out about the world I'd never know. I did… and I didn't, because of what Nell had been through on Enzar.

"If not Enzarian, what language was the message in?" I asked Iriel.

"That's what makes no sense," said Iriel. "Klathican. Classical."

"Seriously?" Klathican was the official language on a couple of other worlds, including Thairon, but I'd never expected Enzar to use it. Maybe they'd figured it was the language I'd be most likely to understand, because it was the easiest offworld language to learn. Nell had taught me how to speak and read Classical.

"How long would it take you to read all of that?" I asked, indicating the papers stacked all over the desk.

"About an hour." Iriel's eye rotated in its socket.

"Seriously? Damn." I looked away, doing my best not to imagine Enzar's possible motives for using Klathican to communicate with me. Maybe they thought I lived there. The message had been redirected to my communicator through the network everyone in the Alliance used. Thanks to the Alliance's confidentiality mandate and the fact that the Enzarian refugees had been relocated to over a dozen worlds, it was possible the magebloods didn't actually know where I lived. They'd never met me in person, and Earth hadn't been the only world to fight back when Thairon and Cethrax had attacked Central. Half the Alliance had joined us.

"Okay," I said, the office suddenly feeling unbearably confining. "Tell me if you find anything new."

I hurried back downstairs to the entrance hall, my mind

reeling. Nell and Alber weren't waiting for me—they'd probably gone back to the shelter. "Shelter" being a loose term. I hadn't known until a week ago Central had its own equivalent of an underground bunker in case of an attack. Kay's mother had set it up, according to the map of Central's lower floors that Elizabeth Walker had left Kay. As Central was a target, half the Alliance had temporarily relocated over here after the attack from Thairon. We were lucky. The battle hadn't damaged the rest of London too much because it'd been focused over here, but it had whipped up a panic I'd never seen before. Rumours flew through the streets, businesses in the general area had closed, and the building itself had drawn a small but persistent crowd of onlookers waiting to get a glimpse of the next catastrophe.

Central was more crowded than I'd ever seen it, and yet it had never felt emptier.

I headed for the stairs to the basement. Luckily, it lay on the opposite side of the building from the cells where the Alliance's former eminent council member was imprisoned. There was half a ton of sciras-enhanced adamantine between us and Lawrence Walker.

Nell, Alber and I shared a room scarcely bigger than a cell. The rest of our corridor was given over to the other Enzarian refugees. There'd been more living in London than I'd thought.

I wondered if the same was true of the world's other major cities. New York. Sydney. Hong Kong. Berlin. Paris. At one slight change, I might have grown up in any of those places, raised to speak another language, been a different person entirely.

No wonder I had trouble figuring out who I *was*.

I found Nell and Alber in the recreation room, if you could call it that. It was adjacent to the dormitories, and the entertainment consisted of a bunch of old board games and one TV someone had brought in. At the other end was the cafeteria. While there were usually a few hundred people at Central, the doubling of the people living here had forced them to hire extra staff, or ask for volunteers to cook, clean, and generally make sure the place functioned as a proper shelter.

"Hey, Ada," said Alber. "Wondered where you'd gone."

"Just talked to my boss. I'm going out tomorrow."

Nell dropped the book she'd been skimming through. One of mine. I'd not been able to bring much, and I had a bunch of books downloaded onto my communicator's e-reading app anyway, but I'd wanted some home comforts. Nell herself had brought nothing beside clothes, while Alber lamented the loss of his Xbox. But it'd probably be stolen or broken within the week. Nell had put most of our valuables in storage.

"You *what?*"

"It's an intelligence mission on Klathica. Alliance-approved." KimaroTech was technically owned by the Alliance, though they wouldn't take kindly to us spying on them.

She shook her head. "Ada, it's not safe out there."

"Don't I know it." I knew Nell never really left Enzar behind. I could see her going to war. If not for me and Alber.

"Hang on a sec," said Alber. "I'm not a kid, and neither's Ada. Let her go."

"That has nothing to do with it," said Nell. "Ada's in more danger than anyone else in the building." Her voice had dropped to a near-whisper. "Too many people have tried to hurt you, Ada."

"I can't stay here and do nothing when there's a war going on out there. I won't be anywhere near Enzar. *And* I'll be invisible. We're using the Chameleons. I *know* it's dangerous, but if I stay here when I could be out there helping, I might as well be dead already."

Nell sucked in a breath. "Whereabouts are you going?"

"Klathica. It's an Alliance world, but since there were links between KimaroTech and T—" I swallowed the lump in my throat. "The Stoneskins. I want to make sure there's no one working against the Alliance."

"Why," asked Nell, "do they need people from Earth, then?"

"Because..." I weighed my options, not wanting to mention the lawbreaking part. "Because we're neutral. And I'm trained to use the Chameleon."

Nell sighed, but all she said was, "Be careful."

"I'm gonna find Kay and tell him."

I knew where he'd be. Kay dealt with a crisis by taking action, and being as powerless as we all were at the moment was driving him as crazy as it drove me, if not more. For the first couple of days, he'd been in a state of shock, and locked himself in the simulator room for so long I'd had to go in to remind him to eat and sleep. If we didn't get offworld soon, we'd both lose our minds.

Halfway out the door, my communicator buzzed. A message. Goosebumps sprang up on my arms. Every time, it was the same words, sent to every Alliance branch.

We are coming, Adamantine. You are ours.

2

KAY

I'd had to see it with my own eyes, first. I had access to the doorway port and a list of all the symbols for the different worlds. Thairon's was still there. So I'd borrowed one of Valeria's protective armoured suits, complete with boots containing oxygen-shields and hover-ware. Before I'd been able to second-guess the decision, I'd carved the symbol into the auros-covered door and pushed it open a half-inch.

A red-scorched wasteland, dotted with black fragments of adamantine, was all that waited on the other side. Nothing living. The smog that had covered the planet's surface had gone, replaced by a semi-transparent red haze. It didn't quite mask the scattered bits of metal, remains of the satellite that had once housed the remainder of the planet's population. They'd lived in simulation, in a virtual reality created by their leaders, and had been trapped there, in comas. They might not even have felt a thing when their world exploded.

I stared. Counted down from ten. Stepped back, and let the door close. And then sank to the ground, ripping off the visor from the shell suit. Gasping for breath. Shaking uncontrollably.

He killed them.

I'd known my father for a manipulative sadist ever since I was a child. He'd tried to turn me into his weapon, a soldier who'd obey without question. He hadn't succeeded. But this time, he'd drawn the Enzarian Empire's attention to Earth. He'd killed the population of an entire world in a misguided attempt to stop them from destroying us.

He was locked up in the cells. He should by rights have been locked up years ago, before he could put us on the path of no return. But no one ever said the Multiverse played fair.

The simulator was set to maximum settings. I'd lost track of time, numbed to everything but the flow of battle. I switched from dagger to guns to bare-handed combat and I always came back to the same place. As though I could wash away the stains of what Walker had done in a field of blood.

"Kay *Walker!*" The voice cut through the simulation. I'd know it anywhere. Ada.

"What are you doing here?" I asked, stupidly without removing the helmet first. The jarring of real and simulated worlds made my vision swim. I leaned against the real-world wall, misjudged, and fell into Ada instead. I caught myself in time.

"Looking for you," she said. "Take the bloody helmet off."

"Why?" But I lifted the visor to find her staring at me, bright-red hair tousled, face flushed.

"Because you're in here all the time, and to be honest, it's scaring the crap out of me."

I shook my head. "Sorry. Lost track of time."

"You've done nothing but lock yourself away in here for

days, Kay. I know why you're doing this. You think you can shut the world out, but you'll never shut *me* out." She blinked, and tears trembled on her eyelashes. "I think about Thairon every day. You couldn't control what your father did. If anyone should have been able to find that bomb, it's me. And I'm the one who closed the doorway. I doomed them all."

I closed my eyes. "It's not your fault either, Ada. I'm sorry I shut you out. I'd rather be fighting them. Not waiting for them to break our doors down."

Sure, I knew I was far from in the right mental state to go to war. But we no longer had the luxury of choice.

"I know," said Ada. "You think this isn't frustrating for me, too? I got another message five minutes ago."

"Crap." I tossed the helmet aside. "What did it say?"

"Same as the last one." She sighed. "Nell has a new theory every day. First she thought they were planning to tunnel from under the floor, then she decided they planned to open a doorway in the sky, Valeria-style."

I'd considered as many theories myself. There was nothing more frustrating than waiting for the enemy to make their move when we couldn't strike first. Not when we didn't know *where* the enemy was hiding. Earth hadn't felt like a prison in so long. Like I was the one locked up, not him.

"They won't get you," I said. "Not if the Alliance has anything to do with it."

"Yeah. About that. There's... something else."

"What is it?"

"Ms Weston told me... about a mission. Offworld."

"What kind of mission?"

"Intelligence," she said. "It's not supposed to be high-risk, just checking up on Klathica. Make sure there's nothing dodgy there."

"Hmm." Logically, going offworld in any capacity was a

risky move, but I'd never been one for making the sensible choice. And I had an advantage no one else did: a built-in invisibility amplifier. "I'll talk to her. But you know, it's not safe."

"Anywhere. I get it." She bowed her head. "I can't use magic on Enzar itself because of the risk, but I'm one of Earth's few trained magic-wielders."

"Yeah, even the Academy didn't have Magic Basics 101." Technically, neither of us were formally trained magic-wielders, but between us we probably knew more than most people on Earth. And right now, we were a rare commodity.

I didn't let myself think about how fine a line there was between *commodity* and *weapon*.

Ms Weston approved me for the mission right away, as though she'd been expecting me to ask. Though she'd lost some of her authority in the leadership changeover, she ran the show in Office Fifteen. Even the offworld council were scared of her, with good reason.

Ada waited for me outside the office. "She said yes?"

"She'll send us the mission details later."

"You're going offworld?" Markos the centaur came out of Office Fifteen, a frown on his face. "Spying on our allies won't help us find out what Enzar are doing."

"Like they aren't spying on us." I looked back at the office. "The hell happened to all those papers, anyway?"

"Iriel." The centaur's eyes narrowed. "She took the ones she said were useful and left the rest. She *ruined* weeks of work."

"Tragic." I rolled my eyes. "She was looking for information on sources, right?"

"Ms Weston said she was looking for anything on Enzar, too," said Ada.

"I thought there wasn't anything in the archives." I'd searched them myself. A brief history record… and the file on bloodrock, which had started all of this. A file my father had logged.

"Don't tell me that's where you're going," said Markos.

"Of course not," I said. "Klathica."

"Ah." Markos nodded. "Have their absurd innovations finally bitten them back?"

"I have no idea," I said, "but they have more information on sources than any other world."

Including the source in my own blood. My father had got some Klathican scientists to come to Earth and inject human 'volunteers' with pure magic sources in an attempt to create his own magic-wielder army to take down Thairon. But thanks to his tendency to arrange cover-ups, I never had figured out how much he knew about the sources he'd used to ruin my life.

How much did *Enzar* know? Something Ada had told me about the StoneKing kept coming back to me. The mage-bloods had made no direct attack on the Alliance, but in the last few weeks, not only had they almost started a war on our doorstep, they'd sent a declaration right into our headquarters. A warning, directed at Ada. The Alliance's entire communications network had been temporarily shut down. But if they'd always had that kind of power, why use it now? They'd been cut off for twenty years. Even Thairon wasn't linked to our world any longer. But Klathica had been the one to supply the weapons for the war in the first place. 'Weapons' might easily be code for magic sources.

"We ought to be talking to other worlds, too," I said. "Enzar and Cethrax are in league. The Allied worlds aren't enough to outnumber them."

"Which other worlds are you talking about?" asked Markos, one eyebrow raised.

"Aglaia."

The centaur frowned. "For what reason? You know my sister's feelings on humans *and* magic. She'll never fight for the Alliance."

"Yes, but your world is high-magic. We never found out who coerced your cousin into giving up the information on the source." I'd been driving myself out of my mind the last couple of weeks, trying to figure out what links we might have missed. Aglaia's source might be gone, but that world had been the only place I'd actually *seen* lustre.

"You've made your point," said Markos. "I will have to ask for a loan of that ridiculous doorway port." He tapped a hoof. "What is it with you humans and overcomplicating things? Doors are useless inventions, if anyone can open them."

"Let's hope it's just the Alliance who can open *that* one," I muttered.

"Tell me about it," said Ada.

We walked back downstairs to the entrance hall. My heart sank with every step. I'd put it off for days, but I'd be an idiot to leave Earth for Klathica without speaking to my father.

With the help of the world-key I'd taken from my father, I'd gone over to Klathica and argued my way through to Walker's offworld accounts to wrest control of his fortune myself. Once I did, I transferred everything over to my own accounts so Walker's cronies wouldn't be able to get hold of it. I hadn't had time to do any more than that, though once the war was over, I'd figure out how best to use it.

The Walker fortune had been inherited, but based on the records, my father had never touched most of it. He'd been Robert Walker's only surviving child, and his mother had died in childbirth. No one else had inherited. Sure, he was a stingy bastard… but what if he'd left it untouched for a reason? The Walker family had been tied to the war in Enzar. I had the creeping sense I was messing with blood money. But that was beside the point. I couldn't let his fortune sit around while Walker was still breathing. If the fucker escaped, he'd have a rude awakening.

Not only that, every police force in the Alliance knew him for what he was. Nowhere was safe for him now.

"Hey," I said to Ada. "You go to your family, all right? I've got something I need to take care of."

"Oh." She gave me a pensive, concerned look. "You all right? It's not…"

"I have to talk to him. Before we leave."

Ada's expression hardened. "Okay." She kissed me, lightly. "Please be careful in there."

After his escape attempt, Lawrence Walker had been given a level of security never before employed on Earth. His new cell had once been a store room, fitted with adamantine bars. I'd need to get the keys from Carl to enter the room, so I went to the guard office first.

Carl, head guard, was one of few people at Central who didn't tiptoe around me after Walker had destroyed Thairon.

"Kay," he said, looking surprised. "I haven't seen you around."

I wasn't on the guard rota anymore, in case someone decided to blame me for Walker's crimes and either murdered me in a dark corner of the Passages or threw me to the monsters. Even Ambassador missions had mostly been halted as the Alliance skipped over the usual pleasantries by using the doorway ports to move between branches. I might be a fool to stay at Central when more than a few people thought I ought to have been jailed, too, but I'd never forgive myself if I walked away.

"I'm on a mission tomorrow, and I need to get information from our prisoner before I leave."

"You do?" Carl's eyes sharpened. "He hasn't responded to any others who tried to question him. The council's been down there twice."

"Yeah. I'm sure." Of course Lawrence Walker would have kept secrets from the council. Our entire life was a lie, for god's sake. Too bad for him being absent for five years had hindered his attempt to rise to power again and won me some credibility. Some of the council members hated me, of course, but others kept asking for my input in issues I couldn't even begin to make a decision on. Should the Alliance mount a direct attack on Enzar? Should we be recruiting other outlying worlds? I didn't know.

My hand clenched over the keys and I turned my back on the guard office. I climbed the stairs down into the basement. My hand twitched towards my gun—I'd be a fool not to arm myself. I wanted to fire a bullet through his skull, but the protection down here wouldn't allow it. It seemed like tempting fate to take a weapon anywhere near him. *Calm down. He's the one behind bars.*

The room was a cell, behind an adamantine door. The walls were antimagic, too, strong enough to make me feel like a weight pressed on my back. He sat on the bed they'd put in there, and his eyes were on me before I'd opened the door. There was one light, a fluorescent strip in front of the prison's bars.

"I wondered how long it would take before you came crawling back."

"Please." It was easier to pretend I talked to the asshole who'd made my life hell as a kid, not the genocidal lunatic who'd killed twenty thousand people this month. "I'm here for information." His eyes were the only thing alive in his drug-wasted face. I made myself stare him out.

"So you're an interrogator? Let me guess." He stood, slowly, like it hurt him. *Good.* "I suppose you got them to pity you with a sob story to wrangle a place on the council."

"Sounds like something you'd do. I'm curious: did *your* father ever decide to throw a bomb at you, or did you come up with it yourself?"

Walker's eyes narrowed. He never talked about his father, only in passing. Of course I knew better than to ask, but I'd always wondered. My grandfather had died before I was born, but given how Lawrence Walker had turned out, I doubted he'd win parent of the year award.

"Fine." Now wasn't the time to speculate on Lawrence Walker's own childhood. "So. KimaroTech. How many people would answer to you, if you gave an order? Even now?"

Of course there would be some. The Walker name had its own way of bending the rules. Some people would happily serve a despot like him if he gave them what they wanted.

"You want a list of names?"

I couldn't tell if he was being sarcastic. Maybe he'd picked something up from my mother after all.

"Yes, that would help."

"For who? The council?" Walker shook his head. "You have no place amongst them. You know nothing of sacrifice. The Multiverse is an ugly place, Kay, and you're a naïve fool to believe otherwise."

"Sacrifice? Like what you did to Thairon? Twenty thousand people died, Walker. You're not the one I feel sorry for." I clenched my hands over the bars. "You think the Multiverse revolves around you, Walker, and if it were true, it's as ugly as you can get." I let magic spark from my palms and hit the adamantine wall. "Lucky for you, you're wrong. You're wrong about the Multiverse, and you're wrong about me.

Elizabeth knew there was some decency left in the world. So do I. And that's why you're going to lose."

"You're a deluded idealist, just like her."

"And who won in the end?" I knew he was baiting me, but damn if I hadn't wanted to tear into him for the damage he'd done. "Who's locked up in here? If anyone's deluded, Walker, it's you. You're the one who thought the Alliance would let you walk away free. The offworld council will decide your fate, but I hope to be the one to kill you, Walker." I managed a faint smile. "I have the duration of the war to decide exactly how and when. So I guess you better hope I don't survive."

"You won't survive," snarled Walker. "You might think magic grants you invincibility, but it's a weakness. You're dependent on a force you can't begin to understand."

"You're claiming to understand magic? You injected me with an unknown magic substance. Don't try and pretend you knew how it worked. If you had, you'd have taken me offworld."

"I told you I had no way of knowing the consequences—"

"Ignorance is no fucking excuse!" I stepped back, breathing heavily. "And you're high up enough in the Alliance, you *could* have actually researched magic before you injected it into people. Do you even know how the war in Enzar started?"

"So that's it." By Walker's tone, my outburst might not even have happened. "That's why you're so attached to the girl. You think she'll accept you because she's the same. Or maybe part of you *wants* to stand at her side and burn the Multiverse to the ground."

My nails dug into my palms. He was trying to wind me up so I'd forget my purpose here. I knew every one of the bastard's games.

"I came to see your miserable face for a reason," I said. "Because we're at war, in case you've forgotten. If you're supposedly on Earth's side, you'll tell me what you know about Enzar, and maybe—just maybe—you won't die along with the rest of us. You're no magic-wielder. They nearly destroyed Central already, and they have magic on their side."

"Magic," said Walker, "is on no one's side."

I froze. He'd not been the one to say that—I had. The image of the Stoneskins crumbling under my power filled my head. I'd destroyed adamantine. It wasn't unbreakable. Could Enzar bring down even the Alliance's headquarters?

"I didn't come here to talk about magic," I said, "but your little project. KimaroTech. You said they didn't create the Stoneskins, but Thairon had your fingerprints all over it." It was all I could do to get the words out.

"The betrayer was a man named Nelson," said Walker.

I stared. I hadn't expected him to answer. "Who?"

"Dox Nelson worked for my father. He decided to use a world-key to pay a visit to Thairon and meet with Enzar's people. He agreed to keep the laboratory running, as long as Enzar paid him and the other traitors he lured over to his side. None of us on Klathica had any idea."

"So you were on Klathica, with KimaroTech? Doing what, aside from making magic-boost drugs and enhancements with dangerous magic sources? Or making more Stone-skins?" That was the one link between the three worlds. Klathica claimed Thairon had stolen their source.

"I told you," growled Walker, his face inches from the bars, "I did *not* authorise the project. I cut Enzar off from their army. I had no idea that Nelson and my father's other allies kept the connection between Klathica and Thairon running. Nor did I have the resources to close the doorway when it was formed from a creature made of living auros."

"Auros." My heart missed a beat. He knew the name. I'd never told him.

"It's nothing you would understand, Kay. You claim I know nothing of magic—"

"I know what auros is." Screw it—he already knew. "The kimaros was a living form of it. So, did KimaroTech know it existed? They must have."

"Few did," he said. "I kept it quiet. Don't you think the Alliance would have tried to stake a claim on it? Thairon knew they would, and that's why they contained the source within a living creature, one under their own control. Sources are power, Kay."

"You think I don't know that?" I had one living inside my blood. Lustre. The amplifier. "You've not been to Thairon in person since before—" Dammit. "Before your wife died. Was that when you realised Thairon and Enzar were linked?" He'd cut Enzar off from the Passages twenty years ago. Seven years later, his wife had died in a failed mission behind the Alliance's back to unplug the simulators imprisoning Thairon's population, and all access to that world had virtually shut down, too. But I refused to believe it was mere coincidence the Stoneskins had been made the same year. Nor that the link between Enzar and Thairon had been there for as many years as it had without Walker knowing.

He arched an eyebrow, as though he'd read the thought that slid into my mind like the keen edge of a blade.

"They killed her." The words stuck in my throat. "The Stoneskins. They were Thairon's security."

"Does it matter?" He waved a hand dismissively. "The outcome's the same."

You'd say that. "If you didn't authorise the project, did you close the link between Thairon and Klathica?"

"I did, as soon as I became aware it existed."

"So you know about doorways." *Damn.* The Walker family had been in the Alliance from the start. And who'd been the ones to build the freaking Passages? But none of this explained how Enzar had got into our communications systems only a few weeks ago.

"The Walker family classified the worlds, didn't they?" I asked, quietly. "That's what your father did. Right?"

"You never expressed an interest in the specifics of our history."

"I can hazard a guess." Alliance history and *our* family history were one and the same. Even if he'd done his best to cover it up. Not just from virtually everyone on Earth, but even from his own family.

"The past is irrelevant," said Walker. "What does it matter, if Earth will fall no matter our attempts to defend it? Whatever technology Central has adapted in my absence, it will never be enough. My father was a fool to think we could survive cross-world warfare. Why do you think the two of us are the last survivors of our family line? The others died, Kay."

I stepped back as his face loomed close to the bars. My heart hammered against my ribs. *You knew they died.* But I'd never known the specifics. How could I?

"Every single member of our family met a violent end because they foolishly tried to defend Earth from enemies we had no hope of overcoming. They tried to ally with others instead of focusing on our defence first. Instead of making sacrifices, they chose to protect their own reputations. And for what? What good is one human against an empire? I taught you what you needed to survive. Alone."

"I was under the impression you wanted me dead. Or to lead an army. I'm kind of unclear on the details here, Walker. And if you really didn't give a shit about the future, why'd you marry Elizabeth? Or that was just for show, right?"

Walker glared at me, pinning me to the spot. "There were rumours," he said. "Unsavoury rumours about our family. I had to give the impression I intended to carry on the Walker family's line."

"You're despicable." My voice rose in volume, echoing off the walls. "Did you really think I'd have walked into that simulation and gunned everyone down like an obedient soldier? You wrecked any chance of that when you shot me up with a pure magic source. Bet you don't even know the name."

Walker's eyes narrowed. He didn't know. He'd not stayed in the room while they'd injected me with three sources—bloodrock, obsidiate, lustre. Only the last one worked. The amplifier.

"Do you know *any* magic sources?" The Alliance had only implemented magic-based stunners in the past few years, after Walker's disappearance.

"Adamantine."

"Yeah? You know antimagic." I crossed my arms. "That's what's keeping us alive. So, do Enzar have any of *that*? Aside from the Stoneskins?"

It was a rhetorical question. I knew they did, but I wanted to know if Walker had more insight into their army than he'd claimed.

"Enzar *are* antimagic," said Walker. "Who do you think brought *this*—" He tapped the adamantine bars of the cage— "to Central?"

"You didn't," I said coldly. "Your father did. Right?" I'd guessed, seeing as the place was built thirty years ago, at the same time as my grandfather had announced the Alliance's existence on Earth. Robert Walker was the original owner of KimaroTech.

"My father decided it would be in Earth's interests if we had the same protection afforded to other more magically-inclined worlds, yes." Walker shook his head. "In the end, our store of antimagic enabled us to close the doorways to Enzar and its neighbours down before they could do any more damage."

I waited for the words I'd expected from the start—for him to say adamantine was what the Royals had injected into people to turn them into weapons. Though maybe he'd got the idea from Klathica instead. When magic was involved, coincidence was by no means impossible, just unlikely. Give a bunch of people a substance marked "instant superpowers" and you could guarantee some idiot would decide to swallow it to see what happened.

Did he not know of any sources beside the main ones? Did he not know what *I* was? Sure, lustre wasn't used as an implant in Klathica. It was a battery, and not a great one. And it didn't help that it *looked* the same as adamantine, sciras, and obsidiate. Only bloodrock appeared notably different. But he'd definitely used bloodrock. His name was on the goddamn file.

Walker didn't say another word. Maybe he didn't know, after all.

"Speaking of damage," I said, "how many people did you kill off and replace with your allies? Like the council members?"

"I didn't intend them to die. They were poor leaders."

"You used magic as a disguise."

"Bloodrock? Yes, it's a favourite trick of the Enzarians."

"And it requires a certain kind of source," I said. "What did you do with the rest? You do realise unless all magic sources are logged, the enemy might get their hands on any of them."

"That is *precisely* my point," snarled Walker, "and the exact reason Earth should never have been involved with high-magic worlds. How many people on the godforsaken planet even know the potential of the sources?"

"Very few, and most of them are in this building," I said evenly. "Bloodrock. Whereabouts is it?"

"Gone," he said. "I used the last of it to disguise the bomb."

Of course. The bomb that wiped out Thairon. My hand clenched on the bars of the cage, as though I could rip them from the ground and make him suffer for the lives he'd taken.

"What was *that* made from?"

Walker blinked. "If you're looking for a lecture on the mechanics of magic-based explosives, I'd suggest you pay Klathica a visit."

Well, damn.

"So *you* don't know." I shook my head. "Amateur move, Walker. What if the bomb had exploded in your hands? Pity it didn't."

"That's enough insolence from you, Kay."

Something snapped inside me, and anger swept away the lingering fear. I pushed back from the bars long enough to call magic into my hand. Even submerged in adamantine, it answered me, the red light reflected in Walker's dead eyes. "Tell me why you logged the information on bloodrock. I've seen the file." I quoted from memory: "As the whereabouts and extent of this source are unknown, bloodrock is to be treated with caution and samples are not to be removed from storage."

"That's what it said?" He blinked at me. "You remember..."

"Everything," I said, coldly. "But you used bloodrock solution on your servants. Where did you get it from?"

"I fail to see how that's relevant."

"Anything with links to Enzar is relevant," I said, "seeing as they declared war on us. Unless you planned to betray us all along, like everyone else."

"I betrayed no one," said Walker, his voice as cold as

frozen stone, "and the sooner you see that, the sooner you might save your own lives."

"Spare me," I said, equally coldly. "Enzar can't attack us directly because their kimaros—auros—can only connect to certain worlds, right?"

That was as much as I'd guessed. But source worlds couldn't connect to non-source worlds. If they attacked anywhere, it'd be a high-magic, high-profile world like Valeria, or Klathica. Ada had closed their link with Cethrax, but that didn't mean they wouldn't try again.

"It is thanks to me the Alliance has remained safe from Enzar," said Walker.

"Because you cut them off."

"You paint me as a villain, but the Alliance would have been obliterated if I hadn't. As it is, I hear Enzar has done a spectacular job of destroying itself. The Royals are all dead, and the remaining nonmages are mostly in hiding. The magebloods are in the process of building an empire of their own, helped in no small way by the monstrosities my father gave them in exchange for…"

"Bloodrock." My heart sank. *So that's how it went. But what did he even want with it?*

"And adamantine," he said. "All the sources they could spare. In return, my father found a way to create those… Stoneskins. I don't believe they have the knowledge themselves, so they'll die off soon enough."

"Seriously?" I stared, before it hit me I was displaying entirely too much of my ignorance to the bastard. "You think they'll die off? Enzar won't figure out how to replicate the technology?"

"The Stoneskins aren't the ones you should worry about. The war covers more than one universe, Kay, and not a single one of them knows what they're fighting for. They know no other life." He shook his head. "They will *never* be able to accept the Alliance. Intervening will mean our deaths, every last one of us."

The truth in his words was poison.

"In case you've forgotten, Kay, I was a prisoner on Thairon for five years. Now I'm a prisoner again, and you come in to ridicule me." Walker stepped back, suddenly looking tired. "I have had enough of your ingratitude."

"Tell that to Thairon, you bastard." Hot rage ignited in my veins, but I couldn't think straight with the bastard staring me down, assessing me for weaknesses. I should have made a plan. I knew his tricks. He was playing the part of the helpless prisoner, pleading ignorance. He'd left me to die once already. Nothing, not even a threat to his life, would persuade him to give me the truth. He was a pathological liar. Why had I ever thought I could get answers out of him?

I turned my back and left, locking the door with shaking hands. Double-locked. Checked again. My spine prickled and I all but sprinted upstairs. Outside. I needed to get outside.

I collided with Ada in the entrance hall. "Shit. Sorry."

"It's okay. Are you?"

"It's fine." I went to hand the keys back to Carl. "Bastard's as close-mouthed as ever. What we need is a freaking lie-detector." But Walker wasn't just a liar, he was a manipulator. He told enough of the truth it sounded plausible to anyone who didn't know him.

I gave Carl the keys, and came back out of the office to meet Ada. She hesitated before saying, "Don't you want to… be normal, just for a bit?"

"Normal?" That almost got a smile out of me. "Think it went sky-high a while back."

"We could go back to your place. Not that I mind bunking at Central, but Nell punches things in her sleep and Al snores like a jackhammer."

"Sure. Just make sure Nell knows, so she doesn't worry about you."

Really, I felt like an arsehole for not intervening when she'd been forced out of her house. But my apartment wasn't exactly made for entertaining guests. It was hardly bigger than Ada's room here. And I was as much a walking target as they were. Nobody had my address, but the same could be said of the shelters, and someone had thrown a brick through Ada's window last week.

After Ada had sent Nell a text message, we left. I'd parked my bike outside the gates, since most of the car park had been destroyed in the attack. The aftermath had carved burn marks into the tarmac and metre-wide dents where magic had struck in bolts of lightning. Ada and I went out the side gate, near the Passages, after showing our IDs to two rows of guards. As if they didn't already know who I was.

Walker. Magic-wielder. His son.

Ada squeezed my hand, her uncertain smile cracking something inside me. Sometimes it was easier not to feel anything at all.

"We'll be all right." She sounded like she was trying to convince herself more than me.

One bike-ride and four flights of stairs later, I remembered I hadn't cleaned the flat in weeks, let alone opened a window.

"Honestly, it's like a bat cave in here," said Ada as we went into the flat.

"It's not that bad." I shut the door and pulled back the curtains, stirring up a flurry of dust motes. I'd hit the punch bag hard enough to knock it off the ceiling the other day, leaving a trail of sand over the carpet. My spare guard uniform was strewn across the floor, along with several broken stunners.

"There's enough dust in here to make a snowman." She shook her head.

"Well, you did want to wind down."

The window shattered in a shower of glass. A metal-plated device clattered onto the middle of the floor, and Ada dived before I could shout a warning. Her hands closed around the device, and the whole building shook as the magic level surged. The hairs on my arms stood on end, and the device—*bomb*—shattered in Ada's hands. Magic sparks rebounded off the walls, burning holes in everything they touched. The wall plaster. The carpet. I'd instinctively raised my arms to shield my face, and now I lowered them, running to Ada. "Shit. Are you okay?"

Ada grimaced. "Wait—hold on." She splayed her hands, palms marked with blister-like burns where stray sparks had hit her. The magic rushed towards her, and within seconds, the sparks had stopped flying from what remained of the bomb.

"I should have done that from the start." She winced. "*Shit.*"

I ran to the window. But the attacker had fled. Whoever they were, they'd somehow scaled a four-storey building. I peered down, cursing under my breath. A familiar shadow-like shape passed by the window, leaving a trail of sparks. *Gotcha.*

"Goddamn kimaros."

I ran out the door and pelted downstairs, drawing my stunner as I did so. I didn't care who saw us—the quicker everyone got out of the building, the better.

Ada followed, gasping for breath, as I caught up to the kimaros at the street's end. Sparks flew from my stunner, leaving sizzling marks on the pavement. The heightened magic level brought magic to my fingertips immediately, lighting the air in red stripes. I didn't care if there were witnesses, not now. The kimaros spun around, hissing, sparks trailing from its indistinctly catlike shape.

"Where the hell did you come from, you bastard?"

Now I really did sound unhinged. Of course, the beast wasn't intelligent enough to reply. I fired magic from my stunner, moving to avoid the kimaros's swiping clawed hands. It was like a living red shadow, magic contained in not-quite-solid form. But it wasn't the strongest beast I'd faced. Ada and I had gone up against a living doorway just the other week. I didn't feel any sense of intelligence coming from this one. It was like a robot programmed to follow orders. Question was, by whom?

The kimaros sent a volley of sparks across the pavement as my attack missed, arching over its head. Most of the sparks fizzled out on contact with my jacket's sleeves. I fired magic from my stunner again, this time striking its vaguely defined face. The beast screamed, then exploded into yet more sparks. A scorched area a metre wide marked the pavement, and the creature was gone.

Weirdly, some of the tension had eased out of me, like a real fight had taken the edge off the impact of seeing Walker again.

I turned to Ada with an ironic smile. "Looks like I'll be moving to Central." And then, "Your hands. I'm sorry. I shouldn't have brought you with me."

"If I wasn't here, the bomb would have killed you." She clenched her fists, an angry light in her eyes. "Whoever did this will be sorry."

3

KAY

I rony was a bitch. With no other option, I wound up having to stay in a former cell under the Alliance's headquarters.

I wasn't about to complain, considering I'd been seconds from being my old room's new wallpaper. Except being in the same building as my father was like living down the corridor from the bastard all over again. No doubt he'd have found that as unamusing as I did.

Saki, the nurse, beckoned us into the medical room. They'd been run off their feet, too, dealing with the aftermath of the battle. As of yet, no one had got into a fight in the underground shelter—a few threats, but not an all-out brawl. I was willing to bet it was only a matter of time, with so many magic-wielders living in close quarters.

"*You're* fine," Saki said to me. "As for you, Ada, try holding onto this. It helped with some of the others."

Ada took the rectangular piece of gleaming black metal. "It's adamantine? Like, the pure stuff?"

"We don't have a lot here," said Saki. "But it'll help."

"Thanks," said Ada, with a slight wince. She gripped the

rock in both hands. "Uh. I never did apologise for attacking you before, when I was a prisoner here. Sorry."

Saki blinked. "Save your apologies. I think you'll need them after the war."

"What, you think it's my fault, too?" Ada's voice shook. "I didn't ask them to attack Earth."

I placed my hand over hers. "You know it's not your fault." I caught her gaze, and she finally nodded.

Saki sighed. "Well, whatever the reason, we're at war. I'd never have guessed Enzar would be the ones to do it. If I had to pick a world, I'd say Klathica."

"What makes you say that?" I asked, taking my hand off Ada's. "Klathica might have provoked skirmishes, but their current council is sound. And they never wanted a war. That's why they agreed to update the Alliance's mandate." I knew it by heart. As much as I knew it had been founded on a lie.

"The Alliance isn't what it used to be."

I couldn't argue with that. "Maybe it just wasn't what it appeared to be."

She scowled. "Of all the times for the council to gain a conscience, it had to be when we're in the middle of a war. Why tell everyone on Earth we're being invaded? The communications network's down again because of all the emergency calls. Any one of them could mean the war's here."

"None of them will," I said. "I've been hearing the same thing from my friend at the New York Alliance. The magic level's hiked up so weird crap's happening worldwide. At least half the calls are false alarms or scare stories started by tabloids. Look at the one about Bigfoot being an interdimensional teleporter."

That got a laugh from Ada, at least. Simon had sent me a photo of the headline from where he'd picked it up at a news stand.

"Magic," said Saki, with a snort. "The world's gone insane."

"You think?" I rolled my eyes. "They'd deploy Alliance guards if the local stories were genuine. All the magic-wielders in London are here, so it's contained." In theory. The rest of the world was having considerable trouble adjusting to the possibility of another magical attack, even though odd magic-related problems had been cropping up for months now, since the first time Earth's magic levels had gone skyrocketing.

"Believe me," I said, "when the war starts, we'll know about it." I knew Ada was thinking the same as me: Enzar could communicate directly with the Alliance if they wanted to.

"Except we're harbouring a criminal." The nurse shot me a dirty look.

"He has information we need. We can't afford to lose our only lead on Enzar."

"Is that what you believe? I carried out that man's orders for four years. If every mission he covered up became common knowledge, there'd be a mob at the door."

"Don't I know it." I stood, letting go of Ada's hand. "Getting answers out of the bastard is like trying to negotiate with the vox-kind."

"Aren't you his stand-in on the council?"

Don't go there. I'd heard some of the guards whispering similar things, saying it couldn't be coincidence that I'd been the one who'd heard his plan. The cameras Ada and I had taken to Thairon had been scrambled in the fighting, and with the threat of the war, some people just didn't want to know there could be another explanation than the obvious one: that I was Walker's pawn. I was well aware the sensible thing to do was go into hiding, and I hardly qualified as an

Ambassador anymore, but I was in too deep to back out now.

My fist clenched. "No, I'm not. In case you've forgotten, he tried to have me killed for getting in his way. And it wouldn't surprise me if it was one of his minions who just tried to blow us up. I can't think of anyone else who'd have gone to the trouble of staking out my home address." I dropped my hand, frustration burning in my blood. "Who-ever they are, they got a kimaros out of the Passages even with all the security. The strip-down searches will stop anything getting in here, but I'm more worried about what's out *there*. That bomb could have killed people."

"Yeah." I'd bet Ada, like me, was thinking of Thairon. "Saki, I know you hate Walker, but really, if you know anything about his plans... we might be able to stop this happening again."

Saki turned to her. "I only know what I observed. When he first joined the council, I heard rumours about his rivals stepping down at the last minute for unknown reasons. People who would have been considered threats. And then there were those medical records."

I nodded. I'd expected as much. "Anything about magic? Or sources? He didn't tell me a thing."

"He really didn't?" Saki frowned at me.

"No, and believe me, I wish he had." I ran a hand through my hair, wearily. "I've had it with trying to untangle the mess he left behind, but it's not like anyone else at Central has a clue what other shit he covered up. Or did they?"

Saki gave me an assessing look, then shook her head. "I think I'm the only person who noticed the discrepancies in the records, especially of Thairon. The only one still working at Central, anyway. You may have noticed we have a high staff turnover rate. Especially since the number of disasters has tripled since the pair of you showed up."

"Imagine that," I muttered. "All right. I'm just trying to find out who might know… anything. We're at a loose end."

"Aren't we all?" Saki opened the door. "Go, the both of you, and for heaven's sake get some sleep. You look dead on your feet."

Ada and I left the room.

"I think I'm growing on her," I said.

Ada rolled her eyes. "C'mon. Let's go face the music. Nell's gonna be pissed enough to lecture me all night."

I expected most of it to be directed at me. But to my surprise, Nell hugged Ada, not saying a word. I got a glare, probably because there were so many people around.

Everyone gave the Fletcher family a wide berth, encouraged by Nell's unfriendly expression. Pretty impressive how a short, non-imposing woman projected an aura of *don't fuck with me* as effectively as she did. As for me, I made sure Ada was okay, then left and climbed the stairs to the guard office, saying I needed to report the incident to Carl.

Not strictly a lie, but I had other plans, too. Specifically, clearing anything from my flat which

I didn't want the enemy to get their hands on—like my grandfather's map, depicting the whole of the Passages and the shelters beneath Central. Within ten minutes, I'd run back to my flat, grabbed everything I might need at Central, and left the room the way it was. The landlord was going to be pissed at the damage the bomb had wreaked, but I didn't particularly care.

I found Ada with her family back in the downstairs recreation room at Central. She jumped up from the sofa she sat on beside Nell, dropping the adamantine piece. "Tell me you didn't go back."

Ada's younger brother sat with several other teenage Enzarians, who all gawped at me. I shrugged and sat next to Ada. "I just went to the take-out over the road." I passed Ada and Nell the pizzas I'd picked up on the way back to cover my mission to search my apartment and make sure there weren't more kimaros lurking around.

"Sure you did," Ada muttered in my ear, but she opened the box and picked up a slice, and didn't ask any more questions until the Enzarians were engaged in their own conversation again.

"Are your hands okay?" I asked her. The magic burn didn't seem as bad as last time, but I should have acted quickly enough to stop her getting hurt in the first place.

"I'll live." She shifted closer, so only I could hear her. "What was so important you had to go running back to your apartment after it nearly blew up?"

"Information on magic-based substances," I said, as quietly as I could. "I had a printed copy from the archives. And the map of Central with these shelters labelled on it. I couldn't risk anyone getting hold of them, since whoever sent the bomb knew my address already."

Ada breathed out. "You're still an idiot, but yeah. Good point."

"Can I see the message?" I couldn't get the damn thing out of my head. It probably had no connection to the attack on my apartment. No way was Enzar directly behind that—unless they had someone tailing Ada. Just one of a hundred other possible enemies.

She passed me her communicator. "It's exactly the same as the others. I wish I could send one back. Every time I try, it gets blocked."

"I've drafted a dozen messages," said Alber from the opposite sofa. "Telling them to fuck off back to their hole in the ground."

Ada stiffened. "A hole in the ground. They can't be…" She cut herself off, but I guessed her thoughts.

"The floor's made of adamantine," I said. "Trust me, nobody's getting in here."

She nodded but didn't look completely convinced. I didn't feel any safer in here than she did, especially not after the bomb.

"What happened to your arm?" Alber asked. I'd removed my jacket without thinking, revealing the wyvern scar on my forearm, and six curious Enzarian teenagers stared at me.

"I pissed off a wyvern." I flipped my arm over to show the other side. "They had to stitch me back together."

"Awesome."

Ada laughed. I half smiled at her. It was worth it to hear that sound, a reminder not everything decent in the Multiverse had gone.

We passed the rest of the evening in silence. Nell didn't even fuss over Ada's hands. I paced behind them, checking my communicator, wishing I could do something other than stay here and pretend not to hear the whispers from anyone who saw me.

"Walker…"

"His father…"

My hands clenched so hard on the communicator I almost snapped the covering off. I went to pace in the corridor instead, to calm my breathing down.

"Kay? You going to your room?"

I turned around to face Ada. "If we're on the mission, we'll have an early start tomorrow. If your hands are all right by then."

"I hope so. Nell gave me sleeping pills in case the magic burn keeps me awake. But last time it was gone in a few hours."

"We'll see what happens."

Her eyes said, *I won't be able to go on the mission, will I?* I didn't want to lie to her. I wouldn't go myself, but they might still have information we needed. I'd be a hypocrite to persuade her to stay behind. Was she any safer here than on Klathica?

"I'm sorry." I pushed the door to my new room open. "I never should have taken you back there with me."

"Don't worry." She gave a strained smile. "Place looked like a bomb hit it anyway."

We both cracked up. There wasn't much else to do.

"You owe me one," she said, between gasps of laughter.

"Yeah, I do."

Ada hugged me and rested her head against my chest. I didn't say anything, just ran a hand through her hair until all sounds faded away except her quiet, steady breathing. I didn't want to talk about Enzar, or Klathica, or the war. I just wanted her.

I wound my hands into Ada's hair and pulled her close to me. "About that favour."

A buzzing sounded, jolting me awake from dreams of battlefields and blood. I grabbed my knife before a second buzzing noise told me the noise came from my communicator in the pocket of my jacket. Ada lay curled up, asleep. The sleeping pills had knocked her out.

Guilt surged as I read the message telling me to report to the Klathican rep for instructions. I looked at Ada again. She'd be pissed at me later, but I'd do everything I could to protect her. Even if it meant leaving her behind. *I'm sorry.*

4

ADA

The magic burn had faded by morning, but Kay had already left. I'd been in too deep a sleep to notice. *I hope that wasn't goodbye.* Because he'd better be alive so I could berate him for leaving me to do the walk of shame through the Alliance's downstairs corridors. Luckily, not many people were around, because I wandered in circles for ten minutes before I found the right way back. Nell raised an eyebrow at my state of dishevelment as I finally walked into our shared room, but didn't comment. At least my hands were barely marked from the magic burn.

Once I'd showered and dressed, I went into the common room to grab some breakfast before sneaking out again. I wasn't in the mood to be stared at, not after what happened yesterday. Kay had never given his address to anyone outside the Alliance. Which meant someone must have been following him… or they'd got the information from Central itself.

Ms Weston had sent me a communicator message telling me I was excused from admin for the day, probably because I couldn't usually hold a pen while suffering from magic burn.

I hoped she hadn't told the council, because if they found out that just touching the sparks of magic from that bomb had incapacitated me, they'd find even more excuses not to let me on missions. I wasn't even on the patrol rota. Even though I didn't look like the other Enzarians, with my dyed-red hair and Alliance guard gear, I still drew too much attention for Carl to feel comfortable sending me close to Cethrax.

Short of begging my way onto a patrol, I had only one way to go offworld: visiting my brother. If I couldn't go to Klathica, I could at least talk to Jeth and see if he'd had any luck tracking where Enzar was broadcasting their messages from.

After telling Nell and Alber I was going to check in with my boss, I marched up to the third floor. Putting on my meekest expression, I knocked on the door to the council's room.

"Uh. Hi," I said, awkwardly. I didn't have to fake it. By the looks of things, I'd interrupted a meeting over coffee between Earth's and Valeria's council members. Mr Shean, Central's only surviving council member, spoke with Ms Greene, one of Valeria's council heads. "I hope I'm not interrupting something important. I wondered if I could use the doorway port to visit my brother on Valeria." I looked at my feet the whole time. For once, constantly being mistaken for younger than my age came in handy. I was a kid thrust into the middle of a war. At least, that's what the council thought. Lucky none of these guys had got close enough to see me fight.

"I can't send anyone offworld without paperwork," said Mr Shean.

"I'll sign something. I… I'm worried about Jeth. So's my mum."

I'd never called her 'Mum' in my life. Nell was Nell.

I tilted my head up and saw the council members

exchange glances. I wore my uniform, which spoiled the effect, but I knew I was the picture of innocence because I'd pulled the same trick on Nell a hundred times. Of course she never fell for it anymore.

"It's okay, never mind." I backed towards the door.

"Wait," said Mr Shean. "Your brother's at Valeria's headquarters, isn't he?"

I nodded. "Yeah, he's helping them. He went through the doorway port yesterday. He said he's staying on Alliance territory. It's safe there."

"As safe as anywhere," said Mr Shean, with a nod to Ms Greene. "I don't see why we can't permit a short visit. You were planning to check in with your colleagues, weren't you, Alexis?"

Greene fixed piercing eyes on me. "Yes," she said. "I suppose I can take Miss…"

"Fletcher." My heart sank as the council members exchanged glances and I almost heard their unspoken words. They all knew my real first name, all right.

"You'll have to leave your weapons behind, though. Ordinarily we allow them for security measures, but given the volatile nature of the substances being handled in the building…"

"I understand," I said quickly. *Oh, hell.* I hoped Greene was one of the good guys.

Relax. You're a walking weapon, for god's sake. They knew that even with the sweet-little-girl act.

But it worked. Within ten minutes, I once again stood on the threshold of the doorway port after signing some paperwork to prove I had permission to travel offworld. Greene watched me from the side. She didn't trust me. The feeling was mutual. We were reluctant allies in the war. Like everyone else.

The other side of the doorway port led into a corridor

lined with more doors, and a window overlooking the Valerian skyline. We were pretty high up, judging by the skyway wrapped around the building's side. Even in a crisis, Valeria's roads were as crowded as ever, hover cars stilled mid-flight at a red light. As we passed by, the light affixed to the building's side changed and the traffic moved again, hover cars and bikes gleaming under the bright-blue sky.

The inside of the corridor looked like any other Alliance building. Walls of black gleaming adamantine and polished floors, and fluorescent lights on the ceilings. Open labs were filled with odd-looking metal contraptions and staff members wearing black shell-like suits with visors over their eyes. Greene stopped by one of the doors and keyed in a code.

Another laboratory lay behind the door. Dr Helm sat behind the wheel of a half-visible car, floating in mid-air. Nearby, Jeth conferred with several others by a set of computers hooked up to one another. He'd pushed the helmet of his suit down, otherwise I wouldn't have recognised him.

"Ada?" he said, eyes widening. "What happened?" He hurried over, putting down the handheld device he'd been holding.

"Uh. Nothing. Just came to see you."

Luckily, Greene backed off so I could talk to Jeth alone.

"So," he said, dropping his voice. "What are you scheming?"

I grinned. He saw through the ruse right away. "I'm thinking I'm going to go mad if I don't get out of Central, ASAP. Not just here, but out there. Do you happen to have a spare Chameleon?"

"Yes, but…" Jeth glanced at the other tech guys. "I'm not sure it's a good idea you running around alone."

I sighed. "I've heard it a dozen times, Jeth. I wanted to be on that mission to Klathica. Keeping everyone safe… you know it's what I always wanted to do. It's why I joined the Alliance, and it's why I spent my whole life in the Passages. I belong out there, Jeth. It's always been dangerous."

He heaved a sigh. "Yeah. All right, Ada, you're not gonna get any more arguments from me. But you need a better way to defend yourself."

"Huh? Isn't magic enough?"

"We've been working on something new," said Jeth. "Your dagger's adamantine, isn't it? So if you use it on a magic-wielder, it suppresses their power."

"I guess it does." I hadn't really thought about it. "They're mostly designed for cutting down monsters, though, right?"

"Yeah. The thing is, it doesn't do you much good as a magic-wielder. You can't use magic at the same time. Not with the same hand, anyway. The adamantine handle would block it."

I hadn't thought of that, either. I'd never had reason to. One weapon was good enough to cut up a monster.

"Okay. You're thinking I need another weapon like the specially designed guns, right?" When I'd run out of bullets, I'd fired magic itself in its place. The magic gun had worked as a conduit—no, an amplifier. "Lustre?"

"Got it in one," said Jeth. "Valeria's donated theirs, and they managed to persuade Klathica to supply the Alliance with some of their source. Because amplifiers aren't much use on their own, nobody's really thought of using them in a weapon before. But think about it. Obsidiate's destructive enough in an Alliance stunner. Add lustre and it's twice as powerful without much adjustment."

"Yeah." I swallowed. *Nobody's really thought of using them in a weapon before…* Lawrence Walker had. If he'd even known what he injected Kay with as part of the experiment. Walker had tested every available source, and lustre happened to be the one that worked. Jeth had a point, though. Lustre wasn't a store of magic, and it could only amplify what was already there.

"We've had some success." Dr Helm hopped out of the car. "If the weapon makes contact with anything, it can be a conductor."

"You mean a power booster," I said.

An amplifier would have no effect on Cethrax's monsters, which had naturally magic-proof protection in their armour. It wasn't designed for that. We were talking weapons designed to kill humans—especially magic-wielders.

"Anyway," said Jeth, also looking uncomfortable, "that's what the weapons team are doing. But what *we're* doing—" He indicated Vic and Andy, the other tech guys who'd transferred from Central too—"is trying to amplify our tracker. We *think* we can get a read on suspicious activity which might tell us where Enzar is broadcasting from."

The messages. My brother had come here for my sake, after all. "Can you?" I asked. "You said the signal's untraceable."

"That's just it. *Nothing* is untraceable when you know what you're doing. And with magic sources, we can do anything. I think they're hiding the signal with a source."

My heart missed a beat. "You do?"

"Yeah, it's all I can think of. They've no shortage of magic sources over there on Enzar, right?"

"True, but I'm not sure that's where the signal is coming from. Enzar itself can't link to the Alliance worlds." The whole world was a war zone. They were most likely projecting from one of the worlds they had conquered.

"Not yet," said Jeth. "That's the issue. But I'm ninety percent sure they picked up our signal through Cethrax. Thairon's... well."

"Gone," I said quietly. He was right. Enzar must be

reaching us through Cethrax. It was impossible for the Alliance to close *all* their doorways—more of them opened every day. Accidental tears in the fabric of reality. The words of Robert Walker's journal came back to me. Maybe he was where this all started. And the first mission to Cethrax.

"Anyway, we'll keep an eye on it," said Jeth. "You'll be the first to know if we find a clue. We have something else in the works, too. Like your magicproof gloves, but even better."

"Yes, we do," said Dr Helm. "Your brother told me something of your… situation."

"Situation?" I blinked, confused.

"Your magic, and how it reacts to you when you're in an unstable magical environment," said Dr Helm. "We're making new uniforms, and your brother requested we make one especially for you."

"What kind?" I asked warily. There was only one reason I'd need a new uniform: for the war.

"An adapted version." Jeth grinned. "Helm's experimenting with altering the ratio of adamantine to sciras—how much you can put into synthetic fabric and have it still be effective. Thanks to—well, we took the materials worn by the… by Walker's servants."

The fake council members. They'd had adamantine protection like Stoneskins, but an enhanced version of guard uniform. My heartbeat drummed, and my palms went sweaty. I wasn't sure I wanted to have this conversation.

"You think something similar would stop magic reacting to me the way it does?"

"We hope to build it into your new uniform, with a barrier," said Dr Helm. "We're trying to find the right balance. We don't want to stop you using magic altogether, just stop it from being a danger to you and others."

"Yeah," said Jeth. "So you can fight. It's what you want, right? This time you'll be ten times as badass."

He was right. And if I did go to Enzar… if my power was muted… I could fight without ruining everything. I could fight for my world, not destroy it.

Fierce determination burned in my veins. "Damn right," I said.

"Not just that," Jeth added. "We're working on chameleon suits."

"What? Chameleon *suits?*"

"Yep. Don't tell anyone. Only Carl and the council at Central know, but we're hoping to use a cloaking device built into the uniform itself which mimics the Chameleon's effect for anyone who wears them, not just magic-wielders. There'll be an activation switch, and three times the battery life…" He and the others excitedly launched into a detailed explanation which mostly went over my head. Chameleon suits. Armour with magical protection. My mind whirled. I was certain the council would find excuses not to let me go to war anyway, but now I had an ironclad case. I'd go to my homeworld, and—

And what? Persuade my long-distance relatives not to blow up my home? I was an Ambassador, true, but I hadn't had the chance to put the few negotiating skills I'd picked up into practise. When it came to magic, there were no second chances.

Jeth stopped talking as Greene reappeared behind me.

"Your hour's up," she said. "You're not authorised to bring anything back to Central, by the way."

"I know," I said through gritted teeth. Did she really think I'd drive out of here in the invisible car or run off with the equipment?

I let her go ahead as Jeth beckoned me closer. "We're working on the new uniform around the clock. We'll get the custom made one to you, don't worry."

"Thanks," I whispered, fervently.

I walked into the corridor again. Greene's expression was wary. Maybe she'd overheard what Jeth and I had spoken about. That, or she'd seen me drop the sweet-and-innocent act.

Before I even considered going to Enzar, I needed to find out what might to be happening over there. I'd have to make sure I was more than ready before risking discovery. If the magebloods wanted me that badly, they must have a plan. Question was, what could we do to stop them with no connection to Enzar other than a few messages from an anonymous signal?

I parted ways with the council members and made my way back down to the shelter, jumping when a giant rainbow-coloured bird flew over my head in the entrance hall. Looked like the Alliance's rules on household pets had gone up in smoke. They didn't want offworld species flying around London and it was unsurprisingly difficult to persuade animals to use the doorway port, so they'd let some of the odd creatures from offworld stick around. I was happy to see they drew the line at griffins, though.

I stopped in the entryway of the recreation room as I spotted Alber talking to Cynthia and some other Enzarian teenagers. She'd sort of been my friend, before I'd joined the Alliance. Before her sister, Skyla, had betrayed us all and died for it, at Kay's hands.

I'd barely spoken to her since. She'd all but blamed me for her sister's death, and she'd be even angrier with me now the world she'd narrowly escaped was attacking Earth.

"They aren't gonna send us to war," said Alber to a younger kid of around twelve. "They just want to keep us safe. Central is the safest place in all London."

"Isn't Walker imprisoned here?" asked one of the older kids. "Isn't his son still walking around?"

I couldn't move. Nor could I catch Alber's eye.

"What, Kay? He's not a villain." Alber's tone was casual.

"You know him?" Now all eyes were on my brother.

"Yeah, he and my sister are madly in love. Trust me, no one could fake that. His dad's a dick, but Kay's on our side."

A rush of gratitude for my brother swept through me.

"Didn't he close our shelter down?" This time, the speaker was Cynthia.

"Nah, that was the Law Division. Some guys in suits." Alber shrugged. "Bound to happen eventually, right? That's what Nell said anyway."

"Nell said we're gonna get out of here, too," put in one of the other Enzarians. "I heard she broke in here once and took out all the guards."

"Oh yeah, that really happened," said Alber.

I almost didn't want to ruin Alber's moment of glory. But at that moment, he spotted me and waved. "Hey, Ada. Jeth's not managed to blow up the lab yet, has he?"

I caught the flash of guilt in his eyes. Maybe it was too soon to start joking about explosions.

"Nah," I said. "Though I don't think I could be around hover boots that long and not take them for a spin."

All the kids stared at me. "Hi." I opted for friendly, hopefully not freaking them out.

"You're Ada?"

"Yeah, that's my celebrity sister," said Alber, casual as anything. "She's saved the Earth too many times to count."

The stares were more curious than hostile, though Cynthia wasn't looking at me. *I can deal with a bunch of curious teenagers.* "Not exactly, but yeah. I wish I could get you guys out of here, but this is the safest place in London. Probably in the world."

"Awesome," said one of Alber's friends. "You used to sneak around the Passages, right? Any chance we could get in?"

"No way," I said. "Sorry, guys, it's way too dangerous. But if you want to join the Alliance guard when you're a bit older, just ask Carl. His office is upstairs, but you might want to get permission before going up there. Or speak to Kay, if he's around. He got me this job."

"Really?"

"Yeah. Tell you what, if anyone's interested in helping out if we need volunteers, they can speak to Kay and he'll put you right through to the guards. He's on a mission right now."

"See?" said Alber. "This is our chance. We're hanging with the Alliance guards now. We're at the centre of the Multiverse."

"Some of us just want to go home," Cynthia muttered, getting to her feet without looking at me.

Oh, crap. I quickly moved to walk alongside her. "Hey, Cynthia. Are you doing okay?"

"Same as anyone." She didn't meet my eyes, but her tone wasn't as unfriendly as the last time we'd spoken.

"We managed to get an Xbox in here," said Alber, from the sofa. "If we're gonna be under siege, might as well do it in style."

"This isn't a siege," said Cynthia, quietly, so none of the others could hear. "They're waiting, I know they are. They'll have a plan. Unless the Alliance attacks first."

"I don't know what the council are planning. I wish I did. I'm…" I looked around the room. "I'm trying to gather clues about their plans. For one thing, how did Enzar get a message right into the Alliance? If they have the technology, why would they do it now?"

"I have no idea," said Cynthia sharply. "I've been through the interrogation already. Do you not trust me? I'm not Skyla."

"I know." I swallowed, a lump rising in my throat.

"They closed all contact." Cynthia looked at her feet. "The people who used to work at the transition points are stuck on Valeria."

"A war almost started here. If we can end it, we can help them…" But things couldn't be the way they were before. Never again.

Looking at Cynthia's downcast eyes, I knew normal had ended for her when her sister died.

"Sorry," I said, ineffectually. "I never wanted this."

Cynthia shrugged, her expression hardening. "Sometimes I think I'd rather risk my neck out on the streets than stay here with her killers. With the people who experimented on kids for fun."

My heart plummeted. "The one who started the whole thing is in jail, and most of the Alliance want him executed."

Cynthia's gaze snapped onto me. "Walker."

"Lawrence Walker, yeah." I dropped my voice. "Nothing like those experiments will happen ever again. I can promise they won't."

"You really believe that?" Cynthia lifted an eyebrow at me. "I can't believe you'd defend the Alliance even with proof they were behind what happened to her."

"Not all of them," I said. "It'd be like blaming *us* for the war, which, by the way, a fair few people do. Me more than you," I added. "Besides, Enzar's not exactly guilt-free. They're the ones who—who gave me magic. They did that to me, same as…"

I trailed off, suddenly aware we weren't alone. Of course, I'd checked no one was close enough to listen in, but I still didn't know if I wanted the whole world to know what the Royals had done. Keeping it secret didn't seem to matter now my homeworld was on the doorstep, but there might still be spies. Not Cynthia. We might not have been close, but we'd had one thing in common: Skyla. She'd betrayed us both.

"I didn't believe her, you know," she said quietly. "I know she hated the Alliance, but I thought she ran off because she wanted her own space. She always used to argue with us."

"She did," I said. "I wish I'd known her better. But I didn't join up here to screw with you, I swear."

A pause, then she nodded. "I know."

I looked at the teenagers again. "I'll come talk to you guys later, okay?" I called to my brother.

"Sure thing, sis," said Alber.

The other Enzarian teens were younger than Alber. Up close, they weren't identical, though Enzarians tended to look pretty similar. Selective genetic breeding, according to Nell. After generations of war, both sides wanted the best warriors. If not for the difference in eye colour, magebloods and nonmages looked the same, too. Medium tanned skin, fair hair, eyes hidden behind contact lenses.

"Hey," I said. "I'm Ada."

"I know you," said the first girl. "Thanks for helping us back then… back in the Passages. I'm… Eva." The slight hesitation suggested she'd taken on a new name when she'd come here. Like I had, though Nell had chosen it. I didn't know the name Nell had been born with. She'd shed it along with her old life.

"Marie," said the other. "And we already know who you are…"

I relaxed inwardly when neither said my real name. "Yeah, I guess everyone does," I said, as if it was no big deal. "You aren't getting trouble from anyone else, are you?"

Marie shook her head, while Eva shrugged. "It's not too bad here. I preferred the shelter, of course, but it's better than the transition point. We were there five years."

"Five years?" I hadn't spent long there with Nell. Within a few months, we were on Earth. Sure, it took longer for some people to be placed, to have a new identity made, but I guessed we were a special case, because I was Royal, with a target on my head.

"Yeah, it wasn't that bad," said Marie. "I liked Earth, at first. I didn't think the fighting would come here."

"Neither did I." I tried to remember what I'd planned to ask. "So you were on Enzar... how long ago?"

"Seven years ago. We were eight when we left. Our dad went to fight in the war, and they got our mum." Eva's lip trembled. "We hid under the floorboards and got lucky, because our house was in the middle of nowhere. We crawled away, lived wild for a couple of days, and ran into a bunch of other civilians."

"Mageblood?" I asked, seeing Marie's eyes had a tint that meant they were purple under her light-blue lenses.

"I think they were." Marie shrugged. "I don't—I don't know who bombed our village. I think the magebloods did it."

I swallowed. "Why?"

She shrugged. "I don't know why they do anything. Maybe looking for the last Royal?"

"I... what?" My heart thudded, twice as fast as before, while adrenaline flooded me. "The last Royal?"

"Their missing warrior," said Marie. "It's something the others have been saying. The mageblood soldiers wanted to wipe out the last of the Royals, make sure they can't rule us again."

"The magebloods are winning," I said. "I heard. Is it true?"

"I dunno," said Eva. "No one's winning, far as I know. A lady came to our shelter last week, she said the mageblood leaders are looking for the source."

"Source?" I said, a little too quickly. "So—wait. The Royals don't have magic. Any of them, right?"

"Nonmages," said Eva. "The Royals are dead. But yeah,

they can't do magic. Some genetic thing. It's why they wanted to kill all the magebloods."

I'd heard similar stories from Nell. Magebloods had natural magic. Royals had none at all. But they had sources. I knew *that* much. I wished I'd paid more attention to the stories Nell had told me about the past.

"You can use magic?" asked Eva. "Can you teach us to do it?"

"I—I'm not a teacher." Anyone with mageblood heritage might have the natural ability, but I was the least likely person to be able to help them.

"You're a trained magic-wielder. For *Central*." Both of them stared at me with awed expressions.

"You're not old enough to fight." Not many people here were. Most were too young, old or injured, or taking care of children. "But I can talk to the others."

And yet... I *did* know some tricks that weren't common knowledge. Maybe I could help. At least I had a talking point now. I made my way through the Enzarians, gathering stories. Mostly, they confirmed what I already knew: the magebloods were at an advantage. No one had even seen the main family of Royals for years, but they'd planted bombs everywhere, and were fighting with "fearsome monsters of smoke and lightning".

So they were using kimaros, or living sources.

The image of the kimaros emerging from the shadows on Thairon came back. Magic trapped in a living form. Angry and destructive. According to the usual rules of the Multiverse, they shouldn't by rights exist, but they weren't the only creatures in the Multiverse capable of slipping into a semi-corporeal form, like a shadow. They also talked about magic-wielder soldiers, who apparently fought with both magic and technology. Nell had told me the Enzarian Empire had once thrived during times of stability, and had developed magic-based technology on a similar level to ours even without any connections to the Alliance. It'd been the bitter struggle between magebloods and nonmages that'd been the world's undoing. Even if Enzar survived the war, it'd take generations to rebuild what was lost. But the stories lived on, and I owed it to my home-world to remember. I hoped the other Enzarians would remember as well.

It never stopped being weird hearing about the Royals as though they weren't my family. The Enzarians here knew I was a magic-wielder, but not who I really was. The Royals had taken their secret to their graves.

Not just that. My suspicions kept coming back. Nell had told me magebloods and Royals didn't intermingle, but the Royals wouldn't have injected me with adamantine if they hadn't been certain it would work...

Oh no. Oh, god, no.

I got to my feet, scanning the room for Nell. She must be in our room.

"Where are you going?" Eva eyed me curiously.

"Sorry," I said. "Gotta talk to my guardian."

My mind whirled. *Why didn't I think of it before?* If nonmages had no magic at all, yet the experiment I'd undergone as a baby had turned me into a magic-wielder, I must have had the genetic potential from the beginning. It wouldn't have worked otherwise.

Which must mean I was part mageblood.

"Ada?" Nell half-stood as I ran back into the shared room, the door snapping closed behind me. "Is something wrong?"

I was tempted to laugh. *Everything's wrong.*

"Am I part mageblood?" I blurted. "Who *were* my parents?"

Nell stared at me. "What happened?"

"This doesn't add up." I sat on the bed. "I heard the Royals couldn't use magic—none of them could. Well, all nonmages. Does that include sources?"

"Why would you say that?" Nell fiddled with her hair. She hadn't swept it into its usual bun, and it straggled loose, revealing blond roots peeking through. She never talked about her life before Earth, only in general terms. It seemed no one's past was safe from resurfacing.

"That means yes," I said. "I knew it. The nonmages *have* sources, but they can't use them internally, only externally. So... so to do what the Royals did to me and for me to be able to use magic, it means I must be partly mageblood, right...?"

The breath stuck in my throat. Nell looked at me, for the first time, like the other Enzarians as we'd helped them to Earth. Like they still watched from behind the bars of a cage.

"That's the reason they kept mageblood slaves," said Nell, quietly.

Oh my god.

I swayed back on the bed, not sure if I was going to throw up or pass out. Or both. She didn't need to spell it out for me to grasp her history as the Royals' servant. But did that mean—?

I forced out the question—"You're not my blood mother?"

Not that it would make this ghastly mess any better if it was true.

Nell shook her head. "Your father instructed me to take care of you. I don't know what happened to either of your parents, but as I said... the palace was destroyed."

"So I *am* the last Royal?"

She bowed her head. With a twist of nausea, I remembered she'd once told me she was younger than me when she came to Earth. A twenty-year-old slave with a baby that wasn't hers, fleeing through the underground tunnels of Enzar.

"So the magebloods fought back with their own magic? Right?"

"They tried, but the magebloods knew the Royals had the upper hand because they'd claimed Enzar's main source. They needed more than magic, so they raided other worlds to build sophisticated weaponry."

Klathica sold them weapons, too. But that didn't explain the kimaros, and why Thairon had taken the magebloods' side. Maybe they'd traded as well.

"Weapons—you mean, stronger than the ones the Alliance has?"

"Maybe," said Nell quietly. "Given that the former council cut off all efforts to intervene in the war… they must have felt they had no choice."

Lawrence Walker thought he was defending Earth. I shoved that thought away. To think I'd once considered the Alliance untouchable. All-powerful.

Impulsively, I checked my communicator. No sign of Kay, and no other messages, either. Nothing to indicate whether the mission had been a success or a failure.

"You spoke to some other Enzarians, didn't you?" said Nell.

"Yeah. They said… they said they lived at the transition point for years." My old suspicions came back. "Is that normal? We skipped the line and came to Earth immediately because of me, didn't we? Did anyone else there know who I was?"

Nell shook her head. "I didn't dare tell anyone I held the last Royal, no. I pretended I was the one they chased. I blindfolded you, told them you'd lost your sight, so they wouldn't look at your eyes."

The lie had probably saved our lives. "How… how exactly did that work? You told me you smuggled me through from the palace."

"Before it burned to the ground," she said. "Yes, it's true. I'd already made arrangements for someone to meet us in the dungeons below the palace. I travelled through tunnels for two days. I was injured and barely conscious. Luckily, I met up with a group of others, who took care of you when I couldn't. If not for them, we'd both be dead."

I blinked rapidly as tears threatened to make an appearance.

"They led us through an underground tunnel, through to the Passages. To the transition point."

I cleared my throat. "And? What about the people there? I don't remember them." Obviously. When I'd helped people through the Passages, we'd always gone through Delta's family.

Delta's family. They'd wanted Enzar's power for themselves. They'd wanted me. But had they told anyone else? Or had our other allies been just like them, waiting to sell me to the highest bidder or use me as a weapon?

"No," I said, half to myself. "The people who smuggled me out... they weren't on the magebloods' side, were they?"

Nell drew in a breath. "Ada... I tried to explain, but the situation is far more complicated than the mageblood and nonmage struggle. Not everyone is involved directly in the conflict. The people at the transition point are dedicated to helping noncombatants escape. Is it really important which side they belong to, if you want to use such simple terms?"

"The magebloods want me dead. So would the Royals, if they knew I was still alive. Delta's family wanted to use me as a weapon to end the war on their own terms. The Enzarians... would they want me dead, too, if they knew what the Royals did to me? Some people here blame me, some don't, but I'll bet they'd hand me over in a heartbeat if they thought it'd end the war."

"They will not," said Nell. "Even if you were the nexus, it

wouldn't end the war, unless they used your power to raze all the worlds in the conflict to the ground. They understand that. The war is bigger than one world."

"So that's it." I clenched my hands in my lap. "I'm a freaking weapon all over again. Was the bomb someone threw at Kay's house meant for me?"

"Ada, if anyone here wanted to kill you, they'd be kicked out. They're angry, yes, but not enough to kill an unarmed girl."

"They know it wouldn't end the war. But the StoneKing seemed convinced I *could*. If I lied to everyone. Would the Royals… the magebloods… would anyone believe it?"

Nell hesitated. "I don't know who controls the Royals' armies now they are dead. It wouldn't surprise me if all the war's instigators were long-dead, too, and the rest fight on, because it's all they've known. They might latch onto an excuse to end it. A ceasefire…"

A ceasefire. After everything, I knew beyond any shadow of a doubt that just handing myself over wouldn't help. But the idea… just the idea of halting the fighting, so nobody else had to die, hung tantalisingly out of reach.

"Unbreakable," I muttered. "No offence, but you were way off the mark."

"I lied to you, Ada," she said, softly. "Adamantine was your birth name. I didn't name you myself."

My breath caught. It'd been my birth family who'd called me *unbreakable*. I didn't blame Nell for the lie. Not knowing the depth of the horrors she'd faced.

"At the transition point, I panicked, and registered you under the name *Ada* instead, but I told you your name as soon as you were old enough. I feared they would hunt you down if they knew the truth about you. And I feared word would make it back to Enzar—to the Royals. When the Stoneskins captured you, I thought the worst had happened.

Even though the magebloods are at an advantage, they would see you as a threat. Only days after our escape, the palace fell, and the Royal family scattered. There were no more children. You were the last of them, Ada. And that means… even if they don't know what you can do, the magebloods want you. You were supposed to be…"

"…the Royals' weapon. The magebloods knew the whole time. We are coming, Adamantine, you are ours. That's how they knew my name."

"They knew the symbol for *adamantine*," Nell corrected. "It's an ancient language. I translated your name to English, but the original language of the Royals was taken from one of the worlds they conquered. As I told you, the magebloods were the original inhabitants of Enzar, but no one knows where the Royals came from. Enzar's Empire once covered half the Multiverse. I never learned much of history at the palace. They told us only that they were the rightful rulers."

And the magebloods would probably have taught a version of history where they were the cruelly oppressed rising to take back what was theirs. Two worlds living in one, and they'd wrecked half the Multiverse.

"They know who I am," I said. "They'll stop at nothing to find me. But that doesn't mean I should hide." I took in a breath. "Jeth and the tech team are making me a new uniform, and it'll stop magic overreacting to me. And it turns invisible. A disguise. The way things are going, they'll attack Earth again. Or one of the other allied worlds. This is who I am, Nell. You know it is. Half the reason I even went into the bloody Passages was to fight things."

Once the words started, they didn't stop. And yet every breath came lighter. Like I was finally unpacking the secrets I'd stored in the darkest, most self-centred part of my heart. All the times I'd gone into the Passages, my mind had always been half-trained on the magic, on the spark in the air, the fire in my blood. The echo of the other lives I might have led. Even then, I'd feared I was like my blood family after all. But I had a choice.

Nell watched me. Silent. Not judging. "Anyone from Enzar will have orders to capture you, not kill you."

"The whole Multiverse wants to get their paws on me. Unless I *die*, I'll never be safe." I looked her in the eyes. "I want to fight for Enzar, and for me."

Slowly, she nodded. "Then fight."

5

KAY

Klathica's main Alliance headquarters appeared no worse the wear for the war. The doorway port opened into a wide meeting room decorated in glass and chrome. Several Alliance members were on the mission, along with Iriel, the only one of the group I'd met before. Two were Klathican, but were skilled in espionage, apparently even against their own original homeworld. I carried a tracker and briefly amplified it to see if there were any nearby sources, just in case any of Walker's people were lurking around. On Klathica, magic was on a high enough level that running into kimaros was more likely than on Earth. On the plus side, with my amplified tracker, I'd know right away if one of *those* creatures was following me.

Someone must have given orders to the one I'd found outside my flat yesterday. My father claimed to have been able to control them because they were creatures made of pure magic, and his antimagic servants intimidated them into serving him. They'd come from Klathica. Even if Walker hadn't ordered the attack on my flat, this was probably the least safe allied world aside from Earth. It didn't help my paranoia that over fifty percent of the population here were plugged into simulators most of the time.

We passed by two mechas—guards stationed at each door, human-shaped with guns built into their hands. They weren't alive; they'd been built in a lab. KimaroTech labs, to be exact. We crossed a glass bridge over to another steel-framed building, wrapped in wires. Klathican sim-tech. Even with a war on the horizon, most of the population remained immersed in virtual havens, which became even more evident when we boarded the drone, a giant bullet-shaped hovercraft-type transport. Last time I'd been here, in the main road, the gleaming strip dividing the city, mechas walked alongside the elite in their sharp suits. Now, barely a soul was on the streets.

The drone landed on a roof and we disembarked, ready to sneak into KimaroTech's lab. One of the guards indicated it was time to activate the Chameleons. Their battery life had been extended since more lustre had been added, but I didn't have to worry about it, because my own amplifier could last indefinitely. Hopefully, nobody would notice when I slipped away.

I'd wanted to look around the labs, but more than that... this was the place Lawrence Walker had come after returning from Thairon. Lilian Greyson, whoever she was, had been entrusted with KimaroTech when Walker went off to Thairon and ended up imprisoned there. If anyone knew if Walker was still plotting against the Alliance, she might.

Another labyrinth of meeting rooms awaited. Here, KimaroTech made enhancements, from cyberware to implants on the less-than-legal side. On the occasion where Alliance laws clashed with a homeworld's laws, that world's laws generally won out. Besides, it was a given that as soon as an enhancement was on the market, there'd be fake ones a street corner away. Often with fatal side-effects.

"Kay, what are you doing?" Dammit. I forgot the Klathicans on the mission had enhanced hearing and had picked up on my retreating footsteps even though I was invisible.

"There's something I need to check out," I said. "Ms Weston's orders."

"It's true," said Iriel, jumping in. She'd probably figured I intended to sneak off. I didn't particularly want any of them to be around when I went to find Lilian Greyson. And I had words of my own to share with the woman who might have been the one to authorise the experiment.

"Be back here at our assigned time," was all the Klathican said. "And don't wander too far off route. Remember: we don't adhere to the same rules as Earth."

Didn't I know it.

As the others left, I headed right. I'd already memorised the map. The others were supposed to look around the labs, not talk to the President of KimaroTech appointed by my father, but she knew my name, if nothing else.

My skin prickled, and I glanced over my shoulder. No one here. Where were the guards? Klathica was meticulous with security. Had the others caused a diversion to make sure nobody bothered us?

I reached a corridor with a glass window in place of a wall, offering a panoramic view of the city—and a bright red streak reflected in the glass.

Blood.

The trail led around the corner to a door, which lay slightly open. Paranoia dug its claws into me—*what if someone's trying to frame you?*

No. Whoever had done this surely didn't know we were coming. Ms Weston alone at Central knew about the mission. And definitely not the Klathican council, though they'd flip a lid when they found out. The Ambassadors had volunteered on their own.

Who...?

I eased the door open, making as little contact with it as possible.

The scene hit my eyes like a punch. Blood—a lot of it—and bodies, heaped on the desk. The metal floor gleamed red. I stared, transfixed, for a long moment. Then I made myself focus on the details. They'd been stabbed, multiple times. I nudged the nearest guard with my foot. The mecha's neck had been snapped clean, and judging by the amount of blood on the inbuilt knife in place of a hand, it was the murder weapon. Of course, it *looked* like the mecha had killed the other humans in the room. But they had no will of their own. Had someone reprogrammed it?

I made myself step towards the carnage. My heart beat so loudly, it'd give me away if any of them were still alive. But they weren't. A woman lay at the centre, sprawled across the desk, blood spattered across her name badge: Lilian Greyson.

ADA

By midday, Kay hadn't come back, and though I knew he was more than capable of handling himself in a fight, I couldn't get the latest close call out of my head. The more I thought about it, the more convinced I became that someone in the Alliance had thrown the bomb at us. Someone already on Earth. What chance did we stand against a world-conquering empire if we kept fighting amongst ourselves?

My communicator buzzed in my pocket. I opened it with shaking hands, expecting another message from Enzar. Instead I found an alert from Carl telling all available guards to come to the office. My heart sank. I wasn't on the guard rota. That he'd sent the message to me either meant they had a shortage, which left Central vulnerable, or something serious was happening.

I found a group assembled in the entrance hall, both Earth guards and offworlders. Carl waved me over with a grim expression.

"There's been an attack," he said. "In the Passages. The guards have requested backup."

"Shit. Is it… them? Enzar?"

"It's more likely to be Cethrax. If you want to stay behind—"

"No, I want to fight." I sent Nell a quick message warning her I'd be back in an hour at most. I should have guessed Cethrax would strike again. Even though the Alliance had blocked the hidden Passage while they tried to determine which part of the territory had been linked to Thairon, Cethrax had hundreds of doorways, and new ones opened every day. Short of torching the entire planet, there was no way to ensure that world wasn't linked to Enzar. *Of course it is.*

I hurried to the changing rooms to put on my guard gear, my heart pounding. I still hadn't heard from Kay. If he wasn't joining the guards, the mission must have run overtime. Or something had gone wrong.

Our group left Central to shouts and camera flashes. Apparently we were a tourist attraction. I supposed to outsiders, the guards looked like a cross between the military and a biker gang, and I was seized with the bizarre desire to laugh at the camera-wielding people pressed up against the gates. Life went on for the rest of the world, even as all hell broke loose elsewhere.

Carl shot the clamouring tourists an irritated look. "Ignore them. We need to get this done."

We ran down the side road to the Passages, where the door was open wide. I felt the rising magic level even through the magicproof gloves, and wished Jeth had finished my new suit already. We were operating on borrowed time, and I didn't dare consider going onto Enzar again without more protection.

The Passage entrance was a haze of red smoke. I blinked the glare from my vision as the guards spread out alongside me, looking for the source. Down the corridor, a volley of sparks ricocheted off the ceiling. It wasn't Cethrax attacking, but more kimaros. Smoke revealed at least six lion-sized beasts fighting the guards. *Damn.* Close quarters was the worst place to fight them without risking magic burn or worse, and you couldn't cut into them with a dagger, even an adamantine one. Lightning flared above them, mingling with sparks from the stunners.

I fired my own stunner and sent one creature tumbling, writhing, collapsing into smoke. The magic level was higher than ever, even in the Passages, and my skin buzzed underneath the glove as my stunner fired. In here, with Enzar potentially watching, I wouldn't dare to use my magic to its full extent.

"How'd so many of them get in here?" Carl yelled through the fog.

"They appeared out of nowhere!" someone shouted back.

"They do that," I said. "They're like Cethrax—they can even get through closed doors." I was willing to bet that was how the one outside Kay's flat had found us yesterday. Question was, had someone set these creatures loose? Or were they flocking to Earth because of the rising magic level?

The smell of burning filled the Passages as the guards surrounded two of the creatures, bringing them down with coordinated attacks. I gritted my teeth and fired magic through my stunner rather than my hand, reeling it in so the magic wouldn't rebound off the Passage walls. I hit the creature on the right while the other two guards brought down the one on the left. Magic sparked from my stunner again, and the beast hissed, shrinking in on itself as it realised it was cornered. I finished it off and ran to join the others.

A collective explosion of stunner-sparks took care of another kimaros. The guards had brought down two others, but the last one slipped through their grasp, climbing the walls like a giant smoky red spider. I jumped, firing my stunner at it, and missed. The shot bounced off the ceiling and I held my breath, but it didn't strike anyone. I fired at it again, driving the kimaros back towards Carl. Between the two of us, we fired our stunners and the creature exploded into smoke and sparks.

I stood back, blinking the glare of red from my vision.

"There might be more," said Carl, pointing down the corridor.

Sure enough, we found the smoky remains of another kimaros a corridor away from one of the staircases down to the lower levels. Even though Cethrax's doors had been closed, I wasn't sure the Alliance *could* keep them out for long.

"That's where it came from," said a guard. "Up the stairs. Too fast for anyone to catch."

My heart thudded against my ribs as another wave of magic made my skin tingle all over. A deafening crash shook the Passages, and the air vibrated with the echo of an explosion. I leaned against the wall, my ears ringing. The guards were shouting, but I didn't hear a word. Everyone ran down the corridor, and I joined them, skidding to a halt at the corridor's end.

Guards had gathered by what had once been a staircase leading down to the Passage where, at the other end, lay the hidden door into London, the one near my old house. *The hidden Passage.*

The shouts became distinguishable. "Get away from there!" someone yelled.

"That's why you don't bring Earth tech into the Passages," another voice said.

"What happened?" I asked repeatedly. Guards hemmed me in on either side, preventing me from seeing into the hidden Passage downstairs. *I thought the noise came from upstairs!*

"Get over here!" yelled an irate-sounding Carl. "Earth's guards, come here."

No wonder the place seemed so crowded. Most of the guards weren't from Earth. Some were Valerian, while some bore the cybernetic implants of Klathican guards. I recognised Simon, Kay's friend, amongst a group of guards from Earth's other Alliance branches.

"Hey! Ada." Simon waved me over.

"What in the Multiverse is going on?" My head rang from the impact of the noise. "Did something explode?"

"Some dingbat decided to fire a gun in the lower Passages," Simon told me.

My jaw dropped. "*That's* what it was?"

"Yeah. Whoever shot that gun managed to block Cethrax's hidden Passage. The whole ceiling collapsed."

"Earth's guards!" Carl bellowed. "Stop obstructing the corridors and get over here. Now."

That was when the second explosion went off. I pressed my hands to my ears as panic erupted down the corridor, and I swore my eardrums fractured as the sound of metal on metal filled the whole Passage.

"What was that?" I gasped.

"It came from upstairs," said Carl, his voice muted oddly

by the echo of the explosion. "There's someone on the second floor."

My blood turned to ice. The second floor was supposed to be closed off, forever.

It has to be them. Enzar.

6

———

KAY

I didn't dare touch anything in the office. Not the bodies, not the mecha lying broken by the door with the murder weapon in its hands. The last thing I needed was to be framed. *Could Walker have ordered someone to kill Lilian Greyson?* I didn't have a clue. It was a messy job, like it had been done in a hurry. I might have more than a fundamental grasp of Klathican tech, but I sure as hell didn't know how to work one of their robots.

The sensible thing would be to call the police, only I wasn't even supposed to be here. The trail of blood was pretty conspicuous. It hadn't been here long. The murders must have happened at most hours before we'd arrived.

Why did no one check? Even if they killed all the guards, other people work here.

I left the room. Further searching confirmed someone had stopped all the elevators, external and internal. Down for maintenance, apparently. The killer had covered their traces. *How did they get out?* More to the point, it shouldn't have been so easy to sneak in. Unless *all* the guards—the mechas—were compromised.

77

I had to find the others on the mission. Now.

On the way downstairs, I considered my options. I hadn't expected Lilian Greyson to talk, but finding her *dead* brought me up short. Walker had appointed her as the President himself. Killing her made no sense, especially in such a conspicuous fashion. With the obvious exception of Thairon, when Walker wanted to take care of an opponent, he used subtle means and connections which would make it impossible for anyone to trace the deaths back to him. Unless he felt he had nothing to lose now the Alliance knew him for a traitor. I sure as hell couldn't think of anyone else with a motive. Except me, of course, but not only did I have no clue whether she'd been the one to actually authorise the experiment, nobody else knew about that aside from Ms Weston. The setup looked suspicious, and Walker *had* known I was coming here. *Damn. I should never have spoken to him yesterday.*

One floor down, and I reached the lab. Unlike Valeria's, the walls weren't reinforced with adamantine. Antimagic was relatively rare here, because their Alliance had opted to trade other sources instead. They didn't want to lock magic out like Earth did. They wanted to embrace it.

The source pulsed in my own blood. Lustre. An amplifier. Walker didn't know it had worked. But who did know? Were those scientists in Lilian Greyson's offices behind the whole thing, or someone else? Did it matter? Now they were dead, I'd probably never know.

My communicator buzzed, and I jumped, cursing under my breath. A message from Iriel: "We're on the roof. Come here. You're late."

Relief flooded me. They were alive. But the message didn't say whether they'd seen the murdered scientists, or any mechas acting suspiciously.

Wait. I'd forgotten I carried the tracker. I hadn't picked up on any traces on the floor where the murders had taken place, but I could track any magic-wielders if they were hiding like I was. Iriel was one, but she was too far out of range. The killers might not have used magic—you didn't need it to reprogram a mecha. I reached into my pocket to amplify the tracker, and found no response. No other magic-wielders nearby, then.

I made for the stairs, and stopped dead when the sound of metal striking metal rang through the building. A whirring came from outside the wall-length window which ran the length of the corridor. A bullet-shaped drone flew by, unsteadily. Its tail-end hit the opposite building's steel façade with another crash. Its swaying motion brought it right into the glass window. I raised my arms to shield my face as glass shattered over the corridor's floor. The drone's side scraped along the building, giving me a close-up view of Kimaro-Tech's logo.

The tracker reacted, magic buzzing under my skin. *There's a magic-wielder on the drone.*

I ran for the remains of the window, throwing myself at the drone-copter's side entrance as it brushed against the building's side. I hung on, fingers scraping metal, and inched along the edge as the drone veered to the side. The exterior panels had the slightest gaps between them, enough for me to wedge my fingers in and turn into handholds. I held onto the side of the hatch, gritting my teeth as the cold air whipped against my face. It took two attempts to one-handedly wrench open the side hatch and throw myself inside.

I landed on top of something solid—a person. My feet caught him in the face, and he yelled, falling several feet down the interior corridor as the drone tilted again. I grabbed him by the throat. "Talk," I said.

He cursed at me in a Klathican dialect and his hand spasmed, a gun protruding from his sleeve. Typical—he'd got one of those stupid enhancements. I went for his weapon hand with my free one, magic sparking from my fingers, and zapped him so he let go of the trigger.

"Now we're on the same page—" I squeezed on his throat, harder—"Who do you work for?"

"Nobody!"

"Yeah, right." Too bad sarcasm didn't work in Classical Klathican. "Did you steal this drone?"

"I had orders."

"From whom? KimaroTech?"

Outside of the logo on the drone's side, it looked like a transportation drone carrying supplies from one side of the city to the other.

"No…"

"What's inside this drone?" I asked, giving him room to breathe for a second. "Did *you* kill the president of KimaroTech?"

He shook his head.

"Fine. Then why did you hijack the drone?"

"I didn't mean to," he gasped. "We're dying on the streets, they needed hired help."

"Who the hell is *they?*"

"They're not… human. But… they have magic. Of a kind. They're made out of armour."

The Stoneskins? Impossible. They were dead.

Not all of them died.

"Which world did they come from?"

"They spoke Classical fluently."

Thairon? Had to be. So some of them had survived the fight. But how did they get here?

The drone tilted sideways with a scraping noise as it connected with another reinforced steel building side.

"What are you doing with this drone?"

"Nothing," he said, in a suspiciously calm voice. I looked

down at his eyes, which had gone oddly glazed. Like… a sim-addict.

Damn.

I drew my gun and shot him in the leg. He dropped his own weapon, and I kicked it away. I punched him on the jaw hard enough to make his eyes roll back in his skull, and ran for the nearest door. The engine room would be at the front, but it might be set to steer on automatic. It had to be, otherwise we'd have already crashed. But I was sure I heard something like voices beneath the deafening noise of the drone's path.

A choked scream came from in front. I ran towards the source, rounded a corner, and was greeted with carnage. Bodies lay heaped beside a collection of crates, and a mecha stood in the centre, his knife-arm impaling a man in what had once been a protective shell-suit. Most of it had been ripped from his body, and the mecha didn't look at me as he tore his hand free. The man fell back, already dead.

The mecha was one of their newer models, with one knife-hand and one normal one. It hadn't seen me yet, but I'd turned invisible. *Someone programmed it. Like the one that killed Lilian Greyson.*

I turned off the invisibility and amplified the sciras instead, grabbing my own knife with the other hand. Magical bullets would probably bounce off it, but Alliance daggers could cut through almost everything, and the mecha's exterior looked like ordinary metal to me.

First, I threw a handful of magic. The first-level shot bounced off its arm, but allowed me to get within close range. I ducked under the knife and stabbed its hand right through the vein—or wire. Its hand fell limp to its side, exposing the mechanisms inside. I stabbed upwards with my own knife, cutting through the metal coating. Sparks exploded outwards and I dropped to the ground, shielding my face. Luckily, the sleeve of my coat kept them from me. It was run on a magic source, all right. The mecha's knife hand came down again, but I'd already rolled out the way, my own weapon poised to sever the wires poking from its neck. It fell in a clatter of sparks.

At the same time, a buzzing noise kicked up. A smokelike lion-sized shape materialised before my eyes, hissing, sparking. A kimaros. Figured.

"Don't suppose *you'd* like to tell me who you're working for?" I said to the kimaros. Of course, it didn't respond.

I grabbed my magic-gun, sending a wave of magic towards the kimaros. The drone jerked to the side as I hit the kimaros, sparks striking the walls. My next attack hit the creature dead on, and it exploded in a shower of sparks.

The drivers—humans—were dead. Which meant this drone would run on automatic until it ran out of steam or crashed. Probably in the middle of the ocean. Unless they had a target they wanted to take out.

Footsteps, then a groan came from behind me. The guy I'd knocked out was back, and he yelped at the sight of the bodies. Not completely addled, then.

"Who do you work for?"

The guy gave me a blank look.

"What are your orders?"

He strung a series of disconnected syllables together that made no sense to me. Like mangled Klathican dialect.

"Tell me," I said, in Klathican, "where are you taking this drone?"

He limped forward, his leg bleeding where I'd shot him. Lucky for him I hadn't fired magic into that bullet. His movements alerted me to an open crate at the side, which contained a block of a familiar-looking black metal-like rock. From here, I sensed the signal pulsing from it. Looked like obsidiate, the most volatile of magic-based substances. If the drone crashed, the sources would collide, and *damn.* The consequences would be worse than if a bomb like the one that had hit my apartment exploded. Especially it if went anywhere near an Alliance or KimaroTech building.

"Where the hell are we going?"

"The... Alliance."

The drone tilted sideways, and the screech of metal filled the air.

"Shit." I ran for the engine room, though I had no clue how to steer one of these things. The closest I'd come was flying an Earth plane in simulation, and one look at the controls told me they were nothing alike.

The drone tilted backwards, and I hung onto the metal chair as the end pointed towards the sky. Swearing, I grabbed for the steering controls, but succeeded only in losing my hold and falling head over heels into the wall. I half-fell into the pilot's seat. The other man crawled after me.

"There's a doorway entrance." He pointed, eyes dilated with panic. "Up there!"

I couldn't see anything, but the view from the front was tilted, and at least I'd managed to steer the drone out of range of the buildings.

I got my hands on the controls and tilted the drone upwards. Whether he was right or not, aiming for the sky would stop us from crashing into the high-rise buildings.

The buildings outside vanished, and the screech of metal reached a new pitch. Hell—those weren't building walls. They gleamed blue, and the noise came from both sides. We'd passed through a doorway into the Passages.

Now we were in trouble. I swore and hit the controls, but nothing made it slow down. The jolting motion sent me crashing into the ceiling. The drone moved too fast for me to control. Where in hell were the brakes? Not that I could hear a thing outside the deafening scrape of metal. As the noise grew louder, I did the only thing I could think of—I fired magic directly into the engine's wires.

The wires snapped, sparking, and I was forced to throw myself behind the door again. The drone's progress slowed to a crawl, and stopped altogether.

I peeled myself off the ceiling, swearing. Everything ached, though I'd be much worse if I didn't have the uniform. How had I ended up in this mess? Klathica was going to kill me. That is, if they didn't blame *me* for Lilian Greyson's murder.

I retrieved the obsidiate and pocketed it. With difficulty, I crawled to the other crates. I activated the tracker, but I didn't sense any other sources.

"Tell me," I said to the other man, who lay in a groaning heap in the corner. "Where are your other weapons?"

"Not here. This drone was... a decoy."

"To damage the Alliance's morale? You know you'd probably have died in the process?"

That left the question of who had murdered the head of KimaroTech. And what else they planned to do. At best, people would have been killed on impact if this thing had collided with an Alliance building.

The man groaned. "They were in my head..." And he slumped over, unconscious.

"Great." I pulled my communicator out and found to my surprise it was intact. *Good.* I fired off a message to Earth telling them what had happened. Klathica was at risk. I bloody hoped this was the extent of it and nobody else had fallen under the kimaros's influence, because Klathica's military was one of the most advanced in the allied worlds. Definitely not an enemy we wanted to be facing with Enzar and Cethrax already threatening us.

I crawled back to the hatch, dropping to the ground alongside the drone. The wide corridor just about accommodated the drone, but there didn't appear to be any guards around. It seemed weirdly quiet, actually. Far too empty. I must be disoriented from getting banged about in the drone, because I knew the Passages.

Wait. I was on the second floor. I hadn't even known Klathica had a door here. Doors 60-70… I was near the stairs down to the Enzar Passage.

My skin chilled. I wanted out of here, but I didn't want to leave the drone lying around. I put another message into my communicator. I had to warn the Alliance.

The stairs were unguarded on this side, but when I tried to climb down, I was thrown backwards with a jolt that went through my bones. My back hit the wall, pain shooting up my spine. Bloody magic shield. Probably made of obsidiate. Just what I needed. I was trapped behind whatever barrier the Alliance had put up to stop anyone getting to the second floor. How to break the boundary down without letting whatever might be behind those doors onto Earth?

A minute or so passed. I glared at the barrier. "Hilarious," I muttered. The one time the Alliance's security system was functioning and I managed to get myself stuck behind it. It felt like even Enzar was laughing at me.

Enzar. Doors 63-9, according to the file I'd memorised months ago. Door 65 led to the transition point. To the place where Ada and her former friend met people and took them through the Passages to Earth. There was nothing on the other side but a tunnel leading to a shelter. The freezing-cold breeze of the Passages swept over me as I paced in that direction, stopping beside Door 65. The door was closed, but something seeped through the cracks. Magic?

No. That wasn't magic, but antimagic. The cold touch of a drained source. Someone had sealed the door, all right… by sucking the magic right out of it.

Footsteps. I whirled around. They came from the stairs, and sure enough, two guards appeared behind the barrier.

"Kay, what in the world are you doing here?" Iriel's voice echoed through the Passages.

Carl followed her, staring at the drone in horror. "What in god's name did you do, Kay? What is it with you and bringing classified transport into the Passages?"

"It was going to crash into Klathica's Alliance headquarters. I had to do something." My hands curled into fists. "Someone reprogrammed a mecha to slaughter people in KimaroTech. Lilian Greyson's dead. They hijacked this drone. A kimaros was controlling them."

"Impossible." Every drop of colour had drained from Iriel's blue-tinted face. "Impossible."

"It's true." As much as I wished it wasn't.

Carl gaped openly at me. It was the first time I'd actually rendered him speechless.

"Are those doors all sealed?" I asked Carl.

"They were supposed to be." Carl shook his head, appearing to recover himself. "Where exactly on Klathica did you come from? Through which doorway?"

"Very good question. That guy—" I indicated the prone form of the man who'd followed me out of the drone—"Told me there was a doorway when I was driving this drone to stop it crashing into the Alliance's place. I didn't think these ones were open."

"Apparently someone forgot to check that one," muttered Carl.

"I'll have words with their security team," said Iriel.

"You didn't find anything in KimaroTech when you searched?" I asked. "The executives were all murdered by mechas. They were reprogrammed."

Iriel shook her head. "It would explain why we saw so few of them. We searched the labs and there was nobody around, and no sources, either. We got an alert from Klathica's Central Headquarters that they were sending people in. That's why we left. I hoped you were behind us. Sorry we left you behind. I figured you were invisible, so you'd be able to hide until you could get back to the Embassy."

"Never mind that," I said. "I found a kimaros on the drone, but it was taking orders from someone for sure."

"A kimaros couldn't have killed Lilian Greyson," said Iriel. "I don't think anyone really *liked* the woman, but nobody—nobody would have dared kill her. What exactly did you see?"

"She and all her staff were stabbed," I said. "A mecha was there at the scene, covered in blood and holding a knife. I'm sure someone framed it. Reprogrammed it to murder all her staff. But I didn't dare touch anything in case it implicated me in her death. We weren't even supposed to be there."

"No, you weren't," said Carl, an irritated expression crossing his face. "Your drone will have to wait. Some of the novices decided to run into Cethrax's tunnel."

"Of course they did," I said.

"Kay!" yelled a voice. Ada ran towards us, followed by Simon of all people. "What—what's going on?" Her gaze went from me to the corridor behind me, her expression somewhere between dread and relief at seeing me alive.

Oh, shit. Enzar. "It's not them," I said quickly. "The leader of KimaroTech was murdered, most likely by the same person who hijacked a drone carrying sources and set a kimaros loose on it. They also reprogrammed two mechas and framed them for both crimes."

Ada took a step back. "And…. and you crashed the drone? How'd it even get in here?"

"A doorway," I said. "In the sky. The drone was meant to hit their Alliance headquarters. I killed the kimaros… but who was it taking orders from?"

7

ADA

"It's stable." Zan Izen glared at the rest of us from across the table in Central's meeting room.

"Don't be ridiculous." Ms Weston had taken the council meeting in hand. "Klathica is plainly *not* stable. The president of KimaroTech was murdered."

"And the perpetrators have been taken care of. We are making every effort."

There was an awkward moment where everyone tried hard not to look at one another or let our thoughts show on our faces. I mean, Izen wasn't convincing anyone he had the situation under control. Even me, and I knew less than anyone in the room about offworld security. Klathica was conspicuously absent from the meeting apart from Izen, as they were busy investigating the murders and the fact that one of their sky doorways was open when it shouldn't be. At the head of the table sat Mr Shean, the only surviving member of Central's original council, who wore a grey line down the centre of his face as a souvenir from his narrow escape from being turned into a Stoneskin.

"Have you switched off your simulators?" Kay asked Izen.

He'd not even bothered to disguise his impatience throughout the meeting. Apparently a major murder wasn't enough to issue a state of emergency warning throughout the other Alliance worlds—mainly because the people who'd hijacked the drone were dead, and so there was no proof of the killer's motives. There were no other survivors on the premises who knew what happened. The enemy had slipped in and out of KimaroTech's headquarters like a ghost.

Like Kay himself. He'd scared the crap out of me, crashing that drone in the Passages, but the alternative might be much worse. He'd been lucky to escape with a few scratches and an earful from Carl—though the nitwit who'd fired a gun in the lower Passages had ended up in more trouble. Besides, we had bigger problems. The leader of Kimaro-Tech had been murdered. And Kay had found the body. Whether it was a setup or not, the whole scenario stank of foul play. Thankfully, Earth's council stood behind us, because Izen seemed set on blaming Kay for the incident because he'd been trespassing on Klathica. Only the fact that Kay's DNA hadn't been found on any of the bodies had kept them from arresting him—though the dark expression on Kay's face told me he had a theory he didn't want to share with the council. I could guess. Lawrence Walker had ordered someone to throw a bomb at us on Klathica only a few weeks ago. But it was way beyond me to figure out the motives of a genocidal madman.

"KimaroTech had a traitor planted in them," said Kay. "A company-wide shutdown of all your security during the murder can't be a coincidence."

I'd guessed why Kay had really wanted to go on the mission, after he'd mentioned looking for the President, who Lawrence Walker had appointed himself. He'd wanted answers about the experiment, and now the one person who might have told him the truth was dead. But hell, maybe there'd been a bug inside the organisation. Or a hornet's nest. Whatever the cause, Lilian Greyson was dead, leaving half of Klathica in a state of shock and the Alliance scrambling to find out who did it. I had a dozen wild stabs at theories, all of them linked to Enzar, but no evidence to back them up. Kay himself had mentioned the man on the drone had described the person who'd ordered the attack in a manner similar to the Stoneskins, but the guy had been addled at the time, and Klathica's own police wore similar enhanced armour.

The idea of the Stoneskins being alive chilled me as much as the notion of Enzar being *there,* on our neighbouring world, a hair's breadth away from Earth.

"How dare you," said Izen. "The president of our most esteemed company is dead, and still you accuse us of conspiracy?"

"I'm accusing no one," said Kay. "I'm trying to establish what happened to make one of KimaroTech's staff reprogram their mechas into turning on the president."

"Clearly, we were betrayed," said Izen. "I'd worry about your own security first. Did I hear there are rumours of spies inside Central?"

Not again. "No, there aren't," I all but snapped at him. "There are rumours about all sorts of crap. People are panicking."

"But there *is* a spy," said Izen. "We're getting those messages, too, to all our Alliance branches."

My blood froze. *Don't.* I'd wanted to get answers about the murder, not be scrutinised because of those ridiculous rumours again.

Ms Weston gave him a sharp look. "Enzar's attempts to contact Ada are her business only."

"She was affiliated with offworld transition points," said Izen. "They're a likely site for spies from her homeworld, aren't they? Isn't that how the Campbell family's smuggling operation functioned, right in front of Valeria's Alliance?"

"Do *not* bring us into it," said Greene. "Those transition points are empty and closed off. There is no communication network there."

"They wanted to *avoid* the Alliance," Kay added. "Not to mention the Campbells got their weapons from Klathica originally, if you want to point fingers at one another."

"The Campbells." Izen turned to him. "Wasn't their attack some kind of revenge crusade for restrictive trade laws?"

"Not just that." I shivered as I recalled Delta's father's calm expression as he'd told me his insane plan. "They said Enzar was capable of taking out the Alliance, so they intended to build a weapon to oppose them."

"Yeah," said Kay, "they got the parts for the bomb from Klathica, one at a time, so it wouldn't appear suspicious. It's all in the reports from last August."

"Yes," said Izen, "we do have those reports. None of them mentioned Enzar... except..."

"Me," I said. "I was the only witness, I guess. And no one knew they illegally helped offworlders escape so they could trade with the worlds excluded from the Alliance."

"I hear tell of a substance which allows a person to disguise themselves," Izen said, his eyes on Kay. "There are some odd stories coming out of Central. This... bloodrock."

"You don't know what bloodrock is?" I probably didn't sound polite enough for a council meeting, but well, who *didn't* know what bloodrock was by this point? Klathica must not use that particular source. Izen was probably telling the truth when he said he didn't know who'd ordered the murder of KimaroTech's President, though.

"Klathica doesn't have any?" asked Kay. "I thought that's where Walker got his from. He used it on his fake council members."

The room appeared to grow colder, the air tighter, at the mention of Walker's name.

"What is this bloodrock?" asked Izen. "If you're conspiring to keep information from me—"

"Bloodrock is Enzarian," Ms Weston interrupted, startling me. "I checked the notes, and bloodrock is unique to Enzar itself. The Alliance's supplies came here twenty-five to thirty years ago."

I stared at her. That was when the file by Robert Walker had been written. So he'd traded with Enzar. Bloodrock for… what?

"I think we're departing from the point," said Greene. "So Campbell was convinced Enzar had a weapon. When speaking in magical terms, we mean a source. Now, in the Alliance, the number of such weapons is small because of the treaty put into place thirty years ago." She turned to Kay, adding, "Robert Walker's treaty."

He knew? Of course he did—Robert Walker was his grandfather, after all.

"You know the details?" asked Ms Weston. "We do have a copy…"

"Everyone knows," said Kay. "It's the updated version of the Alliance's mandate. There *was* a clause involving magic sources. Something Klathica have tried to get around for years," he added. "There's a loophole which lets them get on with making their temporary boost implants."

Greene looked outraged. "That's how they do it? Despicable."

"You are one to talk," said Izen.

"I never said they had their morals in order." Kay gave a dismissive glance at the Klathican council member. "But they're quick to arrest anyone who does break those rules."

"Precisely why we outlawed magic-shots," said Greene. "I would *hope* no one in the Alliance had anything to do with this atrocity. Klathica is a crucial member, despite our past differences. If we cannot trust our allies, how can we hope to defend ourselves against Enzar?"

"You can trust us," said Izen, "because we have *nothing* to do with Enzar."

"I'm in favour of reforming KimaroTech from the ground up," said Kay, once again causing a shocked silence. "Some of their scientists were involved with Thairon, with experiments creating the Stoneskins, and with an attempt to instigate illegal magical implants on Earth."

There it was. Out in the open. Kay's expression was calm, but I was pretty sure I was the only person to see his hands shaking, under the desk.

"The person behind this," said Kay, "was, of course, Lawrence Walker. He hired Klathican scientists to help with his plan. I believe they were involved with the part of KimaroTech that created the Stoneskins. My father claimed to have tried to stop the project, resulting in the Stoneskins' escape... after which they went looking for revenge. But their original purpose was to serve in Enzar's war. In fact, that's where KimaroTech got most of its sources. Enzar. They funded the war, as did Thairon, and it was the reason Lawrence Walker claims he activated the bomb."

The stunned silence continued. Unbroken. Did he mean to imply his father had somehow ordered the attack, from jail? But the callous murder of a bunch of scientists surely wasn't the act of a former Alliance council member trying to protect Earth. Still, who else could have done it?

"So," said Kay, "unless we find out which side Walker is working for, it's difficult to tell who was behind today's attack. It might have been a retaliatory measure, a warning, or someone's misguided attempt to prevent an attack on Earth."

"Send someone to talk to Lawrence Walker," said Izen,

immediately. His tanned face had gone greyish-white. "Kay Walker. You've spoken to him recently?"

Kay's face was unreadable, but what choice did he have, with the entire council watching? "I tried to get answers... for why he did it." I heard the low note of pain underneath his voice. "He seems to think he acted in defence of Earth. There was a living source on Thairon with enough power to wipe out the Multiverse, and he wanted to cut off Enzar, too —he said that's why he ruled noninterference, because they had weapons even the Alliance didn't know about."

"This again," said Greene, with a non-too-subtle glance at Izen. "Campbell claimed the same. What if the enemy is in front of us? In the Alliance? We're the ones with the weapons. Enzar has never tried to attack us before."

"Because they couldn't," said Kay. "Like Thairon, all the doorways were closed, weren't they? I don't know how that's done," he added. "Walker closed the doors himself?"

"He did," Izen confirmed. "Just as we closed our own doors today."

"How did he do it?"

"That information is classified."

"Figures," said Kay. "But Walker knows. Probably everything. Am I right?"

Fear rippled through the room.

"His allies," said Izen. "If anyone ordered an attack, it's Walker. But he is imprisoned. *Here.*"

Izen's tone was harsh. "I have outstayed my welcome here."

He stood, and in one sweeping motion, he left the room. I watched him, my heart sinking. So much for getting answers about the murderer.

"He's not going back to KimaroTech, is he?" asked Greene, looking appalled.

"Where else is there to go?" Another council member

shook his head. "The Alliance won't hold if this continues. Klathica is a founding member."

"This isn't the time to fight amongst ourselves," said Kay. "Klathica is free to handle the situation however they'd like, and there's no evidence connecting the attack to Enzar. Cethrax is known to be the likely site of the invasion, but thanks to the lower Passages being clear, it's entirely possible the enemy is planning an attack similar to the last battle on Central, in which they opened a doorway of their own to mount a direct assault. But there's little reason for them to have murdered the leader of KimaroTech, other than to destabilise our relations."

So Izen thinks Walker did it? I was stumped as to *why*, but then again, Walker had blown up Thairon as a precaution. He didn't do things by half measures. All we'd gained from the meeting was a bunch more questions, instead of answers as to who might have been behind Lilian Greyson's death and the hijacking of the drone, and what they'd hoped to achieve by it.

"Kay is right," said Ms Weston. "I've said before that bickering amongst ourselves will only stir up old divisions. We need unity, to stand against Enzar's army. Need I remind you that the reason Enzar is in such a sorry state is that they refused to negotiate with any other worlds, and destroyed themselves as a consequence."

"I would hardly compare a war to Izen's incapability of seeing the truth in front of him," said Greene. "Klathica's ambitions will get them killed."

"I'm not saying the system doesn't need work," said Kay. "Just that in case you've forgotten, the Alliance nearly went to war within itself only a few decades ago. Think how many people would have died. We'd be another Enzar." He glanced at me. "We're the Alliance, and it's about damn time we started acting on our own principles."

"As long as magic, and its sources, exist, we'll never be able to agree," argued Greene. "Magic puts some worlds on a higher ledge than others. Maybe we should ban it entirely."

"That's not the answer," I said. "I think there's a problem in the Alliance's mandate. Magic is something we claim to understand, but I'm not sure anyone can. We need some kind of training in place." I struggled to pull my thoughts in order. "The Enzarian war started because of magic. Because some had a talent others didn't, and they divided themselves. I don't think we should be trying to cut them off. If they want to take out the Alliance, they'll keep trying. I don't know who the leaders are, or where they're hiding, but if we want to stop the war, I think we should send someone to speak to them."

Everyone started speaking at once.

"Ridiculous—we cannot engage Enzar."

"They're unreasonable. They'll kill us all."

But so many lives had been lost already. Cutting Enzar off had been like chopping the head off a hydra: a million magic-related problems had cropped up in its place. And if they were trying to reach me, maybe it was time I gave them my answer.

Kay didn't say a word until we were out of earshot of the meeting, halfway down the stairs to the entrance hall. Then he asked, "You're planning to volunteer yourself, don't you?"

"To go to Enzar?" I hesitated. "They already know my name, and they want to speak to me. I don't have to go *to* Enzar. There has to be some kind of neutral ground."

"Aside from the Passages?" Kay shook his head. "Ada, I know they're your homeworld, but they want you dead."

"I think they want me alive. That's why they keep sending

me messages." I'd thought it over, and it made sense. If they could really kill me so easily, why hadn't they done so yet? I was more use to them alive than dead—unless they planned to do the same as the Campbells and turn me into a human bomb. But with their own sources, they didn't need to do that.

"We can't risk it." Kay's expression was tight, anger glittering in his eyes. "Unless we figure out where they're broadcasting those messages from, we can't risk letting them gain access to any of the Alliance's worlds. If they have a tracker, it only takes a trace for them to be able to open a doorway directly into any world. They might even be counting on it. We'd be letting them invade."

"I know." We crossed the entrance hall, having to duck a low-flying rainbow-coloured bird chased by a couple of irate-looking guards. "Why did someone shoot a gun in the Passages, anyway? Did they actually see anything from Cethrax?"

"Good question," said Kay. "I'd say the guards panicked. They have reason to." His fists were clenched, his breathing measured, like he was trying to calm down. "We're no closer to answers than before. What the hell use is having access to council meetings when we've no evidence to back up our claims?"

"Do… you mean Walker? Whether he did it?"

Kay turned to me, and the despair etched on his face tore at my heart. "I honestly don't know anymore," he said, in a low voice. "Anything on Klathica *might* be traced back to him, but I've looked into all his contacts and it doesn't seem like he gave anyone orders to follow out in case he was captured. All his creepy servants died when Cethrax attacked. The ones on Earth did, anyway."

We headed for the stairs.

"You don't think…" I hesitated. "Izen. He seemed genuine.

Do you really think Klathica's Alliance might have had something to do with the murders?"

"If they did, it makes no sense," said Kay. "They re-elect their council every year. No one's in who knew Walker, not personally. And he ditched KimaroTech just before he left for Thairon."

"Yeah. Guess all we can do is wait. I'm thinking of taking another trip to Valeria tomorrow, to see Jeth. Maybe he can think of something."

Kay nodded. "If we can talk the council into letting us go. They've actually invited us to their next strategy meeting."

"Guess I should be flattered that they value my opinion." I rolled my eyes. "Next thing you know I'll be nominated for the council."

Kay didn't say anything, and I glanced sideways at him. "That was a joke," I added. "I don't think anyone's going to go out of their way to elect an Enzarian, least of all the one who caused all the trouble. But *you* could do it."

He winced, which kind of surprised me. "Did you really think I didn't spend every second of that meeting wishing I was anywhere but here?" he said quietly. "I have no place even being near council meetings, let alone making suggestions about the Alliance's future. The only reason I'm still at the Alliance is that I have to make sure Walker doesn't get his way. Even if it just confirms what people think of me already."

"Kay..." I took his hand. "They're wrong about you. You're not like him. And your ideas are, well, good. Like disbanding KimaroTech and rebuilding it."

"I don't even have the authority to say that." He ran his free hand through his hair. "But if no one else suggested it, things would go on the same as before and people like Walker would get to carry on as they always do, torturing others for their own gain."

"I know." I squeezed his hand. "I get it, Kay. You aren't seriously thinking of leaving the Alliance... after?" I'd watched as the recent events wore him down, even as nobody else noticed. The strain showed in the hollows under his eyes and the way his hands shook, just a little, when I held them.

"I've done enough to get myself fired a thousand times," Kay said quietly.

"I'd vote for you."

He almost smiled then, bending his head so his lips brushed against mine. "Maybe you're a little biased."

"Maybe I am." I sighed. "Nell is going to flip out on me."

"You're probably right." He turned to unlock the door. "Better not mention how I crashed that drone. And I'm sorry I ran out on you."

"Maybe I'll forgive you." I stood in the doorway, not leaving. I didn't want to think about Enzar any longer. I just wanted the two of us to be alone, away from all of this. War and murder and bloodshed might be on the outside, but here, in the silence, I could believe we were the only people left here in Central.

His mouth quirked up. "Maybe?"

"If we finish what we started last night." I slipped inside, letting the door close behind me. "I reckon we won't get much more time alone for a while."

He closed the gap between us and brought his mouth down on mine, his hands easing my jacket off. The outside world was forgotten as we fell into one another. Just for now, the war faded to a backdrop.

Just for now, I was home.

～

To my surprise, the council let Kay and me go to Valeria the following day to talk to Jeth about the latest turn of events. Greene, Valeria's head, accompanied Kay and me through the doorway port, probably to stop us running off.

"I heard about the Chameleon suits," said Kay. "Carl says they won't be much use on patrol, though. A few magic shots too many and they'll turn visible again."

"I think they're more for the element of surprise," I said. "I like the idea. He's also making me a custom suit with built in extra antimagic."

Kay nodded. "Makes sense." But he didn't look happy that I'd implied I'd be going to war with the others. "What you said yesterday… about negotiating with Enzar. I'm not sure they'll let things get that far."

"I know." I looked away, at Valeria's skyline through the glass window at the side. "They're murderers. But some of them… they don't want to be fighting. Magic doesn't give you a choice in the matter. It's like it's always been. If you have magic, people step in to make your life decisions for you."

Kay didn't say anything for a long moment. "I never said we won't be able to save the civilians. I think the Enzarians at Central should be allowed a say, too."

"Yeah. The kids want me to teach them magic. Imagine. Me, a teacher."

"That's not a terrible idea," said Kay. "I think there ought to be a system in place for earth-born magic-wielders, too. Most have no training at all when they join the Alliance. Maybe at the Academy."

"Good plan," I said. "But—seriously, about the other Enzarians. Some of them want to join the Alliance guard. I said you can vouch for them."

"What?" He looked at me in disbelief. "I crashed a drone

in the Passages yesterday, Ada. I wouldn't say I'm the most responsible person Central's ever employed."

"So what? Come on, you saved Central multiple times now. You were the guards' hero. They all know who your mother was, they know she's the one who made the shelters underneath Central. Once all this dies down, we can tell them the truth about her mission. Right?"

"Once all this dies down," he repeated. "I think we need to prepare for the very high chance that it *won't*."

He turned to the window, to the view of Valeria's skyways. All appeared normal enough, but that was the point, wasn't it? They'd taken us by surprise already. More than once.

I moved to stand beside him. "You can make them trust you."

"Make them?" He shook his head. "You can't rebuild trust overnight." He spoke quietly, half to himself.

"You weren't the one who did any of those things Walker did," I said. "They know that, but maybe they need a reminder."

He didn't meet my eyes. "They don't need a hero, they need someone to call a villain. The person who attacked Klathica yesterday... nobody even saw who they were. I swear it was set up that way."

Greene appeared around the corner, and he stopped speaking. We walked the rest of the way to the lab. There, we had to duck as two figures wearing hover boots shot over our heads and collided with the wall.

"Ow," said Vic, from the ceiling. "Who opened the door?"

"You again?" Andy rubbed his head. "Nothing happened on Earth, did it?"

"Not this time," said Kay. "Klathica. Did you hear?"

"You're back?" Jeth waved at me from inside the lab. "We were—uh. Taking a break. Helm left the hover boots lying around. And in case you've all forgotten—" he shouted at Andy and Vic—"there's an unlabelled magic source here!"

"Did it come from the drone on Klathica?" asked Kay, indicating the piece of black gleaming rock on the desk, which had been cleared of wires and machine parts.

"Yeah. There's no magic in it, is there?" asked Jeth. "I can't tell, obviously, but they said there wasn't."

"None," said Kay, and I moved closer, too. "It's obsidiate. I did wonder what happened to it." He'd handed the source over to Valeria's guards in the Passages after removing it from the drone. "Damned idiots."

He meant Klathica. *Yeah, they are. Look at Thairon.* Klathica had at least been partially responsible for giving the mage-bloods their weapons, too. But that didn't mean they deserved to be infiltrated and murdered in cold blood. I didn't think KimaroTech were innocent, not by a long shot. But everyone was looking for an easy target to blame, to point a finger at. I was with Kay.

"Obsidiate?" Andy touched down and removing one hover boot. "Isn't it magicproof?"

"No, that's adamantine," I said. "I know it looks the same." But even with no magic inside it, the echo of magic from the source was a totally different signal to the other sources I'd encountered. I was starting to be able to sense the difference, though it was easier for Kay, being an amplifier.

"They all look the bloody same," said Vic. "What do you do to find out which it is, throw magic at it?"

Dr Helm appeared from behind a cabinet. "Obsidiate would explode if you hit it. Adamantine would absorb the hit. As for bloodrock... that's the one source that looks a little different to the others."

Kay asked, "This might seem an odd question, but how widespread is the knowledge of individual magic sources?"

Dr Helm blinked. "Not widespread at all, especially on Earth."

"I meant, in the Alliance," he said. "I know new guards have never seen a stunner before, but what about people related to someone who works in the Alliance?"

"Like you?" Dr Helm frowned. "I would say, even then, it's unlikely. I've spoken to senior members here in Valeria who've never heard of auros. But it depends if you're a magic-wielder. People with a particular sensitivity can tell which substance is which by touch."

"Yeah, I got that," said Kay. "I mean the *names*. Everyone knows what adamantine is, right? But I'd never heard of sciras or auros until I went poking around looking for information. And what about… lustre?"

Come to think of it, I'd certainly never heard of lustre before. Even Nell had only heard of adamantine and blood-rock, for obvious reasons. I hadn't known until I'd joined the Alliance a different magical substance was used in stunners.

But it made all the difference to us. As I'd learned at yesterday's meeting, Klathica's council didn't know *what* bloodrock was. So that source hadn't been involved in their arrangement before the war? If so, did Enzar have similar gaps in their knowledge? If they didn't know one source from another, that might give us the edge over them.

"Lustre?" Dr Helm frowned. "Honestly, I can't imagine anyone outside of the technical divisions of the Alliance would have reason to know. Valeria and Klathica are the only worlds that have used it."

Aglaia did. But the source was destroyed. Kay had told me it was rare—really rare.

"It's an amplifier?" asked Jeth. "Yeah, that's why the team thought it'd be a good base for a weapon for magic-wielders. Iriel's working on it. She taught me how to avoid blowing things up in future."

"Don't put obsidiate anywhere near another source and you'll be fine," said Iriel. "I'd have thought that'd be common sense."

"This source looks the same as a battery, doesn't it?" Jeth asked. "We're focusing on developing daggers rather than guns this time around. Less explosive." He pointed to the table, where what looked like an ordinary Alliance guard dagger lay amongst the general chaos. "Normally, they're made out of adamantine, but we figured we could join it with another source especially for magic-wielders. Just to keep the enemy on their toes."

I picked up the dagger. "This is… lustre," I said. "And the other side is made of adamantine. So one side blocks magic, the other amplifies it?"

"Pretty much." Jeth grinned.

Huh. That might be useful. Using the lustre side of the dagger, I'd be able to amplify my magic if I used it to attack, while the adamantine side gave it extra protection and made it difficult to break.

Kay was still frowning at the obsidiate source from Klathica. "So how did the magic get removed? I didn't see."

"Klathica slammed it with adamantine," said Dr Helm. "That's how we usually do it. Isn't that how Earth removes magic from… of course, you don't use sources, do you? Except in your stunners."

Kay shook his head. "No. Most magic sources don't work properly on Earth. Stunners use obsidiate, but are three uses maximum only."

He sounded like he recited from a textbook. So he was covering up for me. Covering the fact I could drain magic out of a source… because of the adamantine in my blood.

Could we use that to beat Enzar? If they have a source… No, it was too risky. I'd have to be standing right next to the source to drain the power out of it.

"Have you made any progress on the message?" I asked Jeth.

"Well…" said Iriel, "there's something odd. The last message didn't use Klathican script, it used these symbols we couldn't translate."

"Enzarian?"

"They… Ada, they looked like those symbols we found on Vey-Xanetha."

I stared. *What?*

Images flashed before my eyes. Evidence of the previous inhabitants of Vey-Xanetha. Before the void. The void linked with Cethrax.

"Are you sure?" I asked.

"Positive," said Iriel.

"Actually…" I recalled, with a shiver, that Ms Weston hadn't been able to get hold of Kevar, who lived in a city on Vey-Xanetha, since Enzar had declared war. "That makes sense. Vey-Xanetha and Cethrax used to be linked, and Cethrax has been hooked up to most worlds through doorways at some point or other. High-magic ones, anyway. What if it's all tied together?"

"What, Enzar and Vey-Xanetha?" Kay frowned. "They've had no contact with other worlds outside of the void in a thousand years."

"There aren't any records of Enzarian history that go back far," I said. "Not ones that are likely to be accurate, anyway."

"Well…" Kay paused, frowning. "Some magical upheaval did happen on Vey-Xanetha—that's where Veyak and the other gods came from. Residual magical aftershock."

"Wait, what?" said Vic.

Now everyone in the lab stared at us. A brief flash of panic flared, then it hit me I was being stupid. Those kimaros were all over the Passages and escaping through every doorway they found. Most guards would have seen them by now, and knowing what the enemy was would be a relief to most people.

"They're called kimaros," said Kay. "They're like magic trapped in a living creature's body, but not corporeal. Ada and the guards fought one in the Passages earlier today. They usually result from third level magic."

"There was one in the void when Central was attacked," I added.

"Jesus," said Andy. "Glad we're under a crap-ton of adamantine here. I'm not going outside.

The Multiverse has gone mad."

I couldn't argue with that. I decided not to mention the mind-control part.

"There have been a few attacks here, too." Dr Helm passed me a communicator—a Valerian one, which was slightly bigger than Earth's and equipped with several buttons I didn't recognise—and tapped the screen. Up came the blurred image of something large and hazy shadowed against the high-rise buildings.

"It has a million hits on the network already," said Dr Helm. "Luckily, most injuries were minor…"

"Magic burn." I grimaced. "It's not serious, but not fun either. I'm glad no one was badly hurt. Where did it come from?" I handed the communicator back to Dr Helm.

"Probably the Passages," said Kay. "But there are so many doorways here, it'd be impossible to track."

"Is that a *face?*" Andy asked, pointing at the screen. "It looks like… it can see me. It's creepy." He clicked off the screen. "It's made out of magic?"

"Yeah," said Iriel. "Raw magic."

Vic shuddered. "Sounds like a horror movie."

"Pretty much." Vey-Xanetha had been almost tame

compared to Thairon and the living doorway, though. I still hadn't told Kay my newest suspicion.

"What, they spoke to you?" Dr Helm's expression told me I'd probably inspired a new research project.

"Kind of." Veyak had spoken, mostly through the summoners it had used as vessels. And the kimaros on Thairon… just thinking about it made me shudder. And there had been another, too. A plant, like decaying magic, on a world destroyed in Enzar's war.

A world that had once been linked to Cethrax. The only other world with creatures that could take on a shadowy form. They were magicproof, but if they hadn't been, on a world where magic could be trapped inside a living being… they'd become kimaros. Maybe they'd even evolved to avoid that happening. I was almost certain Vey-Xanetha's gods, and the kimaros, were warped forms of the giant vox-kind.

"Magic can talk," said Andy. "What next, it starts demanding human rights?"

"It nearly killed us," said Iriel seriously. "A source like Veyak can control magic-wielders. That once happened in London, too."

"Yeah." I nodded. "Veyak was like… conscious, though. And the others had awareness."

"Magic has a *name?*" said Andy, looking incredulous.

"The Vey-Xanethans named the three forces of magic active on their world, as gods," said Kay. "Veyak was the main one—the one the Vox enslaved on the orders of the Stoneskins."

"Them again?" Vic paled.

"No, the ones who captured me are dead," I said. "But… there might be others on Enzar."

"Brilliant." Andy threw his hands up. "We all bow down to invincible monsters."

"You really came from the Academy?" Iriel shook her head at him, incredulous, and Andy went silent, muttering to himself. "They're not invincible. Not even the strongest kimaros—right? You think Enzar are using similar creatures?"

"Probably," I said. "Adamantine's their main source. It would make sense. But that's not the point. Those symbols… Enzar stole the language. My guardian told me the Royals' symbols were taken from one of the worlds they conquered. It might easily have been Vey-Xanetha. This would have been thousands of years ago, before the Alliance's records."

"Really?" Iriel's eyes rounded.

"Yeah. Their own history's pretty patchy and inaccurate. I was trying to work out how they might have broken into our communication network." I paused. "The worlds they conquer tend to be low-technology. Their magic—it overwhelms most tech, or replaces it. Magic sources burn themselves out even on high-magic worlds." I stopped myself before I mentioned the Royals' fate was unknown.

"So how would they have the technology to broadcast a message to the Alliance?" asked Iriel. "Cethrax doesn't have the reach."

"That's what we're trying to work out," said Jeth. "Sorry I can't be more help, sis. I'm almost done with your new suit, though. I've been working overtime."

"You didn't have to do that."

Maybe he did. If the war's this close. I hadn't seen Enzar's latest message. I'd been too preoccupied with the fallout after yesterday. But they'd used Enzar's true symbols this time. To goad me? The symbols, appropriated or not, were used by the Royals, not the magebloods.

Either way… *someone* over there wanted to claim me. And I had absolutely no intention of letting that happen.

Dr Helm scrolled down his communicator screen. "This

doesn't look good. Someone's claiming there are magic-wielder traitors here in the capital."

My heart lurched. "Traitors?"

"There was a disagreement," he said, "between the Alliance guards and the enforcement head concerning whether the magic-wielders who attacked guards were acting of their own free will."

"Hell," I said. "No—they won't have been, if the kimaros was influencing people."

"Damn," said Kay, who'd been on his communicator all the time. "Yeah. Valeria doesn't like magic, so enforcement have come down like a ton of bricks. And there's a rumour on the network about spies on Earth."

"Not again." I pulled out my own communicator. "Shit." My own face filled the screen. "Someone on Earth thinks *I'm* the spy?"

I stared mutely at the screen, unable to believe what I was seeing.

"That came from Earth?" I asked Kay.

"From Central."

8

ADA

I about-turned, fury singing my veins. "I've had bloody enough."

"Ada, wait." Kay put his communicator away and followed me. "We'll talk to them."

"This is ridiculous." I ignored Greene's protest and stormed down the corridor, past the dizzying views of the skyway. "How the hell can anyone think I'd have ordered an attack on Klathica? I hadn't even been there until less than two weeks ago."

"You're right, it's ridiculous." Kay walked alongside me. "Who started the rumour?"

"Doesn't say." I fumed. "For crying out loud. Even if there was a chance I *did* do it, why the hell did Central let a rumour like that go viral? They're supposed to be—"

On *my* side. But maybe some of them didn't think I was on theirs. I was Enzarian, a magic-wielder, from the world belonging to the enemy. I was a wild card.

I'd planned to go after Enzar of my own free will, once I knew whereabouts they were hiding. At this rate, the Alliance would draw them right here. I was furious enough not to care at the moment. Let them come, and I'd show the Alliance I'd *never* fight on Enzar's side.

On the other side of the doorway port, we found Ms Weston arguing with Mr Shean at high volume.

"What's this?" Kay demanded, drawing their attention to his communicator screen. "Someone in the building's spreading this crap around?"

"Kay," said Ms Weston, "of course we know Ada isn't a threat."

"Good," said Kay. "Because we're about to take care of it."

"Yes, we are," I snapped. "If you could tell the guards I don't have a freaking clue how to screw with a Klathican mecha and I nearly got killed by a kimaros the other day, it'd be great." I'd even fought alongside the guards. Yesterday. Some gratitude they had.

My heart sank when we reached the first floor. Through the window over the balcony, crowds gathered in the entrance hall. All eyes turned to me as we reached the bottom of the stairs. The majority of the guards were around the hall's outskirts, most arguing loudly.

"This is ridiculous," I said. "It's all *ridiculous.*"

I flicked an icon on my communicator I'd never used before—the microphone. This was the opposite of what I'd usually do, which was keep quiet. I'd had too many thoughts swirling around in my head lately. Thoughts I wanted to back up with actions. But I couldn't fight alone. I was far from the only person willing to go head to head with Enzar.

I just needed to convince them.

"Hey!" I shouted. "I don't know which idiot decided to spread rumours, but if I was a spy for Enzar, you'd all be dead. You realise the enemy's probably laughing at us while we're tearing one another to pieces? Nobody here caused the war."

"His father did!" a voice shouted, and Kay stiffened at my

side. "You let Walker stay here. You're as good as letting the enemy step in and take over."

"He's not his father," I said, loudly. "Lawrence Walker murdered twenty thousand people on Thairon out of paranoia. But—" I couldn't say what Lawrence Walker had done to Kay. It wasn't my story to tell, and I knew Kay wouldn't want me to broadcast it. "That doesn't make Kay to blame any more than it makes me to blame for—for what my blood family did on Enzar. But there are some things we get a choice in. You picked the Alliance. If you regret that, the door's that way."

"Hear hear!" someone shouted.

Bolstered, I went on. "The Alliance is far from perfect. I know that. But they're the best shot we have for survival, and petty bickering and blaming your own colleagues is the stupidest way to handle the situation." I glared at the guards. "You should know better than that."

"Yeah?" one said loudly. "How about Cethrax? We kill every monster we come across, because they're a threat to Earth. Enzar is just as much of a threat. You nearly destroyed Central yourself, yet everyone thinks you're a hero."

"Cethrax was refused Alliance membership because their leaders told the council that it's not their problem if their monsters kill people as sport." I glanced at Kay. I didn't know the laws inside out the way he did. "There's a difference between kicking the crap of a monster that's about to kill you and blaming me just because I'm a magic-wielder from Enzar. I'm not a spy. Do you really think I'd have fought on the Alliance's side if I was?"

Ms Weston spoke from behind me. "We're not here to debate the finer points of Alliance law. Nor question why Walker was allowed to remain on the council. They were a respected family—not unlike others on the council. Not unlike some of you," she added to the guards, who had the decency to look abashed.

"Exactly," I said. "A week ago, you'd have been worshiping the ground Walker trod on. Judge by actions, not the name. Kay's never given you any reason to doubt his loyalty to the Alliance any more than I have. We don't choose our parents."

"Walker's still alive," someone said. "You all let him live, even after what he did. The council should have ordered him executed."

Muttering filled the hall as Kay inclined his head.

"Kill him!" another voice shouted, and there was a general murmur of agreement.

Kay raised his own communicator, and the whispers were extinguished. "No," said Kay, his voice amplified. "We can't afford to. He might know something that'll give us the advantage. He's the only surviving informant from Thairon, which had ties to Enzar."

"Because he *killed them*," a guard shouted. "The bastard deserves the worst torture on any universe."

Again, agreement swept through the crowd. My fists clenched. I wanted nothing more than to kill Lawrence Walker myself. But Kay was right.

"I know," I said. "But if it turns out there's something he knows which will help us win the war—we'll get the information out of him no matter what."

"Using any means necessary," said Kay, his voice flat, but sharp as a knife. "But the Alliance comes first. Always. I won't make it easy for him. Whatever he knows, we'll know. He's already given us information."

I glanced sideways at him. So he'd spoken to Walker… but what had he found out? A pang hit my heart. Maybe he still didn't feel like he could confide in me.

I distinctly heard a whisper: "What if he escapes again?"

Kay didn't look at the speaker. "Central is the most secure

building on Earth. Walker won't leave that prison unless we say so, and I've no intention of doing that."

"Is he working with Enzar?"

That was the hardest part to explain. Maybe it was easier to lump all the villains on the same team. Walker might have killed Lilian Greyson, but that didn't mean he was on Enzar's side. Considering the extreme lengths he'd gone to protect Earth—or so he'd claimed, anyway—I didn't think so. Didn't make him right.

"At the moment? No," said Kay. "And if he has any history with them, I'll get us answers. Count on it."

"Did *he* bring the war to Earth?"

"That's enough," I cut in. "This is a war that's been going on a thousand years, and it was only a matter of time before it reached Earth. You joined the Alliance not just to defend Earth, but to defend all the worlds and the people in them."

"Exactly," Kay said. He sounded calm, but I heard the tremor of anger beneath. "So I hear some of you decided to blame the nearest target for the war, when I'll bet none of you even know how it started. Maybe I wouldn't fault you for that, if I didn't know it contradicts the Alliance's mandate." He looked at each guards, one at a time. Almost all of them faltered.

"When you joined the Alliance, you agreed to uphold that code. Who's breaking their word in here? The mandate was updated to prevent war between the allied worlds. The magebloods and Royals of Enzar work through discord. The Alliance doesn't, and that's why we're going to survive."

"And," I said, "that means when we confront Enzar, if they agree to a peace deal, we offer them membership in the Alliance."

This time, the silence was punctured by protests. As I'd expected. I hadn't known I'd dare speak the words aloud until they'd come out of my mouth, hanging in the air as shock reverberated through the crowd. Ms Weston's gaze burned into my back, too. She'd be pissed at me for not mentioning it to the council beforehand… but as far as I knew, every time there'd been a peace agreement reached between the Alliance and a non-member world, they'd been given the same offer. Some didn't take it. Some fell into war again. But my homeworld deserved to be given the chance to try.

"That doesn't make me a spy or a traitor," I shouted over the noise. "Most of the people we've saved from Enzar don't want any part in the fighting, and if you bothered to talk to us instead of starting rumours, you'd know that."

Kay raised his voice. "Ada and I are going to fight. Any of you are welcome to join us. But we don't have time to waste. Enzar are going to attack Earth again. We can't afford to argue amongst ourselves, and I won't fight on the same side as anyone who'd turn on our allies. If you're going to leave, do it before we're under attack. I'm not going to stop you."

Silence. My heart beat fast. If they didn't say yes, that was it for us. Maybe we'd both flee. Somewhere safe. Take a world-key and go far away from here. Worse was the lack of a reaction from Ms Weston, or from any of the Alliance members who technically had authority over Kay and me. But it'd bugged me for weeks that some of the Alliance's own employees might easily turn on one of us. If we remained divided, we might fall as easily as Enzar did.

Whispers broke out amongst the crowd. I let the noise wash over me. Who was I kidding? I'd never run away. Never. I'd fight to the last even if it meant fighting alone.

No. I wouldn't be alone.

"Right," said Kay. "We need a verdict. If you want to stay, raise your hands. That goes for all of you—Alliance or not."

For a heart-stopping instant, I thought nobody would. I didn't dare look at Kay, away from the crowd. *Please.*

The first hand went up. Then more. And more. I did spot a couple of people leave the room, but more overwhelming was the sight of one after another committing to our cause. Fighting with us.

I looked at him. His eyes were wide, disbelieving. I turned back to the crowd.

"Thank you." My voice cracked. "I can't promise no one will get hurt. But we'll do everything we can to keep you safe."

"I second that," said Kay, quietly. "Thank you."

And through the fear and dread for the future, hope flared to life like a beacon.

Somehow, the council managed to shepherd everyone back to where they were supposed to be. Either the shelter, or in the case of the guards who'd started the protest, the doghouse. I heard Carl having choice words with some of them.

"What's this?" Markos the centaur cantered through the crowd. "What have I missed?"

"Ada brought the house down," said Alber, and I flushed.

"I did *not*."

"Ooh, are we kicking people out?" The centaur parted the crowd easily, spotting some of the guards arguing near the doors. Evan took one look at him and bolted.

"Dear me." Markos shook his head. "How easily frightened are these new recruits?"

I couldn't help laughing as he waved a hoof and two more of the protesting guards fled for the doors.

"You're awesome, Ada." Alber grinned at me.

"Thanks, Al." It seemed so surreal. I'd spent my life hiding from my heritage, not defending it to a roomful of angry guards. While most of the others had left, Kay had remained in conversation with Ms Weston. I went to join them.

"I think we need an Enzarian representative on the council," I said to Ms Weston.

If she was surprised, she didn't show it. "Yes, we do. But nobody here has any experience of leadership. Except you, Ada."

My heart sank. "No. I don't want to do that. I want someone to speak for Enzar who's seen it all." Would Nell do it? Was it fair to ask her? "Hell, maybe it's wrong that I want to negotiate with them. But clearly someone on one of the sides is trying to reach me with those messages. That suggests at least one side is prepared to talk. They're coming…"

The image of a sky shattered by lightning, of bodies falling, rose in my mind. The people sending the messages weren't blameless. But I'd never forgive myself if I abandoned the survivors.

"I know I can't convince everyone to get along, but we should be looking out for allies, not enemies."

"I'm glad I'm not alone in that opinion," said Ms Weston. "We *have* sent out pleas to every world not actively opposed to the Alliance, but we don't have the resources to send actual representatives. As for Enzar itself… the council needs to discuss the matter further. I agree with your words, but the Alliance as a whole needs to come to an agreement as to whether to extend the offer of a ceasefire or membership, assuming hostilities don't escalate."

I nodded. I didn't expect an easy solution. Maybe I was deluding myself for even thinking there could be an end to this without more bloodshed. Even if we managed to speak to people on Enzar who didn't want to fight, they'd never trust in the council. Not after Walker had doomed their world to destruction. Magebloods and nonmages had been fighting for a thousand years. They'd never known peace. The spark that ignited the latest conflict was just a smaller piece of history.

The slaughter… Nell had told me the story. She'd been there.

"Let me know if anything changes," I said to Kay and Ms Weston. "I have to speak to my guardian."

9

ADA

I found Nell in the recreation room, in the corner she'd commandeered, immersed in a book.

One of mine, actually, an epic fantasy about the end of the world. Kind of appropriate.

"Hey." I sat down.

"That was quite some speech," said Nell.

"Didn't know what else to do." I paused. "Do you know who started the rumour about me being a spy?"

Nell shook her head. "No. Your head guard—Carl—he spoke forcefully to the guards who encouraged the rumours."

"Yeah, he did." I glanced around at the other Enzarians. Words alone couldn't always change everyone's minds. We needed the actions to back them up.

"You did well, Ada. I'm proud of you."

I blinked, surprised. Nell didn't give praise easily. It had to be earned. It didn't mean she was harsh, just honest.

"I—thanks," I said. "But really, all I did was speak my mind. Doesn't always turn out well. I'm no leader."

Her gaze sharpened. She must know where I was going with this.

"If the Alliance does decide to make a deal with Enzar, the people living here on Earth will need a representative on the council. I'd never be as good as you are at helping the others."

Nell shook her head. "No, Ada… I couldn't inspire people the way you did."

"Inspiring? I thought there was going to be a riot back there. Besides, I don't want to be a leader. I never have. I never thought I'd ever be talking about Enzar, let alone out in public in the Alliance HQ."

"No," said Nell, quietly. "I never imagined we would ally ourselves with Central."

The reality was probably harder for her to accept than it was for me. Nell was the one who'd drilled into me that it was impossible, absolutely impossible, to ever expect the Alliance to offer us support.

"Yeah. Sorry. I didn't want to put pressure on you or anything. Just, you know, I'm as likely to mess up and say the wrong thing as anyone. You're the one who—who's been there. I mean, you're speaking from a position I can't put myself in, because I've never had to. Because you saved me. Like you saved all these people…"

"Enough," Nell said sharply. "Don't pretend I'm a hero, Ada. I've killed people."

"But you've saved so many more." I stood my ground. "It doesn't mean you can't inspire the others. You always have. And if anyone can talk the Alliance into doing more for Enzar, it's you."

She exhaled. "They're unlikely to listen to me, Ada, given our history."

"You'd be surprised." I scanned the room. "Unlikely alliances form under duress. And… there was something I wanted to ask, about the mageblood rebellion. I've heard some contradictory stories about what exactly happened back then. But if it explains how the magebloods brought down the Royals—I need to know."

"I would guess the full story isn't in the Alliance's reports," said Nell.

"No—it was twenty-five years ago, right? The whole section's missing from the files."

Nell paused, before saying, "There were no witnesses to the first attack. The nonmages had captured some magebloods who'd killed a Royal. They were to be executed, but unbeknownst to the Royals, they'd found a source, and they used it to make a bomb... with the help of offworlders. I didn't find out until later, as I was at the far back of the crowd, with the other Royals. The bomb killed a hundred people. Within days, the capital was in ruins. I remember watching it from the windows, watching it disintegrate as the magebloods used their weapons to obliterate everything in their path. The war started overnight."

I sucked in a breath, then another. Pretending she was telling me a story. Not her *life* story. Not that these were the people who wanted us all dead.

"You were in the palace. It was made of antimagic, wasn't it?"

"Yes, the major section of the city was. That's how we remained as the rest of the world fell apart. But... the tide turned. The Royals mined their hidden stores, experimented, and..." Her eyes clouded. "Ada, you once told me you wanted to know everything. Once I cross the line... there's no going back."

"I know." But my heart dipped further. There was more? Worse than what she'd already told me?

Seeing I wasn't going to back out, Nell said, "As I said, you were the only survivor. They didn't know how to transfer magic from a source to a person at first. They experimented on animals to begin with, but the aftereffects resulted in horrific creatures storming the city. They tried injecting it into humans, but with no effect. They tried operating, but most didn't survive the procedure. Eventually, they decided half-blood children were the likely candidates. You, Ada... I was there that day because..." A gasp escaped her, and silent tears traced paths down her cheeks.

I looked around, but no one so much as glanced in our direction. Like we were encased in a bubble. I had no clue how I was supposed to react. I'd never, in my entire life, seen Nell lose control.

And I knew worse was coming.

"They took her, too," she said. So quietly. "She was all I had, but they ordered every child in the palace to be taken away. They knocked me out, and when I came to, I knew it was too late. I broke out in the dead of night when it was quiet. They'd left. I had to check, I had to see if she was alive. But instead, I found you. You were barely hanging on, Ada."

My throat was dry, my head pounding like I'd been hit on the skull. *They did that. I was less than a year old, and they...*

"There were no other survivors. Ada... I lied to you. They didn't inject you with magic, they implanted it over your heart."

Silence. She'd stopped crying. As for me, I could hardly breathe. "You told me... you told me it was in my blood. The magic."

"Implanted, not injected, Ada. They put you to sleep and... they implanted it under your skin. Over your heart. So it can be taken out, if they want."

My hand jerked towards my chest. "What? They really..."

"Nothing else worked. It was an experiment they expected to fail."

"I wish I'd killed them," I whispered, the words like glass in my throat.

Silence. She let me stay there, my head on her shoulder. I

couldn't imagine what it must be like to raise the child of an enemy, because they were the only survivor of a cruelty indefinable. I couldn't have done it.

But that wasn't the only reason. Maybe I'd always known it.

"You had to take me away," I said, "because I was their last weapon. Wasn't I?"

Nell's hand rested over mine. "Don't ever think I didn't care about you. I did. But I can't be your hero, Ada. I was mad with grief, mad enough to take a child that wasn't mine. Mad enough to venture out there, where I would have died were it not for the nonmage rebels, for Maena." I blinked at the unfamiliar name. "She saved me," Nell went on. "She risked her life to take one of the Royals' underground shelters and set it up as a safe house. The city was mostly deserted by then. The Royals had left the Palace. I wouldn't have escaped otherwise."

"They left? When I was there? But who…"

"People acting on their orders carried out the experiments," said Nell. "They didn't expect success. If they'd found you before I did, they'd have taken you to be used in their war. But as I made plans with Maena, they must have worked out something was wrong. That night, the nonmages ambushed me in the tunnels. I escaped and hid, with you. I got out, followed the path for days, until I reached another shelter. It's no longer in use. Most of the refugees we've helped in the past few years have escaped from the outer islands, or the other worlds in the Enzarian Empire."

I nodded, trying to bring my thoughts back to our present dilemma. Pushing the horror aside, looking at the facts. To find out what was really happening over there. To stop any similar atrocity from ever happening again.

"So Enzar—the world, Enzar—might not be where they're operating from?"

"The transition point isn't on Enzar itself," said Nell. "It's been going thirty years, before the Alliance announced themselves on Earth."

"Yeah, but to get there, they isolated sections of the Passages, didn't they? Using auros?"

"I never knew the name," she said. "But yes, that's what they must have done. I can promise you nobody at the transition point knew your real name. They don't even know my name, I changed it three times before we settled on Earth. The only people in the entire Enzarian Empire who knew the name of Adamantine were the Royals, and if word has got out, they must have told people."

"Or they're still alive."

A nod.

"Shit," I said. "Well, it's not like I'm hoping for a family reunion, but… if they were going to destroy the Alliance twenty years ago, that was before you left, right? So—do you have any idea how they might have gone about it? Because we were the backup, weren't we? They couldn't have relied on human sources. They must have had a major magic source."

"Ada… I knew nothing about magic back then. I didn't even know what you would be able to do, and although I did everything I could to ensure we were relocated to a world where magic didn't function like Enzar, I feared for you every day. And every single time you went into the Passages alone… I was afraid you might not come back. When I saw you use magic…"

It was like seeing *them* again. Guilt and grief tangled in my chest, constricting my lungs.

"It's not your fault. I would never have burdened you with this if I had another choice, and… don't ever think I didn't love you as you were. I never for an instant saw you as a burden, or a danger. And I *always* wanted to keep you safe. That was my priority."

I nodded. "I know. Nell, I—I wish I didn't have to talk to you about Enzar. But someone's trying to get at me *here*. They can access our communications network."

"The technologies they had were mostly destroyed or scattered," said Nell. "The Royals' strategy has always been to conquer and steal whatever they found, but none of the outlying worlds had any connection to the Passages. Even if they had higher technology than the Alliance, it's impossible to join Inter-World communications without using one of the Alliance's signals. Jeth told me."

"So… they must be working through Klathica."

"Perhaps. This latest murder… it sounds very suspicious."

"Kay thinks it's Walker. He's not working with Enzar, but on his own agenda."

"I've no doubt he is. However, if the time comes, you can't give yourself up to them. Not just because *I* want to keep you safe, but because of what you are. You… you were supposed to be the nexus of the Enzarian Empire."

Nexus. The StoneKing claimed Enzar was looking for it —the centre of all magic on their entire world. His claim might been mad raving, but now, nothing was certain.

"I have something, by the way." Nell handed me a folded-over piece of paper, thick and yellowed. I'd probably call it parchment, though the rough texture was unlike anything I'd ever felt before. Symbols covered one side.

"Is that…?"

"Enzarian." Nell wiped her eyes. "You probably don't remember, but I told you the story when you were small… about the Enzarian sky-goddesses."

"The stars." I smiled, though more tears crept out. "I do remember. It's the only story you told us about our homeworld."

"Because I decided it wouldn't do any of us a bit of good to dwell on the past. It was selfish of me, Ada."

"No, of course not." I ran my hand over the page, hoping, for one stupid moment, something in my DNA would react and I'd be able to read it. But no. The swirling glyphs were unreadable, even if part of me thought I'd seen them before. A memory or imagination, I had no idea.

"I'll be right back," I said to Nell, folding the parchment again and slipping it into my pocket. She nodded.

I walked over to an Enzarian woman who I'd helped through the Passages so long ago. She smiled at me, recognising me immediately.

"Hey," I said. "You remember me?"

"Of course, I do, Ada. You saved me."

I blinked yet more tears from my eyes. Back then, I'd never have imagined just days later I'd be in the Alliance's hands, my life would have turned inside out and I'd almost have caused the deaths of everyone I'd tried to save.

"I never got your name."

"Elzith." She pointed to her children, the little boy, then the girl. "Nihn and Magho. Say hi to Ada."

"Hi, Ada." They blinked up at me. The level of cuteness was more than I could take.

"Why are you crying?"

I shrugged helplessly. What was there to say? "I hoped you'd be safe here. All of you. But…"

"Ada…" Elzith shook her head. "You're not to blame for the state of our world. I've spoken to some of the others."

I managed a smile. "Thanks. Believe me, I really needed to hear that right now." I glanced around the room. "So you talked to the others? I—I'm looking for information. On Enzar." I weighed my chances. I felt like I could trust her. "I heard they're searching for some kind of weapon. I've not been there since I was a baby, so I don't remember. But the information might help us end the war. Does anyone know about the weapon? Or a magic source. I don't speak Enzarian. Or read it, but…"

"Magic source?" Elzith hesitated. "There were rumours before we came to Earth. In the Passages."

"The transition point?"

She nodded. "Yes, there was talk of labour camps on some of the outer worlds, the ones the magebloods took. They were no longer destroying, but enslaving. Digging in the ground."

"Digging," I said. "For a source. Right?"

The nexus. Might it really exist? Not me—it wasn't possible for a person to contain the magic of an entire world. But maybe there was truth to the rumours after all.

I thanked her and left the room, thinking hard. Nobody here would know the word *nexus.* Aside from the council, maybe, and I didn't want to tell them, not when it probably wasn't true. Even if Enzar had been digging for a weapon, that might have been years ago, and that knowledge wouldn't help us if it turned out they really had infiltrated Klathica. All doorways directly to Enzar had been closed… thanks to Walker.

Walker. Might *he* know? He'd caused the war, directly or indirectly, through Klathica. If he'd cut Enzar's doorways off because he feared they'd attack Earth, he must have been confident in his methods. More to the point… he was high up enough in the Alliance to know how to *close* doorways, permanently. Izen had refused to say at the meeting.

I had a feeling we might need the knowledge. Soon.

Carl had the keys to Walker's cell. I knocked on his office door, heart thudding in my ears. I wasn't as good at hiding my emotions as Kay was, and from what I'd seen of Walker, he'd be able to play games with me even from the other side of the cage. But when I thought of doorways, I thought of

Robert Walker's report on the Cethraxian mission. Did Lawrence Walker know every detail of his father's missions? Or had he been kept in ignorance, like Kay? Because Kimaro-Tech was embedded in the war. Sure, Walker claimed to have nothing to do with them. But he claimed a lot of things.

"Ada?" said Carl, answering the door with a look of surprise. "Are you okay?"

I'd tried to hide the evidence I'd been crying, but for once, the question didn't rub me up the wrong way. Maybe I'd heard it enough times to know everyone meant it differently. "Yeah, I guess. I was hoping I could talk to him. Walker."

Carl frowned. "We can't do that without authorisation from the council, and they're in a consultation right now."

"Please," I said.

His expression softened. "I really shouldn't. Technically, someone else has to be present during questioning, too, but Kay… well. He's Walker's son. I figured the guy might be more likely to give information away if he doesn't think we're spying on him."

"You have hidden cameras in the room, right?"

"Yes. Walker probably knows about them."

"This is really important. Walker was involved with Enzar in a major way, and I have a feeling I've thought of something he might know about the war. It might help us end it."

He nodded. "Okay. But only because I trust you, Ada. Does Kay know?"

"No, but this… it's different. I'll be quick."

"Sure thing, Ada." He retrieved a key, unlocked a drawer in the desk and pulled out another bunch of keys. "I can come down with you and stay outside the door, just in case. There's no way for him to get out from in there, but I'm told it's an uncomfortable experience."

Tell me about it. It wasn't that I feared what he could do to me. I was more afraid of involuntarily giving *him* information. And if he so much as mentioned Thairon, I knew I'd try to kill him, cage or none.

Carl and I walked downstairs to the cells. There were no other prisoners here. The people Walker had locked away had been freed, and Walker's accomplices had been killed in the fighting.

Walker's cutting eyes fixed on me as the door closed behind me, Carl on the other side. My hand was on my dagger. If my aim was on point, I *could* hit him even through the bars. An instant kill.

I took a calming breath. Stepped forwards, ignoring the screaming instinct to run away.

You need answers.

"You," Walker said softly. "Ada Fletcher."

He doesn't know my real name? Or maybe he was taunting me, using my Earth name against me. I narrowed my eyes. "Glad you remember me. I'm not as good at first impressions as you are, Walker."

"Kay put you up to this?"

"You don't even know what *this* is." Magic seared my veins, even in here. The level must be climbing again outside.

"You're frustrated with the council's inaction, so you decided to come and talk to someone who used to take action and get things done."

"Like genocide?" I cursed myself as my voice shook. "I don't want to hear your excuses. I don't give a crap if you live or die, Walker, but I need to speak to a higher-up member of the Alliance. Someone… with knowledge of doorways. Does anyone else in KimaroTech have that knowledge?"

"I have no idea what you're talking about."

"Someone on Klathica killed Lilian Greyson. Wasn't your last request, was it?"

Walker's eyes sharpened. "Someone *killed* her?"

From his surprised tone, I guessed it wasn't him, after all.

"As I said, yeah. I figured, seeing as murders are your thing, you might have something to do with it."

"No," said Walker. "You're mistaken there. Klathica has far too many volatile offworld substances. The Balance wouldn't take it."

I half-laughed. "You *what?* Who blew up a freaking planet? Where'd the backlash from *that* go?"

"Into nothing. If a world is cut off from all others, there is no target but itself. Earth was spared."

"Don't you make excuses for all the people you slaughtered. I'm not going to listen to them."

"You think I made that choice because I'm a calculated killer? My actions were a last resort, just like closing Enzar."

Wait. He'd landed on the point I wanted to bring up. "So that *was* you. I knew you issued the statement saying Enzar was too dangerous to interfere in, but you closed the doorways yourself?"

"What does it matter if I did?"

I crossed my arms. "How many people in the Alliance know how to close doorways?"

"Few, because the council is sorely lacking in basic common sense," Walker said. "The doorways are made of magic. What stops magic?"

Adamantine. So he'd used adamantine? Like when I'd drained the magic from a source. It *was* common sense. I should have known. The Passages were made of auros, so closing a doorway would be a simple matter of using adamantine to drain the magic out of them.

"Right, so you used antimagic," I said. "Got it from Enzar itself, I'm betting."

"How did you know?" Walker's eyes flashed dangerously. "You weren't even born."

"You don't know anything about me." *And never will.*

"I know you weren't there at Earth's last stand on Enzar,"

he said. "There were no survivors of that first attack. My blasted father got himself killed there."

My mouth fell open. "What? Your father died on *Enzar?*"

"Are you so surprised? You know my family were involved in the war from the start. I assumed Kay told you, if he trusts you."

The room spun around me. *Impossible. No way the Alliance don't know! They created the freaking Passages!*

I knew he read my shock and horror and delighted in it. That was enough to ground me back in reality. "So you lied to everyone… again. I can't say I'm surprised."

"And you've always told the truth?" He raised an eyebrow in a sardonic gesture that looked so disconcertingly like Kay, my concentration scattered.

"No," I said. "But unlike you, I was trying to protect people other than myself. So why was your father's death covered up? Was he as big a bastard as you are?"

"Throwing insults at me won't get you the answers you want," Walker said coolly. "The Alliance saw fit to conceal the shady circumstances of Robert Walker's death because they did not wish to tarnish the reputation of Central's hero, the man who enlightened Earth to the possibilities of the Multiverse."

"So you decided to do that for them. You trampled over everything he did. I get why you stopped his stupid project, but why not at least tell someone else in case Enzar decided to attack the Alliance? What if you'd died, and the Alliance had fallen because no one else out there knew?"

"There were other council members who knew, my trusted advisors," Walker said. "Thairon killed them, five years ago."

What? "You weren't alone there?"

"Of course not," Walker snapped. "They were magic-wielders, the best of them. Why do you think the Alliance turned a blind eye to Thairon? They thought we were handling it."

"So… they're dead." That explained… a *lot*. "So that's why the whole upstairs Passage was cut off—no one actually knows how to close the doors."

Hell. They needed a source to absorb the auros…

They needed me.

If I told them, they'd use me to cut off my homeworld. Forever.

Walker assessed me. He knew. That's why he'd told me— the bastard knew deep down, my distrust of the Alliance lingered. I didn't trust them not to sacrifice my homeworld, or leave it to ruin. They'd destroy all access to it forever if it meant stopping the war.

I stumbled over my feet in an effort to get away from Walker's cage. *I can't tell them.*

Even if the Alliance is destroyed, the worlds overrun, the Balance wrecked and Earth turned into a new Enzar?

Worse, I saw how Walker had turned out the way he had. He'd had the fates of worlds foisted on him from birth, from *his* father. Not that in any way excused what he'd done to Kay. But oddly enough, it *had* spared Kay from having the same fate.

Enzar's not your responsibility. If they're using those doors, if there's anything you can do to stop Earth falling…

I had to tell the council.

10

KAY

While Ada was talking to the Enzarians in the recreation room, I left. I turned invisible to walk to the training complex, to be on the safe side. For an instant, watching the traffic stalled at a red light, I wondered if given the option, I'd keep the invisibility up even after the war. It was the only time I didn't feel Walker's eyes on my back.

The simulator brought no answers, but at least it alleviated the sensation of being trapped. My focus was scattered, though. I couldn't stop thinking of how the people who'd created the simulator had known about the void. Klathica had started the first simulator, but who had thought of the idea? Of course, I knew who'd popularised it. Robert Walker.

I abandoned the simulation and headed back to Central, thinking hard. Walker hadn't talked yet, but the simulator was *his* area of expertise. As was KimaroTech. Despite my thoughts always coming back to him, I couldn't think of a reason he'd kill Lilian Greyson. He'd been the one who'd appointed her in the first place.

Carl's office was open. "Kay," he said. "You've seen Ada?"

"Not since the meeting."

"She was on her way upstairs to speak to the council. She looked pretty upset."

"The council aren't talking to anyone now." Damn. Indecision halted my steps for a moment. I wanted to know what had upset Ada... but I needed to talk to Walker first. Just in case some of those protesting guards did come back here to kill him. "Anyway, can I have the keys to Walker's place?"

"Again?" He handed them to me. "You did great up there today," he added. "Talked those guards down. I've set a couple of them packing. They weren't cut out for this line of work anyway."

"Yeah. Suppose not many people are, least of all now."

"Except the Academy," said Carl. "Some of the final-year students qualify. But parents are raising objections." He shook his head. "As if they won't be out there in the Passages in a few months anyway."

"Yeah. The dropouts will have gone by now." The Academy. Another place I'd sent a donation via Walker's account. If I survived the war, I'd pay them a visit and tell them to invest the cash in scholarships for people who couldn't afford the tuition. And in magic-related training for those who needed it.

Walker had never set foot in that place. He hadn't wrecked the whole Alliance. But right now, I had a strong suspicion he—and his father—were at the heart of Enzar's conflict. With the Alliance, at least.

Maybe it was paranoia. God only knew it was justified given his presence had crept into every area of my life and shattered it to pieces...

Ada's face flashed before my eyes. My hand clenched on the key. No. Not everything.

"I'll only be a few minutes," I said, and left for Walker's cell.

"You're back," said Walker, as I closed the cell door behind me. Once again, the walls seemed to press in on me. "First the girl and now you."

My heart missed a beat. "Ada was here?"

"You just missed her." His teeth gleamed in a smile. "Does she often speak to your enemies behind your back?"

What the hell had he said to her? If she'd gone to the council, it must have been serious.

"Don't push me. Was KimaroTech—was Robert Walker involved in supplying Enzar's war effort?"

"You already know the answer."

"Say it. Say what your father did. Tell me the facts, don't shroud them in half-lies. I'll know if you do."

A bluff. But he'd lost more than half of his confidence, much as he tried to hide it. I'd never seen it in him before, but I could tell. Maybe it was the absence of whatever drug he was hooked on. The absence of the simulator.

Or maybe it had finally started to sink in: Lawrence Walker was losing at his own game.

"My father was the leader of Earth's Alliance," said Walker, in a bored voice. "Mostly because he was one of only a handful of people on this world who knew the truth about the Multiverse. While most thought it should remain that way, he persuaded others it was in Earth's interests, for the sake of future advancement, for the public to know. The almost-war between Klathica and Valeria cemented the decision to reveal the truth, because Earth could have easily been collateral damage. We weren't prepared. We still aren't." His dark eyes flashed. "The Walker family flourished before the exposure, but once Earth was out in the open, he made his billions. There's not a world in the Multiverse he hasn't had a stake in. Not a single branch of the Alliance that hasn't experienced the results of his *brilliance*. Robert Walker, the genius —and a liar."

"Your point being?" There wasn't a word of this I didn't know already.

"My point is the entire Walker name is rotten to the core. Robert Walker not only financed Enzar's war, he helped start it. He created the sim-tech that reduced Thairon to a vegetative state. He created the magic-source-fuelled implants and drugs that addled Klathica's population. KimaroTech ruined the Alliance, sank its teeth in and spread its insidious poison to every corner."

"I'm here to talk about Enzar, not whether your father was a crook or not. He got the adamantine from Enzar, right? And he gave them weapons in return."

"If you already knew, why ask me?"

"Just for confirmation. Now, let me get this straight. When you cut Enzar off, how did you know they wouldn't retaliate?"

"I didn't," said Walker. "There was supposed to be absolutely no way for them to get back into the Passages. Every single door was sealed tight. Of course, Cethrax was a problem, but all the doors on Cethrax to Enzar were closed. With no auros left on that world, doorways can't open, even naturally."

"Well, it didn't work," I snapped. "Cethrax is with Enzar, somehow, and Enzar's sending threatening messages to Earth. Know how they might do that?"

"An Alliance-run communication centre is compromised. Surely the council must have thought of it?"

I clenched my hand around the bars. "Yeah, I think there's a traitor. I think you know who it is."

"You are mistaken," Walker said coldly. "If Enzar has, as you claim, had no connection with the allied worlds over the past five years… But there's that girl."

My spine turned to ice. Ada had come here twenty years ago, through the hidden Passage.

He gave me a calculating look. "Ada Fletcher isn't her real name, is it?"

"I'm the one asking the questions here."

"If you want to know why I closed all the doors to Enzar, at the time, the Royals had conquered seven worlds. Both sides were searching for a nexus, a magic source at the heart of their world, and that their ultimate aim was to find Enzar's. Given the nature of the nexus on Thairon, I would be inclined to believe one exists. Robert Walker was on Enzar when the magebloods unleashed their weapon… and there he remains."

"That's where he died?" Disbelief entered my tone, but maybe it shouldn't have surprised me. All I knew for certain was the two of us in the room were the only survivors of the family line. Robert Walker's death had always been a mystery. I'd assumed it was classified, and I'd guessed right.

"Correct," he said. "My father died when the magebloods' weapon turned out to be a little more than they could handle. But I watched the situation for five years. I knew the Royals had a weapon never seen before on any world. I had a few educated guesses at the nature of that weapon… the Royals were known for their distaste for natural-born magic-wielders, but they plainly had designed something that could reduce a thousand magebloods to dust in a single attack. I'd never seen devastation like it. Eventually, I worked out the truth: they made up for their own lack of magic by using people as the vessels for sources. Human beings—the one weapon that cannot be controlled, unlike their kimaros. A weapon with free will. And they were searching for a nexus, a power without limit. Most of the doors were already sealed, but I knew beyond all shadow of a doubt once they found that source, they'd destroy everyone who stood against them. So I sought out every possible entrance to their world and sealed it. World-keys are unable to connect to

Enzar now, and every piece of auros in the known worlds belongs to the Alliance."

"So what you're saying is someone did a really good job of working around it?" I made my face go blank, like my heart wasn't racing at a million miles an hour. Like it wasn't becoming increasingly clear someone linked to Ada was the logical connection to those messages directed at her. And they were based on Klathica—or at least able to communicate through their network.

"I'm saying, Kay, the Alliance will die before I do."

I instantly tensed. "What makes you so sure?"

"Because it's clear my father found a way around the locked doorways, after all. There's nobody else who was on Enzar in the decade or so before the doors were closed, with access to auros. How old is that girl? Younger than you? I closed Enzar's doors more than twenty years ago."

My heart dropped. *No. It can't have been him.*

"There are other Enzarians here, aren't there? I saw the recent records. A large number of offworlders were registered at once, a month ago. There were also a number of documents with allusions to a place known as the *Offworld Transition Point...* you wouldn't happen to know anything about that, would you?"

I stared him out. "Yes. The Alliance has needed an outpost for offworld aid for a long time."

"You'd say that," said Walker. "I'd pin that one on Elizabeth, but I suspect it was before her time. Based on the records, that particular transition point opened not long after the war started, but existed before as an Alliance outpost for contact with hostile worlds. I naively assumed it was cut off after the war started. They hid it well—too well, for non-Alliance members. They could only have known how to hide it if they'd had contact with a higher-up member of the Alliance... and the last such person to set foot on Enzar was Robert Walker."

Impossible. But it was true—no other council members *could* have gone there since then. And if Enzar knew how to link to the Passages and had the means to do so, they could easily have attacked the Alliance by now. But they didn't know. The transition point had been closed off, but until now, it *had* been the only way off that world. It hadn't originally been a sanctuary at all—more like a means of transporting weapons behind the Alliance's back. I was willing to bet what was left of his fortune that Robert Walker would have done just that. But I couldn't be sure it was true. Not yet.

"Of course," said Walker, "the reason I assumed that particular transition point was inactive was because there is to my knowledge only one world in the Multiverse where it's safe to open multiple doorways without causing the world itself to collapse."

What? He had to be lying. The image of the void came to mind, the collapsing blackness, the three-way doorway hinged between Thairon, Earth, and...

"Cethrax?" Disbelief coloured my tone, but I didn't care. "You're seriously saying the safe zone was based on *Cethrax?*"

He had to be lying. Yeah, the Alliance rarely sent extended missions into Cethrax, and most of the swamp looked pretty similar. If the Stoneskins could use it to transit for years without being picked up on, then it *was* possible.

Never mind that now. I'd consider later just how the Walker family had covered that particular detail up. Either way, we were fucked. Enzar had control of the transition point, on Cethrax, or they'd *already* infiltrated the Alliance.

"Wait." I'd been so goddamn *stupid.* "After Thairon, you said your servants were waiting at KimaroTech. You didn't use the world-key to come to Earth. You went from Thairon to Klathica."

Which meant Earth's trace had, until the battle, never been near Thairon. But Klathica's had, and their trace had brought Enzar to them.

My communicator buzzed, making me jump. *Does he know?* Surely not, if he'd gone to so much trouble to keep Enzar away.

Another buzzing noise, then an alarm rang out, echoing off the walls. I stepped back, my heart thumping. That was the emergency alert.

"Aren't you going to answer that?" he asked softly.

I lifted the communicator screen underneath the only light in the room.

A message from Carl: "Vey-Xanetha is under attack from Cethrax."

11

KAY

Vey-Xanetha. The world where three gods lived and shaped the lives of the people there. Aktha, who moved the continents, Xanet of the forest who could heal... and Veyak. Living magic, a living source. I wasn't likely to forget the abyss that had opened between Vey-Xanetha and Cethrax, through which the StoneKing had drawn Veyak's power and enslaved the Vox. Now the Vox was working with the magebloods... I should have guessed it'd be a likely target. And from there, Cethrax could get at the Alliance.

Not if we stop them first.

All the magic-wielders from Central joined Ada and me, led by Carl. Other guards from the various Alliance branches came to fight with us, but Klathica was noticeably absent. The chameleon suits were in beta testing mode, and we also had one each of the double-sided daggers. Ada's brother had said they were mostly made of sciras with a coating of lustre on one side and adamantine on the other. Meanwhile, our guard boots now incorporated hover-tech, thanks to Valeria. If nothing else, I was glad Valeria was on our side.

But was it enough to push back Cethrax? From the reports, it sounded like the vox-kind had appeared from nowhere. They must be using a doorway, or several. Which meant they'd figured out how to link to Alliance worlds.

If they got Veyak under their control again, we're screwed. It was a miracle Ada and I had both walked away from that one alive.

Ms Weston put me in charge of the world-key. Given my penchant for flaunting Alliance laws, it was further proof of the end of days. Though for Vey-Xanetha, the apocalypse wasn't exactly an unfamiliar prospect.

I used the world-key to open a doorway to Vey-Xanetha a few feet into the Passages. Ada stood at my side, gloves pulled on, dagger already drawn. The glint caught the light as the door opened. The world-key was the one we'd used before and it was drawn to sources, so I gestured to everyone to stand back as I completed the last symbol.

A blast of magic shook the Passages even before the door fully opened. I tensed, instantly raising the adamantine side of the dagger. The doorway tore open from floor to ceiling, and another burst of red light blinded me for an instant.

The world was on fire, or so it seemed. The sky was boiling red, the ground scorched and broken, and opposite the door where we stood, the void stretched across the horizon.

We're too late.

"I'm gonna check what's happening." I crossed the threshold of the doorway, hover boots activated.

Magic swirled around me instantly. The shapes of Cethraxian monsters became visible through the haze in the distance. Huge, hulking vox-kind alongside smaller dreyverns. Too many to count. Just like the time they'd invaded Earth alongside Thairon, except this time, they'd pitted themselves against a world where the very forces of nature conspired to keep them out.

Problem was, it also didn't want *us* there. Throwing ourselves into a war between forces of nature was generally labelled 'bad idea'. Worse, I had no clue whereabouts we were or where Cethrax might have opened their doorway. *Focus, Kay.* I scanned the surroundings. Behind the outlines of Cethrax's army was a faint glow, a horizontal line in the distance. There was our doorway. Just like the last time Cethrax had been linked to Vey-Xanetha—preferably without the Stoneskins this time.

Ada's hand clenched on mine, startling me. "Veyak's angry," she whispered. "I—I don't think we should use magic.

Shit. The new uniform probably muted the effects, but it was only a matter of time before the god noticed one of us again. Though I'd escaped Veyak's wrath last time, I'd damn near died, and so had Ada. Cethrax had picked the wrong world to terrorise. My magic was pretty much useless against their armour, so we'd have to go hand-to-hand and hope the god didn't decide to take out its wrath on us instead of the intruders.

I glanced behind me. "Guys, we'll have to lure Cethrax away from any targets. Ada can destroy what's holding the door open. Like last time." But before, there hadn't been an army of vox-kind in the way. Then again, the gods were more dangerous.

"That?" Carl said from behind us, indicating the line on the horizon. "That must be connecting the two worlds."

"Cethrax and Vey-Xanetha," I muttered. "Whatever you do, everyone, do *not* go through the void. It leads to Cethrax or the abyss, and you don't want to be there."

"Right," said Carl. "We'll split into two groups. One by the void to stop the monsters coming out, and one to chase down the ones already on Vey-Xanetha."

I nodded to Ada. If Veyak was overpowered again, she wouldn't be able to drain the magic right out of the source, but it was worth a try, and the quickest way to close the void.

Only it meant splitting up. On a battlefield.

"Activate the suits," Carl commanded. "Stay in line until I say so."

I hoped he'd picked the best of the bunch for this mission, because invisibly tripping over one another would be potentially suicidal. Together, our army moved forwards.

"I'll come back," Ada whispered in my ear, already invisible. I activated my own chameleon suit as the doorway I'd opened closed behind us.

Magic lit up the sky again, though I couldn't tell where from. The illumination was enough to draw the monsters' attention in our direction even with the chameleon suits active. So much for sneaking up on them.

A whirring sounded as our small army activated our hover-ware and converged on the enemy, and the battlefield erupted. I used my own hover boots to aim for the nearest target, a smaller vox-kind. Magic wouldn't help against any of these creatures, so either the gods were pissed off and raining lightning down on the world again, or there were magic-wielders involved.

My dagger found its mark, cutting the ferver vox's throat, and I moved onto the next target. A larger vox-kind spun stupidly on the spot, clearly realising someone was attacking it but unable to see the enemy. I left the creature behind and made for one of the biggest chalder voxes I'd ever seen. Seven feet or more high and almost as wide, it moved slowly but shook the earth wherever it trod. I silently crept up, dagger in hand, and aimed at its weak spot.

The creature shot out a hand and I barely activated the hover boots in time, flying high out of reach. Its comparatively tiny black eyes scrunched up as though searching me out, but I'd already used my hover boots' speed to circle it from behind. I threw the dagger, which sank into its shoulder. Damn. I'd just missed the weak spot, and the vox bellowed loud enough to shake the earth. Wait. The ground shook again. *Aktha.* The god of the earth.

Even the vox's pained roars were lost in the clamour as the ground trembled in a roar. All over the battlefield, vox-kind fell as though struck dead by an invisible force. I moved closer to the flailing chalder vox and threw my second dagger. This one sank to the hilt behind its neck. The vox screamed, its legs buckling, and fell in a bone-shaking crash. I retrieved my weapons and joined the others in the larger battle. Hoping Ada was on her way to end it before the chaos spread beyond this world.

Using magic was out of the question. Every time I considered it, lightning flashed behind my eyes and a static tingle against my skin told me I'd be a slave to the god again if I dared. Veyak was here somewhere, all right.

I couldn't see Ada. Couldn't see any other people, either, but nobody would deactivate their chameleon suits when it gave us such a significant advantage. Any semblance of formation was scattered, and only the cries of the monsters gave a clue as to the others' whereabouts. The bodies of goblins and vox-kind littered the ground, but there were still far too many of them. A faint flickering in the air told me some guards had been hit with magic, which weakened the invisibility in the chameleon suits.

I'd moved closer to the doorway by this point, where it divided the land from the sky. Behind, the canyon we fought in stretched back to the jungle. But that wasn't the doorway I was concerned about. A cliff bordered the army on my right, and one look confirmed my suspicions—that was the cliff where the door which led to the Passages was hidden. The cliff might be steep, but the smaller dreyverns had already begun to climb up. The smoke of the battle had hidden them from view. The bastards. The Alliance had shut them out of the Passages, so they'd found another way. And I was willing to bet Enzar would follow.

I tapped the earpiece. "The Passage door's on our right. Cethrax are heading that way."

Ada's voice, a second later. "Crap. I'm coming."

So she hadn't been able to remove the source of the void and close the door to Cethrax. But the priority had to be keeping the monsters out of the Passages, then closing the doorway. And whenever I so much as considered using magic, the presence of Veyak brushed against me, sharp and raging mad.

I wasn't about to get taken out by the god again.

As I reached the foot of the cliff, I kicked the hover-boots to life and shot into the air.

I collided with something heavy, scaled, and sharp. A freaking wyvern. At least I was invisible, which bought me enough time to put myself between the monster and the doorway at the clifftop.

Below, the battle continued, monsters crawling out of the void, magic striking the ground. More guards ran around, some visible, which meant the second world-key had been activated and backup had arrived. But no sign of Ada.

A brief flash in the air, lit up by the magic. The wyvern dived, and I launched myself at it, slamming down on the monster's back. Ordinarily, the scaled beast wouldn't have noticed, but I hit it at the highest speed and stabbed my dagger into its neck at the same time. The adamantine side of the blade cut through its scales, but they were thick enough I couldn't reach the tip of its spine in time for it to throw me off.

I free-fell, a roaring in my ears. The air rushed past, magic lit up the sky. My left heel dug into the brake and I stopped inches from the ground. Above, the wyvern flailed and snapped at something in the air. A person. *Ada?*

Cursing, I propelled myself upwards again, aiming my gun and firing at its gaping mouth. The wyvern dived at the last second, the bullet glancing off its scales. I'd already kicked up speed again, my dagger aimed at its eye, but it flipped over, claws swiping madly at the air. I dug the blade into its side, dislodging a couple of scales, before it struck at me with its barbed tail. Dodging, I pulled the dagger free and moved out of harm's way.

"Distract it!" Ada's voice echoed in my ears, as her blurred figure passed by.

I switched off the invisibility, directly in front of the wyvern as it slashed the air again. My dagger slashed, too, just missing its claws. Another strike knocked several scales loose. I aimed for the mouth next and missed, my blade glancing off its teeth. Even though I'd used the adamantine side of the dagger, the impact rattled through me. Damn, the bastard was tough. But it did have weak points.

Ada and I circled it, striking out with our daggers and turning invisible to avoid its counter-strikes. My blade sank into flesh. Blood poured from its tail, and it screamed as I fired a bullet into the open wound. Ada appeared in the air behind it, face set, dagger dripping blood. As the wyvern's jaws stretched in a bone-shaking scream, I extended the dagger to its full length and stabbed it through the roof of its mouth.

The lizard screamed again. Swearing, I tugged the dagger free and tumbled through a fountain of blood, regaining my balance a foot below.

Another scale fell free, and another, and its scream became a death rattle. Ada appeared again, above its head, dagger buried to the hilt in the top of its head. I flew up to join her, but she'd already pulled the weapon free, hovering beside the cliff's edge as the wyvern fell, wings splayed.

Ada braced herself against the cliff, breathing heavily. "Kay." She looked around with wide eyes. I switched off the invisibility, leaning on the cliff, too. The wyvern's scaly shape disappeared into the red mist rising from below. Beneath were the tiny shapes of Alliance guards and the bigger shapes of the monsters. They hadn't stopped coming.

And we needed to close the doorway. I hit acceleration again and rose a few feet, to where the door to the Passages rested in the side of the cliff. The door was closed. The monsters must all be coming from the doorway opened on ground level. But why would Cethrax invade this world if not to come to the Passages, and through that, the Alliance?

I pushed at the door, wondering if they had backup waiting behind it. Locked. The Alliance must have sealed the door as a precaution.

"So they locked it after all." My hands tingled underneath the gloves. Magic. Where *was* Veyak? For all the times I'd sensed it in the battle, I hadn't seen the creepy malevolent red shadow fall over the earth. Aktha was visible in the aftershocks trembling through the earth, swallowing monsters into the depths, but there was no sign of the lightning god.

"Come on," said Ada. "We've got to get rid of the door Cethrax opened. I couldn't see the source."

"I can fly through it," I said, as we flew back down the cliff.

Her eyes rounded. "What? Fly through the void?"

"We need to find out what's powering it. You got a better idea?"

"If the door closes, you'll be trapped wherever the hell it leads. Kay—I don't think that's is a good idea."

I looked down at the seemingly never-ending army

crossing the void from Cethrax. "I think we're out of options at this point. I have the world-key, right?"

"Be careful!" she shouted, as I hit the super-speed switch and pelted at the void, and the swampland waiting on the other side.

But there weren't two sides. There were three. Just like when Cethrax had invaded Earth alongside Thairon…

Wait. On the other side of the void was the Vey-Xanethan jungle. They were attacking both sides of the continent at once.

I flew right through the smoke and emerged in a tangle of tree roots. A second battle raged around me, with vox-kind swiping at the platforms suspended above the ground, goblins climbing the trees only to be pushed back. The summoners had formed a line across the walkways between the trees, hands raised to the sky. I kicked off the ground again when the earth shifted, and the trees extended branches to beat off Cethrax's forces.

Vey-Xanetha was holding its own against the invaders. Once I was sure, I crossed the void again, this time aiming for Cethrax. For an instant, I was suspended in red smoke, the tingle of magic making itself felt even through the magicproof gloves.

The voltage went up, like a pressure on my skull, and a bolt of magic lit up everything—all three sides of the void.

On Cethrax's side, the monstrous form of the god—Veyak —fought the vox-kind. I could do nothing more than stare for a moment. That was why I hadn't seen Veyak in Vey-Xanetha. The god had crossed the border to Cethrax and fought to defend its world from the invaders.

But what was powering the void?

I turned back, to look closer at the part of the void which bordered on Cethrax. For a moment, the swirling currents of red smoke remained opaque. Then a face looked back at me from within the pit.

I froze. It wasn't Veyak. But I'd only seen one other kimaros that size, with that much power.

Impossible.

It was the monster from Thairon. The one which was supposed to have died when my father activated the bomb.

For an instant, I hesitated, hovering at the edge of the void. Then common sense kicked in and I backed off. I was no match for that. Not without Ada. Maybe Veyak could take it, maybe not. The creature holding the void open was a nexus—and it was supposed to be dead.

"Shit," Ada whispered, appearing behind me. "It's powering the doorway. I can't get a handle on it."

"Nor me."

Chills raced down my back. We couldn't leave the doorway open, but if the kimaros hadn't died when Ada and I had combined our attacks *or* after my father's bomb, could even a living god overcome it? Bolts of lightning sizzled over Cethrax, striking the monsters down, but Veyak hadn't directly engaged the beast holding open the void yet. The aftershocks tingled in the air, making my whole body shake.

Without warning, Ada grabbed my hand. "There's a source behind us!"

Next thing I knew, she'd dragged me alongside her into Vey-Xanetha—not the jungle, but the canyon we'd fought in before. The kimaros disappeared as we left the void behind, but I still felt its presence, a pressure building on my skull.

"What source?" I looked around, but saw only the doorway cutting the universe in two, and the thin layer of smoke separating us from both the jungle and Cethrax.

"Not the kimaros." She gripped my hand. "It's stronger. I—"

An explosion tore through the air. We were both flung

back by a blast of magic from the void itself. I raised my hands to shield my face and the gloves disintegrated before my eyes, the antimagic stripped away. Next thing I knew I was on my back, a ringing noise in my ears. I tried to say Ada's name, but no sound remained but the aftershock. *Did someone set off a bomb?* Or had one of the kimaros—?

"Kay!" yelled a voice, cutting through the ringing in my ears.

The air flickered, and Carl stood in front of me, dripping blood everywhere. The chameleon suit had deactivated—and his wasn't the only one. The other guards had been thrown back by the blast, too, and the magical aftershock must have killed the batteries in the suits. Some of the fighters had been hit by debris. I tried to get up, but my body was shaking too much to stand. The whole *world* shook, trembled like an earthquake had wrenched the earth.

"The hell just happened?" I couldn't see Ada anywhere, and panic kicked in as Carl staggered back. His right arm— or what was left of it—was drenched in blood.

"Shit." I grasped the world-key in my pocket. I needed to draw a way back—

Another blast of magic ignited the sky, and the void lit up in fire. Veyak's presence pushed against the back of my head. The god hadn't been responsible for the explosion—and now Veyak was on our side of the void again. Red clouds gathered overhead and bolts of lightning rained down, striking at Cethraxian soldiers and Alliance guards alike.

"Cut that out," I shouted, raising my hand to the sky. Magic flowed into me, burning against my exposed hands, every nerve lighting on fire.

Whatever pissed off the god, it was angry enough to kill the lot of us.

I managed to get to my feet and hit the heel of the hover boot. Miraculously, it still worked—good job, because my legs didn't seem inclined to walk in a straight line. I moved closer to the void. The explosion had knocked us back a good twenty feet, and now the god had crossed over…

I frowned. I didn't see the jungle *or* Cethrax on the other side. The army had stopped coming. But the doorway remained. It hadn't been closed. Instead, another sight greeted me: a city with cable-wrapped buildings and grid-like streets, viewed from above.

Klathica had hijacked the doorway from their own side.

As the thought shot through my head, the god's presence pushed at me again, and a blast of magic split the sky in a rain of thunderbolts. My vision blurred, the magic level reaching a fever pitch. I tumbled back to the ground, shaking uncontrollably with the charge. Second level, building higher. I tried to get my hand on the adamantine side of the dagger—it sliced through my palm, and my vision disappeared entirely in a haze of red.

Then I felt nothing at all, like all sensation had been snuffed out.

Strange how I'd stared death so many times in the face and yet when the real thing arrived, I couldn't quite believe it was happening. As if I'd earned the chance to cheat it yet again.

This was the second time I'd died here. And this time, there was no god to save me.

~

ADA

Magic surged through me, and that was all the warning I got before the world flipped around me, as I desperately tried to use the hover boots' brakes to stop myself being flung twenty feet into the air. The blast had thrown everyone else back, too, but the overwhelming presence of the kimaros, and Veyak, muted all sound and feeling but numb shock.

Someone had created a magic-based explosion on the other side of the void. I knew that sensation. I'd felt it before when I'd handled magic-based explosives, but never like this. The whole world had shaken. More than one world. The swamp was *gone*, as was the jungle, to be replaced by a bird's-eye-view of a city.

Klathica. They'd somehow tapped into the doorway and shut off the link to Cethrax—by setting off a bomb, right at the kimaros. And… and it looked like it *worked*. The sky lit up again. Thunderbolts struck the ground. Veyak was pissed. *Oh, shit.* I steadied myself, using the hover boots for balance. There were bodies on the ground. Humans and monsters. Some stirring, some not.

I kicked up the hover boots and moving to the nearest body. Iriel. She'd pushed herself half-upright.

"What—?"

"The god's angry. We need to get off this world." But I wouldn't trust Klathica, either. *What the hell were they thinking, blowing up a freaking kimaros?* Where was Kay? Aktha's magic had altered the earth, and there were patches of burned ground everywhere Veyak had struck. And bodies. *Please don't let them all be dead—*

Another blast of lightning shook the earth. Now Cethrax's army had gone, the god had only one target—us.

My gaze snagged on an unmoving body amongst the debris. *No. Please, no.*

"Kay!"

Nothing. His hands were burned red, a sign of third level magic, and when I lifted his right palm, there was no pulse.

"Shit. No. Kay. Wake up."

Panic clawed up my throat. Panic, and rage, and other things I couldn't confront right now. My hands tingled with magic, like a second pulse in itself.

Magic. The gods.

I reached beyond the lingering presence of Veyak, reached for the other I knew was there, though dampened.

Xanet answered.

The shock vibrated through my bones as my hand gripped Kay's wrist and the other pressed to the earth. Xanet's power, amplified, shot through the sky and earth, which trembled again.

Aktha's presence pushed against Xanet.

I *was* Xanet. I saw through the god's eyes, the terror of the torn-up earth, the world ruined by the monsters from the void. I couldn't feel my earthly body, just the pulse of life through the earth, through this world.

We can stop this, thought the part of me that wasn't in shock. *We're here to stop this. We can end it. Help me.*

The pulse beat through me, through everything, healing all the damage it could reach. Holes in the earth sealed. The soothing presence pushed Veyak's wrath aside, and in my own body—

In my hand, a pulse thrummed to life against my fingertips. I gasped as Kay's hand twitched, and I swore my own heart stopped beating.

"Kay." As he sat up, I flung my arms around his neck. "I thought—"

His voice was a whisper. "How did you—?"

"Xanet was still there. The gods wanted Cethrax gone, too. And—it wanted to heal the world. I… I felt it. I spoke to it, and… and it listened to me." I spoke to Xanet. Or *as* Xanet. I wasn't completely clear on that one.

"Damn." He stared at me like I was a ghost. Like I was the one who, for a few seconds—maybe longer—had been *dead*.

I shook all over with the adrenaline, locking that thought away until I had time to deal with it. Veyak was still here.

"Come on." I stumbled to my feet, and he followed suit. Not all the fallen guards were moving. I kept one eye on our path and the other on Kay, like part of me couldn't quite believe I'd saved him.

A figure on the ground shifted, groaning, and my insides lurched when it registered it was Carl, and he was lying in a pool of his own blood. And—alive.

Xanet. The god had performed a genuine miracle.

"Shit," said Kay. "Shit. Don't move. We have to get you out of here."

"It's all right." Carl shifted and I almost overbalanced—his left arm was *gone,* torn away. "The wound sealed itself. I thought… I thought I heard your voice, Ada."

"Uhh…" I tried to focus on his face, not the bloodstained mess where his arm used to be. *It sealed itself. Xanet can't regrow limbs.* But the god had tried. Magic had tried.

Kay's arm went around my shoulder. Good job, because my knees chose that moment to give out as shock set in. "Leave me," I muttered. "Help him."

Two other guards were already here, offering help. Now the ground had settled, and everyone was stirring, and the sky had darkened already.

"We can't guarantee the other god won't come back," said Kay. "Come on. We have to get out of here."

12

KAY

That was close. Too close. Five guards had died in the fight, swept into a nothingness even the healing god couldn't bring them back from. *I should be with them.*

Don't go there.

I couldn't do any more than help with the others. Get everyone back to Central. A nagging sense told me I should search the Passages in case Cethrax had taken their army elsewhere.

And that didn't even cover what Klathica had done. Only Ada and I had seen both sides of the void, and what had happened. Apparently, Klathica's new bomb had antimagic at its core, and had closed the doorway.

For now. If the kimaros was linked to Cethrax and Enzar again, all bets were off.

To nobody's surprise, Ms Weston called an emergency council meeting there and then, for anyone who was in a fit state to attend.

"It seems we have Klathica to thank for their quick intervention in a situation which might have been a lot worse than it was," said Mr Shean.

"Yeah, because they decided to set off a *bomb*," said Ada. Even though we weren't touching, I could feel her trembling through the few inches separating us. We were lucky there were so few casualties. Carl had insisted he was fine, that the wound was cauterised, but had been hauled off to the medical division anyway. I was fairly sure Ada was in shock. Maybe I was, too. But I knew if I shut down now, we might be taken off guard again. Despite all our preparations, Enzar had blindsided us. Cethrax was still under their control, *and* the kimaros—nexus—of Thairon.

"Was it authorised?" I asked, now every eye was on us. "Given the suspicious murders on Klathica this week, I have to ask."

"I told you," said Izen, through gritted teeth, "we are strenuously working around the clock to catch any miscreants. However, when we learned of the attack on Vey-Xanetha, it was our duty to intervene on the Alliance's behalf in an appropriate way."

"Evidently." I couldn't keep the sarcasm out of my voice. Apparently, they still hadn't learned their lesson about messing with magical sources. Even after the murder of KimaroTech's top executives, they'd decided to throw a bomb at a living source. I hoped the gods wouldn't take it out on the Vey-Xanethan people. "You do realise you were facing two living sources, right? They don't react well to being blown up."

"No harm came of it."

"Had you even tested that bomb before?" asked Ada. "Because it made one of the living sources angry enough to try and strike us down. It nearly killed us."

"Angered?" Izen's eyebrow arched. "Magic creatures are not truly living, are they?"

"I think that's a debate for another time," said Ms Weston, who, I was gratified to see, looked at least as pissed off as I was, much as it barely showed on her face. "That was a dangerous move on Klathica's part, one that could easily have done as much damage to our side as the enemy."

"The guards were backed into a corner," said Izen. "Nobody out there, nobody in the *allied worlds* has the ability to stand up to a force like theirs." His eyes fell on me, and a chill shot through my whole body. He knew I was aware what the kimaros powering the void really was—and where it came from originally. So the nexus of a world didn't have to remain living *on* that world. The kimaros must have ended up on Cethrax when Ada and I had cut off the doorway to Thairon.

It was on Enzar's side. And we hadn't even *seen* any of the magebloods. Somehow, that made them seem even more dangerous.

My hands balled into fists. We'd nearly been wiped out. And an illegal, dangerous weapon had saved us. Not Ada and me. Being a magic-wielder had been a curse, not a blessing, in that fight. Small mercy Xanet had healed my magic-burned hands, too. The dead were less fortunate.

Izen was still speaking. "You all need to understand this was a last resort. The KimaroTech labs did run some tests on similar bombs, so we were reasonably confident it would behave as predicted."

KimaroTech. Of fucking course. More than one Klathican bomb had been used in the name of stopping the war, at any cost.

Did he order it?

Sure, Walker was in jail, but I never had managed to track down everyone who worked for him. He had his claws in Klathica, and they wouldn't so easily be ripped away. Izen himself wasn't guilt-free, though, not by a long shot.

"We are on the alert for another attack," said Ms Weston. "Vey-Xanetha was an obvious target, but it might have been a diversion. We are working tirelessly to ensure no enemies find their way into Central—or into any of the Alliance branches."

"And what of Cethrax?" Izen's eyes narrowed. "That place breeds doorways like it does monsters. Are there no spies there?"

"No, there are not," said Greene. "Certainly not human ones. They wouldn't survive." It was difficult for the average person to blend in with a bunch of monsters. Even with bloodrock solution or Chameleons.

"Then you can hardly complain you didn't see the attack coming," said Izen. "I suspected Cethrax would strike, and I stand by my actions."

He refused to say another word. The council finished discussing our next steps, none of which involved Ada and me. We'd been lucky to survive the fight, but if Cethrax had attacked one world, they clearly weren't hiding any longer. Any other world might be the next target.

Even when the meeting broke up, half the offworld council stayed behind, in conversation. Izen, however, was the first to leave. I glanced at Ada, then moved after him, waylaying him by the door.

"Did you take the order from Lawrence Walker?" I asked, before I could question whether it was a wise decision.

"I beg your pardon?"

"What I said." I switched to Klathican. "Walker used a bomb just like that to commit genocide on Thairon. Forgive me for being a little suspicious when it was detonated without warning in a dangerous manner. *Who* was in charge?"

"Klathica's own weapons division," said Izen. "We don't take orders from traitors."

"Did he leave instructions?"

I was grasping at straws now. Those bombs were manufactured by the biggest company on Klathica. It needn't be related to Walker at all. What he'd done had been unspeakably evil, but his motives aligned with Klathica's own, however misplaced. And they *had* closed the doors between Cethrax and Vey-Xanetha.

Maybe Walker had been telling the truth. There was more than one side to the war.

"No instructions," said Izen. "We had the weapon, and a reason to use it."

"Yes, but you opened a doorway directly into the void. How did you know to do that?"

"You're accustomed to keeping secrets, aren't you?"

What? "If you're suggesting I'm hiding information that could potentially bring down the Alliance from the inside, you're mistaken."

"If you had the bomb, the only means to close the void, would you not have used it?"

"Not in the presence of a living source." I stood my ground. "That creature nearly killed all of us. It's a being which almost destroyed the Balance. There'll be repercussions no matter what."

"This so-called god is nothing but a magical force." Izen shook his head. "I thought Central were beyond such superstitions."

"You're not a magic-wielder," I said, "are you? If you were, and you'd been there, you'd have felt it."

He regarded me with a cold look. "Fortunately for both of us, we'll never have to find out."

Dickhead. My hands clenched at my sides as he left the room.

Maybe I *wanted* to blame Klathica, because that was *his*

stomping ground. But how could they have been the site of high-profile murders yesterday and heroes today?

One of the mysteries of the bloody Multiverse.

The long-ass day wasn't over yet. Those uninjured were organised into patrols, not just in the Passages but around the outskirts of Central itself. By the time my shift finished, it was midnight, and I found Ada waiting in the entrance hall.

"You don't have a shift until the morning, do you?"

She shook her head. "No. There's something I wanted to tell you. Before—before the attack on Vey-Xanetha."

"What is it?"

She glanced over her shoulder as we made for the stairs. Nobody else was around at this time, aside from the guards inside and outside Central's doors. "Nell said... she said the kimaros were created on Enzar."

My heart missed a beat. "I knew, I think. Walker told me as much."

Cethrax's foot-soldiers had believed Thairon's kimaros was their Great Undergod, so it made sense that their army had continued to serve the magebloods even after the doorway had blown up. But the fact that the magic-creatures might have been created on Enzar in the first place... it explained a lot about the nature of the conflict.

"The Royals... they experimented on animals, first," Ada said. "So they were linked with Enzar from the start. Cethrax, I mean. It might have been going on for hundreds of years."

"Walker said kimaros can be intimidated, if threatened with antimagic," I said slowly. "Enzar has that, in abundance. I should have thought of it before."

But Enzar didn't only have sources. They'd once had *people* carrying those sources within them. Like Ada. Maybe that was how they'd dominated the kimaros. Didn't explain how the magebloods were in control now, but magic-creatures were temperamental as hell. And apparently unkillable.

"Yeah, about that," said Ada. "I think the Royals might have passed through Vey-Xanetha, too."

"You don't think—the gods?"

"I saw some Enzarian script," she said. "You know back when we were on Vey-Xanetha, I thought their symbols looked familiar? I've seen it before, but not for a while. The Royals used to appropriate languages from worlds they conquered. Maybe they lived there once."

I stared at her. Was it possible that the Royals could have created the god capable of bringing someone back from within inches of death?

"Hang on," I said. "There weren't any sources on Vey-Xanetha, and the Royals aren't natural-born magic-wielders, are they?"

"No, they aren't," said Ada. "But all the worlds have been linked at some point or other. The gods might have been after their time. Anything could have happened. I honestly don't know." She sighed. "My world's history's a total jumble. No idea what happened before the Royals and magebloods started their mad race for magical supremacy. Except... the Royals were only a small group. They just happened to gain power on Enzar through sources... through the kimaros, I guess. But now the magebloods are using Thairon's kimaros, the living doorway."

"Yeah, they are. They must have... antimagic."

Ada's breath caught. "Yeah. I thought so. There's no other way they can dominate a creature that powerful. Unless it just has a taste for killing, after being enslaved for so long."

"Guess we have our answer about how Enzar conquered so many worlds, too," I said.

"Magebloods and Royals. They both did the same. They're equally bad, and I… I can't even consider negotiating with them any longer. If they use that kimaros again, someone's going to die. People already have."

"Yeah." I took her hand, wishing I knew what to say. Her whole world had turned against her—a world she'd never been allowed to claim as hers to begin with.

"There's something else I should tell you," said Ada. "I totally forgot to mention it after everything that's happened lately, but Ms Weston showed me a file. It was a record of a mission into Cethrax, the last one, and—your grandfather wrote it."

I stared at her. "Robert Walker? You sure?"

"Positive. It was dated 1986, and it mentioned a mission to investigate the doorways in Cethrax. And that was right before KimaroTech was formed. I'll find it."

"Well, I'll be damned," I said.

"It said they were looking into auros, and why Cethrax doesn't obey the rules. You know, with doorways opening everywhere."

Oh. I hadn't told her about the latest I'd heard from Walker, either, and that would drag up an entirely new problem. Cethrax being the home of the transition points… Walker might have lied, but if it was true that the last extended mission there had been my grandfather's, who else would have the resources to set up a cross-world outpost?

"Where's the file?" I asked. "In the office?"

"Yeah. Last I checked, Iriel was going through all the files with her bionic eyes."

"Okay. We'll look at it tomorrow, assuming Klathica don't blow anything else up."

"Hope not," she said, shuddering. "At this rate, they'll end the Alliance before Enzar has the chance to."

"That won't happen," I said softly to Ada. Even though I suspected she might be right. That kimaros had nearly wiped out the both of us, and though Klathica might have been reckless by throwing a bomb at it, they *had* closed the doorway between Cethrax and Vey-Xanetha. But the kimaros was still out there. What could stand up to it after two bombs hadn't killed the creature?

We walked in silence until we reached my room, and I closed the door behind us.

Ada sighed, leaning against me. "God, Kay... I thought I lost you."

"I think we both owe that god." I wrapped my arms around her.

"Don't let go," she whispered. "Just for a second."

I listened to her breathing, her heartbeat. Wishing I could hit pause on the world, on the Multiverse, even. Ada's breath hitched, and then she was sobbing into the front of my shirt. I froze. "Ada?"

"S—sorry. I can't stand it. *Unbreakable*, it's the stupidest name ever. I'm in a million pieces right now. I couldn't save the others."

"Don't be ridiculous," I said. "You saved everyone you could. You did something nobody else could have done."

"Why couldn't they have named me after a plant?" she muttered, with a half-hearted laugh. "At least expectations wouldn't be so high."

"It's just a name. It only matters what it means to you, not them. I forgot that, to be honest. Own the name."

She wiped her eyes. "Own it. Adamantine. They're powerful enough to let my name justify their war. What am I supposed to do?"

"I don't know," I said quietly. "I spent my life trying to

figure out how to deal with it. All I could do was use the name to my advantage when possible." My hand cupped the back of her head. "I know it's not the same, but your name could do some good to our side. To people who've given up hope. Unbreakable is better than the name of a killer."

"You own it," she said. "Before he came back, you owned the name *Walker*. You can do it again. I know you can."

No news materialised overnight, apart from patrol rotas from Ms Weston. But she hadn't heard from Vey-Xanetha yet. Klathica were refusing to volunteer any more information on the weapon they'd used to blow up the doorway, and Valeria were refusing to speak to them since two of their guards had been killed in the battle on Vey-Xanetha, even though the weapon hadn't directly caused any of the deaths.

Ada's guardian seemed to have the Enzarians under her wing, judging by the crowd gathering around her in the recreation room as we left for the offices.

"Nell's taken my words to heart," said Ada. "First time that's ever happened, I think."

"What'd you say?"

"That she's the best person to speak for the others. It's true. Didn't mention she could probably beat the hell out of most guards here, but that doesn't hurt, either."

"I suppose it doesn't."

Ms Weston wasn't in her office. Probably speaking to the council. Nobody was in Office Fifteen except Iriel, who was surrounded by a mile-high stack of papers.

"Hey, Iriel," said Ada. "I forgot to check whether you'd finished reading those files."

"I did," she said. "And I found something interesting. It looks like the first quest to Cethrax happened around the same time as the Alliance's last visit to Vey-Xanetha. I mean, before *we* went there."

"So it *is* connected," I said. "This was what, thirty-odd years ago?"

"Yeah," said Iriel.

Markos came into the office. "What are you all so serious about?" he asked.

"The incoming war?" I said.

"There's no reason to expect the worst. I have good news."

"Yes…" I said, warily.

"I spoke to my sister and it didn't end in a fight."

"It really is the end of the Multiverse." I rolled my eyes. "Wait. Weren't you supposed to be asking her if she'll fight with the Alliance?"

"My delightful cousin came up in conversation."

"Wait, Tryfon?" I asked. "Didn't he betray everyone by sharing information…" *On the lustre source?*

"He learned about magic sources offworld," said Markos. "It seems he had a few friends on Valeria. Klathican rebels."

"Rebels?" I said sharply. "From KimaroTech?"

"She didn't say the name," said Markos. "But I'm willing to bet we face a common enemy."

"Too goddamn true," I said. "So did she say yes?"

"Surprisingly, she did," said the centaur. "I can't promise she'll send a whole army, but I think the attack on Vey-Xanetha shook her up. Even the non-Alliance-friendly worlds know they might get caught in the crossfire—"

The door hit the wall as Ms Weston ran into the office. "We're under attack. Upstairs. The doorway port. Mechas from Klathica found it, and they aren't working for the Alliance."

For an instant, everything stopped as all eyes turned to face the boss. Then Iriel was on her feet, and all of us grabbed our communicators.

"I already sent out a warning," said Ms Weston, "but something's blocking our signals."

"That message," said Ada. "Shit. I've got to warn my brother." She tapped the screen frantically.

Ms Weston ran into her office, and came back with an armful of weapons. Guess she'd been stocking up. I had one dagger already, but she passed me another, and a magic-gun. Ada shoved a spare dagger into her weapons belt one-handed, still typing on her communicator.

Ms Weston loaded her own weapon and led the way from the office, with Iriel close behind. "We need to close the doorway port first. We can't let them take the building."

"I'd like to see them try," said Markos, who'd produced a crossbow from somewhere and was loading it with a rather manic grin. "This isn't going to end well for them."

Ms Weston hit the button for the elevator while I waited for Ada to catch up. She stowed her communicator away, dagger already in hand.

"Good luck." Ms Weston let Ada and me in front. "I know I can count on you two to keep those monstrosities out of Central."

"Glad you have faith in me." I smiled back despite myself. "I was the most irresponsible Ambassador who's ever worked for the Alliance."

"Perhaps," said Ms Weston from behind as Ada and I turned to the stairs. "But you've always done what's right."

Crashing sounds came from the stairs. With a glance at Ada, I ran, stopping as a metal body flew past, hitting the stairs with a deafening crash. It whirred to its feet, blade-arms swinging. A modified mecha. Klathican.

"Shit," I said. Lucky we had the hover boots—the stairwell was the worst place possible for a fight, especially when the enemy was impervious to most damage. I shot it in the chest and it flailed, sparks flying out, but didn't stop. I shot it again in the legs, hitting the wires holding it together. The mecha collapsed onto its front and I used the dagger to cut off both its knife-hands. Then I ran after Ada, to the third-floor stairwell. She stopped dead as a guard was thrown across the stairs—unconscious or dead. The attacker followed, this one human, and with a gun embedded in his arm. His blank eyes locked onto me, and he fired. The stairwell left no room to dodge, but a person slammed into him from the side, causing him to misfire. Izen? He must have already been in the council room here. Which meant he hadn't ordered the attack.

Another bullet burned a hole into the wall. The attacker and Izen wrestled on the stairs, but before I could intervene, the attacker threw Izen into the wall with such force, he had to be using an implant. The Klathican council's leader crumpled to the ground. *Dammit.*

I activated the sciras and took his place, striking the attacker's weaponised arm with the heel of my hand and knocking off his aim. I twisted his arm behind his back, trying to figure out how to disconnect the damn thing. Wires snaked up his arm, under and over the skin, to the back of his neck.

Bang.

I leaped back, but the bullet had hit the ground instead, and Ada's foot slammed down on the end of the gun. The force knocked all three of us sideways, but the gun itself crumpled. She'd used a sciras booster of her own.

My fingers found the wire and yanked it out, sending blood flying everywhere as the gun disconnected. He yelled in pain then fell silent as I struck him on the temple with a sciras-enhanced punch.

Sorry, dude. His own fault for getting the stupid implant. I turned to Ada. "That was brilliant."

"I do my best." We both looked at Izen. I checked his pulse. Alive, but unconscious. "It wasn't him. Then who…"

"Come on." Ada ran ahead, switching on her hover boots.

We headed down the third-floor corridor as three more mechas came the other way. I aimed for the one with the gun-arm first, while Ada kicked another in the leg, knocking it down. Those things weren't made of strong stuff. I fired my gun, the bullet piercing the shoulder above the gun-arm. No blood this time—it wasn't human.

Another shot had its arm limp at its side. I was within a foot of the mecha now, my dagger ready to slice it to pieces.

With its free hand, it yanked the dead gun-arm from its socket and swung it at me. I blocked the swipe with the adamantine side of my own dagger. I stabbed it in the arm, causing it to drop the appendage, and cut into its neck. Each stab exposed more wires until its legs buckled underneath it. As the mecha fell, I looked up to see Ada had managed to disable her opponent by removing its weapon-arm. Trusting she had the situation in hand, I tackled the third mecha. As my dagger found its mark, the elevator slid open and Markos and Ms Weston came out.

"Izen was on our side." I gave the mecha one last kick. "He was already here."

"I just heard from the council," said Ms Weston. "The attackers went through other doorways, too. They're attacking Valeria. I should have listened to Izen. He said he'd tried to get KimaroTech to switch off the simulators, that they'd been hacked, but his decisions were overruled."

The simulator. I stared stupidly at Ms Weston for a moment—I should have guessed.

"Shit." Ada kicked the mecha's struggling arm away from her as it stopped moving. "It's Thairon all over again… they must be using the kimaros to control magic-wielders. How many people in Klathica?"

"A hundred million in Venn alone," said Ms Weston, a touch unsteadily. "We'll close the doorway on this side first to cut off their access to Central."

"But how are they attacking more than one world at once?" I asked. "A doorway, or—the kimaros. *Dammit.* I knew it."

Ada's horror-struck expression told me the same thought had occurred to me. The kimaros—the nexus—could link up any world. Klathica had activated a bomb right in their doorway. Of course the beast would be pissed with them and target them first.

"I'm going to Klathica," I said. "We need to figure out what the hell's happening."

"And me," Ada said quickly. I couldn't argue, because if the kimaros really was there, the two of us were the only people who might walk away alive.

I stopped, readying my weapons as footsteps echoed ahead. Shit. More mechas were on the way, and from the sound of it, they outnumbered us by a mile.

"Move aside," said Markos.

"What?" All eyes turned to the centaur.

"I don't want you idiot humans getting mowed down."

At the corridor's end, a line of mechas appeared, followed by another. At least twenty. A metallic click sounded as their gun-hands trained on us.

"Don't you die, humans," said the centaur, and I knew that like the others, he'd sacrifice his life for the Alliance, same as the rest of us.

"Centaurs," I said, with an eye-roll. "Making assumptions because we have two less feet than you do."

He charged at the mechas, moving too fast for them to hit him. A metallic crash sounded, and all hell broke loose. Ada and I ran into the fray, disabling and killing every mecha we came across. *Get to the doorway.* If we closed it, we could stop them from taking the whole building.

If not for the sciras, I'd probably have broken something by now. The mechas were tough, but their wires were flimsy and easily exposed. I cut three down, as the centaur carved a path through the fighting. The door to the boardroom was wide open.

Inside, mechas and humans fought one another, and through the doorway was the sky of the Klathican city. I kicked a mecha aside, not daring to use magic myself in case I hit anyone. Machine parts littered the floor, making it hard to manoeuvre. The centaur charged right through the crowd, knocking mechas and humans alike flying with those hooves, and into the boardroom, aiming right for the doorway port. Looked like he intended to carry out Ms Weston's command no matter what.

I stabbed a mecha through the eye, kicking it aside and running through the door into the boardroom. A gun-handed mecha moved between me and the doorway port. Both its arms had been disabled, but it staggered forward, its face disconcertingly human-looking.

"Walker," it said, in a voice more machine than human. "We have orders to kill you."

"From whom?" I lunged and stabbed him through the back of the neck. "Enzar?"

"Dox Nelson."

The guy my father said betrayed him?

"Walker betrayed us. The magebloods will have their revenge."

"Kay!" Ada shouted. "The doorway—it's closing."

The mecha lunged at me, and I stabbed through the wires in its neck. As it crumpled to the side, I ran to Ada.

Markos had left a trail of machine parts in his wake, and the doorway port was in the middle of closing. *The mage-*

bloods will have their revenge, the mecha had said. They were with Enzar, all right. And apparently Walker's former henchman Dox Nelson was, too.

I made up my mind. Hitting the accelerator on the hover boot, I crossed the room in one sweep, and Ada and I flew out into the Klathican sky.

13

ADA

Even though I knew it was coming, I held my breath as the ground gave way to nothingness until the hover boots steadied us in mid-air. We hadn't come out the other side into Klathica's Alliance branch at all. Someone had opened a doorway in the *sky,* and hooked it up to Central's doorway port. As I stared in disbelief, the pocket-sized patch of air we'd come through sealed up entirely.

"Are they opening doorways everywhere in the city?" I stared around, looking for more patches in the sky, or signs of the kimaros. None. The magic level felt normal for Klathica, but then again, I wore my magicproof suit.

"Maybe." Kay scanned the city below. Buildings covered in cables. Grid-like streets dividing the city into districts. We dropped a few feet in the air, to get a closer look. At first, I'd thought the streets were all deserted. But a crowd gathered on the main street. Hundreds—thousands—of people, yet totally silent. None spoke, and the only sound was the thunder of their footsteps. All marched in lines towards one building in the centre. Not one I knew—but once I dragged my eyes away from the crowd, I recognised the logo.

Kay swore. "That's the place Klathica's simulators are run from."

"They got in there." My throat went dry. "Enzar." The simulator. No way could the people on the streets be acting of their own free will. They were too quiet.

"Thought so. One of the mechas mentioned the mage-bloods… and revenge."

The air suddenly felt like it was made of water, dragging me down. "On who?"

"Me. Or the Walker family."

"We can't go inside there," I whispered to him.

"There's a back entrance. I know the place. We'll go invisible."

"If they haven't already seen us." We dropped several feet until we were on a level with an upper-floor corridor. The glass-and-chrome structure had one of those walkways on the side which linked up with the bridges running across the city. We landed on it, and I fired magic from my fingertips at the window. I'd broken into the Alliance's headquarters a dozen times using this very method, and the magic level was higher here on Klathica. Three attempts later, and the floor-length glass door opened.

Kay's touch was feather-light on my arm as I landed on the floor. For a moment, I made the mistake of turning around to check nobody had noticed us, and my gaze snagged on the crowd below. There had to be tens of thousands out there. Maybe more.

"Please tell me you know where you're going," I whispered.

"This is one of the Alliance's places. I've seen maps."

"You'd better be right." We had no time to waste.

"We need the control room."

"For the simulator?" *If something's controlling it, the people responsible must be in here.* As we entered the corridor proper, I felt it. Magic, pulsing through the building, and through me, like a drumbeat. A heartbeat of something huge and forbidding. Something I'd felt before. On Thairon. *We're too late. They have control over everyone already. How can we stop it this time?* Back on Thairon, the magebloods hadn't shown up in person. If they were here—oh god, what if they knew I was coming? Had they seen Kay and me materialise from the doorway before it closed? If they were attacking other worlds, too, they must have the kimaros, but not here. I'd sense the creature if it was this close. But the beat of magic in my veins didn't slow. Wires running along the walls pulsed with it, and I stopped, magic sparking to my fingertips.

"Ada?"

"It's in the wires," I whispered. "Magic."

"If it's like Thairon, shutting it off might not stop them." So he'd had the same thought I did.

"Maybe not, but…"

"They'll know we're here. We need to find the control room first."

"Follow the wires." We did, moving swiftly, our hover boot clad feet not touching the floor. My heart thudded in tandem with the buzz of magic in the air. I'd sensed it on Klathica before, but never this close. *How many people have they captured?*

"Goddammit," muttered Kay, drawing my attention. A rattling sounded from the nearest door. "It's the control room, and it's locked."

"You sure?" Wires ran underneath the door, but they ran everywhere here. Like a cage.

His hand closed around mine. "We'll have to make an entrance. There's no other way."

"All right." I took aim.

Our combined attack knocked the door right off its hinges, sending it clattering across the floor. I braced myself, calling magic to my fingertips again—but there was no one in the room. Only machinery, and monitors, and a nest of wires encasing every wall. I stopped dead, suspicion prickling my spine. I hadn't expected to find the kimaros in here, but something—a sign, or the person in charge of the machinery.

"Be careful," Kay whispered.

"Speak for yourself."

I'd done this before, but I still hesitated before carefully approaching the monitors. A screen dominated the back wall, but it appeared to be switched off. I aimed for the wires first, using magic to sever each one. I didn't know which ran the thing, so destroying them all seemed a safe bet. Reddish-purple sparks filled the air, and if anything, the buzzing noise grew louder. *It's powered by another source. We need to find it—*

The screen lit up without warning, then went out as another shower of sparks erupted from the corner. Kay must have disconnected it.

My communicator buzzed. Words flashed across the screen, at the same time as a voice sounded overhead, as though from a loudspeaker—

"We have a request for Earth's Alliance Central Headquarters." The voice spoke in Classical Klathican. "Three Alliance bases are compromised. You cannot win this, but we will consider an agreement. There is a girl who belongs to us, rightfully. Adamantine. Return her to us, and we will stop the attack."

My breath caught. The words burned into my eyes, and my hand trembled on the communicator. "They know we're here. Even if they don't—they're looking for me."

The screen lit up, and I gasped. It was still functioning. Now it showed a cliff's edge, zooming in until we could see three sides of a doorway, rotating like it had on Vey-Xanetha. On one side was Cethrax's swamp. And the others…

Cities. Towns. Some mountainous, some islands, some huge metropolises. And each one had split down the centre, monsters spilling over the boundaries. Wyverns. Vox-kind. Rampaging, flying, spitting fire and hurling rocks at everything in their path.

Enzar was using Cethrax to invade the Multiverse.

"Fuck," said Kay quietly.

"If the Alliance hands over the girl," said the voice. "All of this will stop."

The screen went back to reddish purple. Magic sparked against my hand.

"So consider your choice carefully, Adamantine."

The room exploded.

I hit the heel of my hover boot just in time, as the momentum of the blast carried me out the door, arms raised to shield my face. Glass shattered. Kay appeared inches away, reaching for me, and we flew through the shattered window over the bridge seconds before another blast went off. And another. The noise ripped through my ears, and yet the crowd below didn't seem to hear it. *There were people in that building!*

Of course there were. It was a warning there'd be worse unless I gave myself up to the enemy.

But why? Why would the magebloods ask me to turn myself in now? They'd said *we are coming,* but now it sounded like they wanted to give me a choice. That, or they'd been waiting to take Central and the other Alliance branches down first. To prove we never had a chance against them, and that I had no option but to turn myself in. Either they wanted to kill me in person—or use me as a weapon.

And now the magebloods were coming for the rest of the Multiverse.

My communicator buzzed so intensely, I almost fell out of the air. Then it buzzed again, and again, like a hundred messages crossed at once.

Kay and I touched down in a street far from the crowds. A chill wind swept shredded advertisements and other rubbish down the street. Eerie silence smothered everything. The controlled crowd made no sound. Kay checked a map on his communicator while I pulled mine out with shaking hands. The same message, again. On repeat. I clicked it off, slipping the communicator back in my pocket. "Is there a door into the Passages—or the Embassy?"

It'd be too late. Either we'd get stuck in Klathica's never-ending security system, or the whole place was compromised.

"The Embassy." Kay took the lead, and we ran—or rather, flew, turning invisible again. I knew where we were by now. I'd been here the first time I'd come to Klathica, except I'd never seen it from the outside. Kay led the way to the bridge overlooking a river between large warehouses. At the end was a tall building bearing KimaroTech's logo. Like everything else. We might have ridden the lift-like contraption on the building's side, but it appeared to have stopped. Looked like the lights had gone out, too. Kay landed on a balcony outside, and I fired magic from my fingertips to knock open the large window. This was one of the meeting rooms, like the room someone had thrown a bomb into not so long ago. Silence pervaded, and flickering lights followed us into the corridor and across the bridge until we reached the Embassy. No mechas guarded the way into the Passages. They must be elsewhere, on Enzar's orders. Maybe attacking the rest of the Alliance. Nobody staffed the desks, and even the people testing the sim-ware were absent. A ghost town.

The main Passage, too, was silent in a way it had never been before. Because all the guards must be on their own worlds, fighting the invasion. Enzar had succeeded in dividing us after all.

Even Central's doors had nobody on duty outside. The Passages felt confining, and the breath squeezed in my lungs. *Please don't let us be too late.*

I ran through the doorway to Earth. The invisibility wore off as we hurried down the street to Central. I fired magic from my hand to knock the gate open, not caring who saw me. If they were already inside the building, no external security would matter. We were losing. Maybe we'd already lost.

"I'm gonna have a look through the windows first," he said. "If Central's compromised, there's no way to tell from out here."

Of course not. Ice gathered around my heart. If we really were too late…

Kay turned invisible and a faint whirring told me he'd activated the hover boots. I waited a minute in breathless silence, getting out my communicator to check the messages. Ms Weston: *They're asking for you. Don't give yourself up.* And a similar message from Nell.

That had to mean Central was okay, right?

Kay appeared again, beckoning me after him.

"The doorway port's still closed. But Enzar's planning for an attack. Some of the other Alliance branches—they're already compromised."

"It's true." I swallowed. "I—I can't let it happen. Not here. They won't stop until they find me."

What was one life compared to the millions who would otherwise die? If not for the power in my blood—no, implanted over my heart—I *would* have handed myself over. As it was, if I went to them, I'd still doom the world. The Multiverse. They'd fixed it so I had no choice in the matter.

"It's not your fault." Kay swiped his keycard. "Whatever

they tell you, it's not your fault. You didn't start the war, you didn't ask them to make you into their weapon."

"I know." My heart dropped as I set eyes on the crowd in the entrance hall. "But they won't see it that way, and I can't argue with the whole Alliance. Most people don't even know —what I can do." I hadn't even had a chance to tell Kay about the theory of me being a nexus, in the end. Not that it was true. They had one nexus already. They didn't need me to fulfil that function. Only to ensure nobody ever challenged their empire again. But the Alliance didn't know, and I had no time to explain. Everyone would want a piece of the Alliance's only remaining bargaining chip.

"I'll back you up," he said. "As much as I can."

"If we get out alive, I'm retiring from the human-weapons division to a beach somewhere."

"I couldn't imagine that."

"Nah, me neither." I cracked a smile that was more like a grimace. How many people had died today? How many more would die in the hours—minutes—before I made my choice?

The doors slid open. And all heads turned in my direction. I instinctively raised my hands in surrender.

"Ada?" Ms Weston appeared from the shadow of the door.

I tuned out the whispers. I couldn't look too closely at anyone. Not at the people who might give me up to the magebloods.

"They want me gone," I said to her, as she met us in the entryway. "I get that. But if I go, the enemy gets the weapon. They could murder me and the magebloods would burn the place down to get first dibs on my corpse." The source was inside me. It was sick and horrible, but I wanted to shout it to the crowd, tell them exactly what the enemy had done to me. Why giving up myself would only make things worse for all of us.

"Ada, we're not going to give you up," said Ms Weston.

"I've told them, and everyone here knows the war won't end if we hand them one person. The majority of people are on your side, Ada."

"Enzar are killing people. They'd kill everyone in the hall, if they could. I'm the Alliance's only shot at stopping them."

This time, I did look at the crowd. The hostile faces seemed more numerous, but the others weren't looking at me at all. Nell was arguing with someone. Alber hovered at her side, met my eyes, and mouthed, *Jeth's alive. He's okay.*

My heart twisted with guilt. The part of Valeria he'd been in must have been attacked, too.

"How many people have they killed now? I can't sit around and do nothing. Unless you know a way to suck the magic right out of me. Or send a clone."

Ms Weston's mouth twisted, and I spotted Nell making her way towards us, parting the crowd. Her expression made me freeze. She used to wear that expression when terrible news came out of my homeworld. My heart started thudding louder.

"What…?"

"Nell has the last of the bloodrock solution," said Ms Weston. "We're preparing to march on Enzar no matter what."

"On Enzar?" I echoed. "But that's suicide, without magic."

"The Balance is finished," said Ms Weston. "And Enzar leaves traces. We have trackers, and they opened a dozen doorways on Earth, effectively ending any chance of ever keeping them out again. Other Alliance branches are on the defensive, as is the military. But we need an offensive attack before they cut off our resources."

"*Where?* If we knew where they were coming from…" Even then, could we really stop this?

"Some Klathicans have formed a team," said Ms Weston. "The enemy took the simulators and the mechas, but there are army units who have never been near a magic implant and are resistant to the effects on the population. They should be able to find where Enzar is creating the doorways. But we have little time, before they attack again. We need a decoy."

Then it hit me what Nell had said. "Bloodrock solution?"

"Yes. Enough for one person."

The truth struck my heart with the force of a physical blow. "No." I shook my head. "You can't be serious."

"I don't see any other option, Ada," Nell said, gently. "They've given us a limited time to hand you over. If you don't go to them, they'll attack a dozen worlds at once. And once you're in their hands, they win. But they don't know you. They've never met you face to face. They only know your name."

"You," I whispered. "You're saying—you want to be the decoy."

14

ADA

"No way," I said.

A shout across the entrance hall interrupted before I could protest further. Nell's arm wrapped around me, steering me away from the crowd, Alber behind us. In an empty side-office, she faced me.

"But—"Alber's eyes were wide. "Neither of you should have to die. It's not fair!"

"He's right. This is absurd. You can't sacrifice yourself for me. Like you said, that isn't the point. The war won't end even if I die. They have the means to conquer the Multiverse already. They don't *need* me, they want to take power away from the Alliance, and the only people who could possibly oppose them."

"Nobody can oppose them directly," said Nell. "The magebloods have control over every magic-wielder on Klathica. I am willing to bet the same applies to Enzar."

"Then I give myself up," I said. "Give myself up, and then get to Enzar, and try and take as many of them down with me. The Alliance can offer a peace treaty to the survivors.

Unless I die, but they could draw the source right out of me. Right?"

Nell inclined her head, and my last, desperate hope died. If they wanted, they could cut the magic right out of me when my heart was still beating. I wasn't the source, I was the conduit for it—like magic itself. Even dead, I'd be their puppet.

I gripped my chest as though in an attempt to hold myself together. "Then throw me into the void to some dead world where they'll never find me."

Horror crossed her face. "Absolutely not."

"I won't stay here while you give yourself up to them." I looked her in the eyes. "It's out of the question."

"You told me you wanted to fight." She drew in a breath, and pulled something from her pocket. A pendant, one I'd never seen before. But the carved metal disc-shape exuded a familiar buzzing sensation even before I closed my hand around it.

"Auros. How long have you had this?"

"That isn't the name they used," said Nell. "This was in the palace. I took it. I knew they used it to move between locations—I'd seen them do it. And I knew it was my only chance to escape and ensure I wasn't followed. They had a larger source buried under the palace."

"A source." I turned the pendant over in my hands. "You think that's what they might be using? But it belonged to the Royals."

"Yes, but the palace wasn't entirely destroyed." She paused. "Nobody knows, but the capital wasn't completely evacuated. There were rebels, hiding in the palace's ruins after the Royals fled, and who managed to escape the carnage. They... they stole a source and buried it there, where the magebloods will never find it. Rumour has it they've been digging in the capital, but not recently. There's only one way left to Enzar—via the rebels' escape tunnels, the same way I escaped."

"But… how is that supposed to help beat the magebloods? Why not tell me this before?"

"Because the source isn't the important part—it's not powerful, but it is a beacon. It's owned by the rebels, who stole it from the Royals themselves. They saved my life and yours, and if they survive, they're the only people on Enzar who stand a fighting chance against the magebloods' army. The magebloods will go looking for their source again eventually, but now they're attacking the Alliance, their eyes are away from Enzar itself."

"You think *I* can find the rebels?"

"I know you can. And they know your name."

My mouth dropped open. An army… a secret army, trained to fight Enzar.

"But… how am I supposed to find this source?"

"With that." She indicated the pendant. "You said auros works by linking to a source on the world you're trying to get to?"

"Yeah. That's how world-keys work, anyway." To link with another world, you needed a signal to follow. The pendant had Enzar's essence bound inside it.

It was a way back home.

"I don't know about world-keys, Ada, but the Royals never knew I took this. They won't know you have it, and I doubt the magebloods know what it can do. They have none of their own."

"But this source under the palace—are they looking for it?"

"Not anymore. Now the enemy is watching the Alliance, the rebels will be preparing to strike."

She was right. This was the best chance we had. And for all my fear of the magic taking control of me again, people on Enzar had learned to harness it. In another life, I'd have been trained as a soldier since birth.

But no more people would be turned into vessels for magic. I could drain the magic from any source, thanks to the adamantine inside me. Maybe even the kimaros, the living source which must be controlling their army. If there was any way to break that hold, I might be able to do it like I had on Thairon—but it'd make no difference if nobody knew where they were actually operating from. But if anyone might, it was the rebels who'd fought them since before I was born.

"All right," I said. "So Kay and I go into Enzar—"

"No. You'd have to go alone. Only one person can use the source in the pendant."

"I…" I looked at Kay in desperation. If he stayed here, he might die. We might never see one another again. "But you. You can't pretend to be me. They'd never buy it. You'd die."

"It's a risk I'm willing to take," said Nell. "Because Earth needs defenders. I'm no magic-wielder, Ada, but if I can fool them for a little longer, you can win the war."

"Nell, they can probably trace my magic signal."

"No," she said. "They won't be able to, not when they aren't actually on Enzar."

"But—" She was right. The only way to stall the magebloods was to make them think they'd won, then attack them from behind. They'd forced our hand. And thanks to what they did to me, they'd made me into the only weapon that could oppose them. If I went with the magebloods, maybe I'd be able to get away, use my magic to self-destruct and take a few of them down with me, but it wouldn't end the war. It wouldn't destroy the stranglehold they had over the Multiverse. There were too many of them, and one wrong move might destroy everything.

Adamantine was implanted in my heart. I was the nexus,

if not in a literal sense. I'd always been a walking weapon. I'd been fortunate enough to avoid the consequences up until now.

Which meant if I didn't rip the power out of me, if I didn't die, the backlash of their weapon would find me no matter where I was. In any universe. There was nowhere to hide, nowhere to run. I had to seek them out myself, and use the adamantine inside me to tear the magic from their own source.

Or watch the worlds burn at my hands.

Truth or not was irrelevant now. They would believe the words Nell spoke. I'd fight to my last breath to save her. But some battles had to be fought alone.

"You won't die, Ada," she whispered. "Don't waste your chance by giving yourself up."

I choked on tears. This wasn't the time to break down. We had to make a plan *now*. Which meant I had to tell Kay.

Everything.

Wiping my eyes, I left the room. Kay and Ms Weston waited outside the door.

"I have to talk to you," I said to him.

"My office," Ms Weston said, immediately. "But you don't have long. Have you decided?"

I nodded mutely. Kay's arm wrapped around my shoulder and steered me upstairs. I let him, because I wasn't sure my legs would support me any longer. But if I collapsed, gave up, no one would take my place. I wouldn't let anyone else risk their life on Enzar.

We reached the first floor. There was no one in the office, though Markos and Iriel talked further down the corridor. Kay and I went into Ms Weston's room and closed the door.

I breathed, slowly. Kay's hands rested on my shoulders. "It's okay, Ada."

I shook my head. "It's not okay. It'll never be okay. They

aren't going to give up looking for me. If I stay here, they'll tear the Multiverse apart. If I give myself up, they'll use me to do it anyway. Nell has enough bloodrock solution for one person left. She wants to be a decoy to divert their attention so I can find the rebels and the source they were looking for inside the Royals' palace. There's a way for me to get back there, but just me." I held up the pendant in shaking hands. "It's pure auros. Linked to Enzar."

"Alone?" Kay's eyes were wide. "You can't do that, Ada. It'd be suicide, even with a decoy. Using magic will draw their attention, right?"

"Apparently not," I said. "They aren't even on Enzar, and they're too preoccupied attacking the Alliance. Anyway, with adamantine, I can kill them, even if they're Stoneskin. I can stop the kimaros the way I did before."

"But if not? If it's a trap? We can't count on them giving in so easily to a decoy."

"They don't know me," I said, my voice shaking. "They only know the name. The StoneKing said I was a nexus, and he was going to tell the magebloods so they would stop fighting, and I'd be able to—to rule over them." Even now, I could barely get the words out. "It's not true. I've been gone twenty years. But the StoneKing said they don't know, they're so desperate for a solution they'd believe anything."

Kay stared at me. "A *nexus?*"

"It's not true," I repeated, like it would make the whole thing easier to accept. "Nell told me it isn't. Not like the StoneKing said, anyway. He said the nexus is the heart of all magic on a world, the Royals and magebloods are—or were —all looking for Enzar's."

"And they'd actually think that was *you?* One person, at the centre of all magic on a single world?"

Despite everything, my heart lifted, just slightly. He believed me. Believed it couldn't be true.

"The StoneKing was convinced of it," I said. "He was absolutely convinced both sides were desperate enough to end the war they'd stop the fighting if I showed up, because killing me would wipe out all the magic on their world. He *was* crazy. It's impossible. For one thing, the magic level there's so high, it'd be obvious from first glance I have zero control over my own magic, let alone all the magic on Enzar. But if it really was him the magebloods were talking about, he'll have told them for sure. I don't know if it means they'll want to kill me or not, but... there's no way I can go near them. Nell wants to be a decoy, but she's not a magic-wielder. And they have a source. More than one."

"I get it," he said, softly. "She wants to give you a fighting chance to bring an end to the war. She believes you can do it." He leaned closer. "I believe you can, too."

"If I can't, we all die. Every one of us on every universe. And Nell—she'll be lucky to get out of there alive no matter what. Klathica's a death trap. She knows what she's doing, but what if I *can't* do it? Or if I'm really the cause of all this?"

"It's not true," said Kay. "Not only is it the illogical claim of a madman, but the magebloods don't know a damn thing. They didn't even know what was in the weapons they bought from KimaroTech."

"Really? For sure?"

"Yeah. Seems my grandfather made his fortune that way. I'm sorry, Ada. I should have told you. He's the reason the magebloods were able to start the war. He gave them the means to do so."

"I guessed. I went to talk to your father before. Kay... he said your grandfather died on Enzar."

"I know." His tone was flat. "He told me. After a fashion. He also told me the name of the traitor who kept up Klathica's link to Enzar's people on Thairon. Apparently, this guy named Dox Nelson is in league with the magebloods."

"What? Someone from Klathica?"

"From KimaroTech," he said. "This Nelson guy kept the Stoneskin project going on Thairon even when my father cut it off. He also sold Alliance secrets to them, by the sound of things."

"So someone *did* betray the Alliance?"

"A long time ago," said Kay. "I think Enzar got the link to Klathica through Thairon when Walker used the doorway to come back after he escaped the simulation. It left a trace. Can't think why they've waited until now to use it. They went after Vey-Xanetha first..."

"Because they're on Cethrax. Not Enzar. They must be." I swore. "Cethrax is linked with every world, with or without the kimaros. If I can find a way to break it, I will."

Kay nodded. "He also said the magebloods were looking for a nexus. Now it makes sense. But... he said the Royals were searching for it, too. That's why he cut them off. He thought whoever found it first would destroy all the worlds."

I stared at him. "That makes sense, but did they mean me, or—something else?" Had the rebels had it all along?

"The magebloods already have the kimaros and the Stoneskins."

"But they don't have auros." I ran my fingers over the symbols carved into the pendant. Compared to a living source and an adamantine army, our own forces seemed insignificant. Maybe I really was going to my death. Nell's sacrifice wouldn't win the Alliance more than a few hours, which might not be nearly enough.

"We can use that against them," said Kay.

"Yeah, well, I'm not sure one person's sacrifice can end this war." I closed my eyes and opened them again. "But I'm going to try. I'll find the rebels under the palace, and I'll do my damned best to stop the magebloods doing any more harm to the Alliance."

"I'll do everything I can. If you need an amplifier..." He tapped the earpiece.

"I'll reach you." I took a steadying breath. "I'm sorry I didn't tell you about... what the StoneKing said. I didn't believe it. I still don't. But I think *they* do, and if that's the case, they'll tear the worlds apart to find and destroy me."

He nodded, his face set. "You sure you know how to use that thing? Because if you need a boost—"

"Yeah, I might," I said. "If it's as powerful as it's supposed to be, I can use it from in here. But Nell... I have to say goodbye to her."

It can't be the last one. Nell had outwitted the Enzarians before. This would be no different.

It couldn't be.

Ms Weston knocked on the door. "Not to alarm you both," she said, "but you have half an hour before the time limit is up and the Enzarians will attack again."

Crap. I turned to Kay. "I'll say goodbye to Nell first, and then..."

And then we'd have to part. Kay's expression reflected my own anger and pain back at me. His jaw tightened. "Sure, Ada."

Nell waited on the stairs to the third floor. The doorway port. Easiest way. No sense wasting time in the Passages again.

The path into the room containing the doorway port was clear, and Nell herself turned the dial with steady hands. Kay waited a few feet back, leaving Alber and me to stand at Nell's side as the doors turned transparent, revealing the main street of Klathica, a sea of blank faces. The crowd. Not our enemies, but their puppets.

Where the hell are they?

The sim-controlled humans were the magebloods' eyes.

Of course they'd be hiding out of sight. They weren't even on Klathica at all.

My hands clenched around the pendant. I didn't have much time. Every second I wasted would be one more chance for them to see through Nell's ruse.

I turned to her. "Are you sure this will work?"

"Even if not, I couldn't live with myself if I didn't try," she said, softly, turning something over in her own hand. A bottle filled with faintly glittering liquid. She tilted it, and a few drops dripped onto her hand.

I swallowed. Nodded. Guilt and rage rose, but I pushed them down. I didn't have room for that now.

"I'll do it. Ada, I've always had faith in you. I know you can end the war in your own way. They won't break you."

If only I believed it. If there was one thing the war had taught me, it was no one was invincible, and anyone could break.

Or self-destruct.

Before my eyes, she changed. Grew four inches so we were the same height. Her newly blond hair came loose from the bun. Her eyes, without the lenses, turned white, sparkled as they looked into mine… as my own face stared back at me. Myself, but not myself.

I couldn't breathe.

She looked at Kay with an expression that somehow managed to be half-smile, half-glare. "If you hurt her, she'll break you."

And that was when I burst into tears.

Nell embraced me, and her face was wet, too. "I'm sorry I never told you the truth, Ada."

"I'm sorry I didn't listen," I said. "I'm sorry I was so freaking immature, and…"

"You forget lazy and slapdash." Alber grabbed Nell for a hug, too.

"Watch it, you." I wiped my eyes. "I'm the parent for now. But Nell's going to come back."

"Of course," she said quietly. "But just in case I don't… take care of your brothers, Ada. And take care of yourself. You deserve a full life, here on Earth or otherwise. Don't let this war take everything you are."

Like Nell. She'd given up everything for me.

No. That wasn't true. They hadn't broken her. She was the bravest person I knew. I had nothing greater to aspire to.

"You're the best." I swallowed over the lump in my throat. "The best person I ever met, and I hope you give those mage-bloods a good smack in the face."

"Kick them for me," said Alber. "And again, for Jeth."

"Jeth." Nell closed her eyes. "Tell him I love him. As I do all of you."

"Of course." I smiled through a fresh wave of tears. "Dammit, Nell. Stop making me cry and go kick their arses."

We moved back, out of sight, as Nell stepped over the threshold. Alber made a strangled noise and pulled away from me, but the door had already closed.

"Get downstairs, Al," I said. "I'll see you soon. Promise."

Wiping his eyes, Alber retreated. I crossed the room to Kay, willing myself to stay calm. I could break down later, when the war was over. I had to dig for the strength for one final goodbye.

I turned to Kay. "I think you're right. Enzar doesn't know what you can do."

Kay nodded. "Yeah. I've got the tracker and world-key. I'll figure something out. See if I can track them on Cethrax. The world-key still has Vey-Xanetha's trace on it, and I know the symbol. I don't think they've had any more trouble, but their world's still tied to Cethrax and Enzar through that. Enzar left traces everywhere through those doorways. And… I have your signal, too." He looked me in the eyes, and it became difficult to breathe. My heart hammered as the saddest smile crossed his face. "Reckon I can find you on the other side of the Multiverse?"

"I know you can," I choked on the words, throwing my arms around him. "But I was never like the other magic-wielders. I still don't know if I can control it. I didn't understand before, but I do now. They *implanted* it over my heart. It can't be drained out of me."

"Yeah." His breath caught on the word. "That's why you're..."

"The only one who can end it all." It wasn't fair. We should have had more time than this. "Even if it turns out to be a lie." I held onto him tighter, my face buried in his shoulder. I heard his breath catch as his lips brushed my ear.

"I'd tell any lie to the whole Multiverse if it meant I got to see you again."

Swallowing, I drew back. "You know I'd never live with myself if I stayed on Earth. I *need* to help them—Earth, Enzar, all of the Multiverse. And Nell."

"Of course," he whispered, tracing my lips with one finger. "After the war is over, I'll find you."

"Same to you," I whispered, and my arms folded around him, and we shared one last kiss. It tasted of desperation and hope, and my heart thudded wildly in tandem with his. We might both die. There were never any guarantees. What we'd had had been an oasis in the desert, a brief light in a life starved of sunlight. I'd never forget him, even if our hours were numbered.

I was the nexus of the war, like it or not.

I turned the pendant over in my hand, and he placed his own hand over mine. The auros blazed blue-white, magic burned in my blood, and the world around us disappeared.

And he let go.

Magic surged through my skin, and the lenses melted in

my eyes, a pressure gripping my skin where the antimagic in my uniform reacted against the atmosphere. This time, I didn't try to hold the magic in. I breathed out and opened my eyes on a world dyed in reddish purple, burning under a sky equally bright. Magic streamed from my hands, and somehow, I knew what to do. I pushed at the magic. The antimagic protection streamed from my uniform, leaching the black colour to grey.

I could breathe again. Magic held me like a second skin. I hadn't even realised I'd been floating until I touched down.

On the edge of a cliff.

15

KAY

I stared at the spot where Ada had vanished, the ghost of her touch imprinted on my hands. Blinking hard, I stepped back, the noise from downstairs finally filtering through.

Get back. You have to do something.

The roaring in my ears rose to a crescendo as I climbed down the three flights of stairs. The crowd remained in the entrance hall, all eyes fixed on a screen projected onto the wall, which showed a split view of several Earth cities, where the military joined Alliance guards to fight in the streets. There was something chillingly familiar about those images.

Wait. I wasn't imagining it—all the images on screen showed the *exact* same sites of the previous monster attacks when Thairon's army had come to Earth. Because once a doorway opened, it left a trace. That was how Cethrax and Enzar were opening the doorways. They had a tracker, somewhere in their doorway port with the kimaros tied into it. Not on Thairon this time. *It has to be Cethrax.*

Goddammit. I shouldered through the crowd to Ms

Weston. "The transition point," I said, in an undertone. "I think they're operating from there."

Even with the Passages closed off, the transition point had been in contact with so many worlds, it'd be flooded with traces. If someone wanted to re-open a door, all they'd need was a tracker and knowledge of the symbol and they'd be able to open doorways anywhere at will. It *must* be how they were doing it. My father had said they were located on Cethrax, after all.

Ms Weston frowned at me. "Kay, as I told you, we closed the doorways."

"Walker told me. He said his father must have set up the transition point. I can't think of another way for them to have got at Klathica. The transition point was linked to the upper floor of the Passages." Which was closed off, but it didn't matter now their kimaros had picked up the trail.

"Which door was it?" asked Ms Weston. "Every tracker at our disposal is working to pinpoint this illegal doorway port of theirs. It's not Klathica's. That living source of Enzar's can only exist on a high-magic world, and Thairon is in no state to hold it."

"Cethrax," I said. "That's where the transition point is. With a tracker and a world-key, I can find them." I pointed at the screen. "They're opening doors to places that already have traces left on them from last time. No way Central won't be a target, whether they believe Ada's guardian or not." And the kimaros had damn good reason to be pissed off at Central, considering Lawrence Walker had tried to blow it up. And Klathica, more recently.

"We're already prepared for another attack, but we're short on magic-wielders, until backup arrives."

Ada. I pushed the image of her face away and concentrated on the buzz from the entrance hall and Ms Weston's pinched, worried face. "Yeah, but if they're operating from

Cethrax, they must have another source there. Something to contain that kimaros. Even Ada couldn't do it."

The screen flashed purple-red, and I froze. All the images merged together into one: the vista of a familiar swamp, with blade-like trees and burned-out ground… and a monstrous face filled the sky, so vivid I had to check it hadn't materialised inside the entrance hall itself. The world on the screen split in two, the swamp on one side, a stretch of desert on the other. Between them, red smoke swirled, and a pair of eyes gleamed within.

The kimaros. The living source.

"Alliance," said a voice—a mechanical toneless one like the voice that had spoken on the loudspeakers on Klathica. "You have seen what we can do. I hope you decided to send us the girl, otherwise things will become unmanageable for you."

Silence. Panicked whispers filled the room. "Who is that?" Most people in the room could understand it, even though the voice spoke Classical Klathican. It must be a person speaking through a computer. Unless…

Was the kimaros using someone as a puppet? Or was it the other way around? The creature had *hated* being imprisoned on Thairon.

"Your attempts to police magic across the Multiverse are over. Now, your magic-wielders will serve our army. Your quick thinking is admirable, hiding your last weapon so soon prior to our arrival on Klathica, but you can't hide it forever. We will take your amplifier, Alliance. We will take everything you have."

The voice faded, the echoes remaining.

"Madness," said Ms Weston, eyes fixed on the screen.

"Yeah." I stared, numbly, at the screen. "What in the Multiverse did they mean by an *amplifier?*"

Lustre. It couldn't be anything else. Klathica was the only world with it in stores, which meant someone had acted quickly to hide it when Enzar had taken control. But the magebloods already had one source. Add that to an amplifier, and there would be nothing left for their god to destroy. And that didn't just mean the level would climb on Earth and a thousand other worlds, but the aftermath would send those dark, forgotten worlds crashing right into ours. It had started on Cethrax already. The world was breaking apart. How many doorways would it take before the same happened to Earth?

"An amplifier?" Ms Weston shook her head. "I never heard of such a thing."

I had. And right now, it hit me: Ada wasn't the danger to the Multiverse if they got hold of her power. Hers had a limit, and could be drained out of her if need be. Ada hadn't wiped out those Stoneskins on her own. She'd used…

Me.

I was their nexus. The amplifier they needed. They couldn't tell one source from another, but it was a miracle they hadn't already found out. Sure, they had adamantine and bloodrock, the most powerful of sources, but an amplifier would make all of that go apeshit.

Words appeared on the screen, at the same time as my communicator buzzed again: "Bring us Adamantine." And underneath: "Bring us the amplifier. Bring us Lawrence Walker."

What?

"No way," I said, conscious everyone was looking at me. "What do they want him for?"

Revenge? Or did he know something? He might be the biggest asshole this side of Cethrax, but I wouldn't give anyone up to Enzar if it meant giving them more power.

"Bring us Lawrence Walker, or we will kill everyone on Earth. We know you have him, we know you have the amplifier."

The hall exploded with noise. I turned invisible, and ran for the guard office.

~

ADA

I stared into the void, like it might give me answers. Nothing. *It can't be here!* But it was, an empty gap where *something* should be. This should be the palace. Or the source, buried underneath.

My feet rested on burned ground. Slowly, I rotated on the spot, transfixed. Pieces of black stone lay scattered, charred. No. Adamantine. The palace was adamantine.

Someone had already destroyed it.

Had I got here too late? I turned the pendant in my hands again. From here, there was only one way back. But if the source was gone, why had it brought me here?

I activated the hover boots, moving closer to the cliff's edge. Careful. Good job, too, because when I passed through the smoke at the edge of the void, I screamed.

The drop surrounded me, plunging down into darkness without end. Icy cold air battered me, and I gasped. A whirring came from the hover boots, telling me the oxygen shields were working overtime. No breathable air here. Or even magic.

Instead, was… nothingness. A hole in the centre of the Multiverse.

The invisibility wore off, knocked out by the magic drain. I was acutely aware I was a tiny figure on the brink of nothingness, a pinprick in the sky.

Get away…

"I wouldn't do that if I were you, Ada."

My heart dropped, right into the void. It seemed to take an age for my feet to get the message to turn round, to get out of the void and face the inevitable—a familiar voice which shouldn't exist anymore.

The StoneKing stood on the edge of the cliff, by the ruins of the palace. If not for his voice, I wouldn't have recognised him. Scaled black armour covered him from head to toe, including his face. The eyes that stared at me were painted-on.

He can't exist anymore. I killed him. I'd fired magic into his eyes. Nobody could survive it.

"You're dead," I said, stupidly.

"You did your best, Adamantine. If not for Cethrax, I would be."

"You fell into the void," I said. "There's no way you can be alive."

"You forget I have a tracker built into my skin, even beneath the adamantine. When you pushed me into the void, I picked up on an unusual signal, and when I followed it, I found myself in an… interesting place. A world ruled by magical forces, in which there exists a *conscious* magic source able to heal even the fatally wounded. I was saved within inches of death."

Xanet. Oh, hell.

"You do know of this place?"

"If you hurt anyone on that world," I whispered, "I'll kill you."

"Now, why would I do that?"

"You're kidding me," I said. "You killed a hundred people, and tried to blast the worlds apart. Did you make this?" I indicated the void.

"Do you know nothing of your history, Adamantine?" The StoneKing shook his head. "This is the chasm that was created when your fellow Royals decided to dig their source out of the earth and use it in battle. Unfortunately, they destroyed themselves in the process."

"All of them?" I blurted. *Get out of here*, a voice whispered in my ear. I had to find the rebels—wherever they were— before Nell...

"They're responsible for generations of war, are they not? Or were you hoping to meet your real family?"

My hands fisted. "No. I didn't want to see *you*, either. I'm here to end the war, whatever side you're working for."

A heartbeat's pause, then the Stoneskin laughed. "There *is* only one side. Magic is all there is, and all there ever will be."

I shook my head. "Like I'm going to fall for any of your mind games now."

My hover boot clad feet touched down on the ground, my fist swinging upwards in a perfect uppercut. I caught the StoneKing on the jaw with a blow that would have dislocated it, had he been human. Lucky I'd had the forethought to activate the sciras first. Even then, my wrist and hand throbbed in pain.

The StoneKing stood stock still a moment, then laughed, a quiet noise that raised the hairs on my arms.

"Apparently, I need a constant reminder not to underestimate you, Ada. You and I might have achieved so much."

I looked him in his sightless eyes. "And just what do you mean? I'm out of patience here. My *real* family's in danger, unless you'd like to tell me what the hell happened here." I indicated the gaping hole into the void.

"What do you think? Your family destroyed their own source when they opened the void."

"They did *that* on purpose?" I hovered in front of him, desperation clawing up my throat. Maybe the rebels were already dead, but I wasn't about to lead someone potentially working for the enemy right to them.

"Yes." The StoneKing tilted his head on one side. "The fools realised the source they owned was cursed to doom them, but they were too late. The magebloods had already found a superior weapon, and now they have everything they need to rule the Multiverse."

I hit the heel of my hover-boot, tapped on the sciras, and shot like a bullet across the three metres separating us, crashing into the StoneKing with enough force to knock him back onto the burned ground. Magic sparked around me, lighting up my skin, and the world brightened, flashing to white. I knelt on his chest, my whole body alight with magic I'd suppressed forever—power I'd never felt so intensely.

"Tell me," I said to the StoneKing. "Tell me where the magebloods are hiding, and I might spare your life this time."

White lightning cloaked the world, as the StoneKing's mad laughter echoed in my ears.

"Adamantine, I do wish you hadn't destroyed my sight," he whispered. "I would give anything to see you now. Adamantine, killer of worlds, with all the magic in the Multiverse at your disposal. Too bad…" The laughter faded as my hand clenched around his armour-covered neck. With the sciras *and* magic, I knew I could break it with a single movement.

"Well?" I asked, ignoring the chill that rocked my bones. *Killer of worlds…*

"There are no sides in the war," he said. "Only magic, and the Alliance has dominated it for centuries. The *Balance*. It's their biggest joke. The magebloods showed me the truth."

"I thought you hated them. You were planning to use me to assassinate them, and to become your *queen*, because you're a deluded megalomaniac. Did you want a little part of their force for yourself?" I drew on the sciras with all my strength, and his armour cracked under the strain. "This is your last warning."

"Killing me is a waste of time," whispered the StoneKing.

A white glow suffused him, his armoured body shaking. I backed off, and his body floated into the air, trailing black smoke. Like a shadow.

"This world is broken," said the StoneKing. "Thairon is, too. Klathica will be the first of yours to fall… then Earth. It's too late for you to save them, Adamantine. Magic rules. It has taken the magebloods, it has taken their minds, and it will take every magic-wielder…"

The StoneKing's body cracked down the centre. Black lightning radiated out, and a blast of magic slammed into me. I hit the hover-accelerator in time to steady myself at the edge of the void, but the StoneKing had already crumbled into scorched, blackened fragments.

Breathing heavily, shaking, I touched down again. My hand was bleeding where the pendant had dug into it. And it wasn't gleaming blue anymore, but dead-black. *Shit.*

I tapped into the auros. Nothing.

"Oh, god," I whispered.

I was stranded.

16

KAY

"I knew you'd come running to me." Walker's eyes gleamed in the near-darkness.

Upstairs, the rest of the Alliance prepared Central for war. I heard Ms Weston barking orders even from here. I'd rather die than let Walker out of his cage. But we'd *all* die if I didn't.

"Spare me," I said. "You probably know we're being threatened by Enzar. They have Klathica, and Central will be compromised within the hour. They've asked us to hand you over." I jangled the keys in front of him. In my other hand, I held a pair of handcuffs I'd grabbed from Carl's office. "If you want to live, you'll help me or I'll spare the Enzarians the bother." If I didn't kill him, Enzar would. I had no reason to fear the consequences. Not any longer.

"Is that so?" Walker raised an eyebrow. "What if I told you I know another way into Enzar, right to their source?"

What? *He's trying to distract you.* "I'd say it's too late." I slid the key into the lock.

"And what then?" asked Walker, his expression challenging. "You take your magic-wielder powers against an

Empire? Or will you dare to do what I did, and close the doors?"

"It's too late for that." But there was no time to think. No time to make a better plan. I had the chameleon-earpiece on, but was all too conscious of the silence on the other end. From Ada. What if she'd been transported straight into a trap?

She's all right. She has to be.

"There is another way," said Walker. "A route into the heart of Enzar."

"A likely story. I know you're the one who removed Enzar's symbol from the world-keys, too. I'm not about to blindly jump into a war zone."

"Enzar is dead," said Walker. "It's irrelevant. If they have a doorway port, it's on Cethrax. But I can take you directly into Enzar from the Passages. I have Enzar's symbol memorised."

"You're lying," I said. "If not, tell me the symbol." Hot anger sliced through my veins. "I know every inch of the Passages. I know every lie you've ever told, Walker."

"There are only a select few of us who can use the symbol," said Walker. "Nobody else can."

"Yeah, right. You probably just want to escape."

"No." Walker's mouth twisted. "It's only right I get to have *my* revenge, Kay. The doorway will lead me to the enemy, to Nelson. I'll kill him with my own hands."

"I don't believe you," I said. "Draw the symbol. I have your DNA, unless you're about to tell me I'm fucking adopted on top of everything else." The key clicked in the lock. "Is this to do with why they asked us to hand over the *amplifier*?" I'd thought he didn't know lustre had given me my abilities. He definitely had no magic of his own.

"They meant the source once stored at Central." Walker

shook his head. "It disappeared thirteen years ago. Imagine that, Kay…"

I froze, my hands gripping the metal cuffs. "What?"

"You didn't think I guessed? When I read over the research… it was the only source that *could* have worked. Lustre. If I know Dox Nelson, he'll burn the world to the ground to find it, but he won't. Klathica has hiding places. They were almost the site of a war with Thairon. They won't give up their sources easily even with Enzar invading them. And the Enzarians will never have seen an amplifier before. They would never have guessed it was you."

Despite myself, my grip slipped on the cuffs. "That was your plan? Set me against Enzar?"

"If I'd known it *worked*." Walker's eyes closed, like he was in pain. "If I'd known, we might have ended that war thirteen years ago."

My heart missed a beat. "You *what?*" He'd planned to use me as a weapon all along. "You were going to do it to other people, too."

"We needed our own army to match theirs. Klathica tried it, and nothing worked. That's how we knew we needed to use it on a non-natural-born magic-wielder. And Earth was the most likely candidate. No other sources worked, not even adamantine."

I held my breath, but he went on, "Adamantine is an absorbent. It has no effect when injected into humans. Klathica have known it for years. If anything, it has the *opposite* effect on a magic-wielder."

So it was true… there was literally no one else like Ada out there. No wonder she hadn't drawn his suspicions. He'd thought she had magic because she was mageblood. Not because someone had implanted it over her heart.

"Lustre, on the other hand, is supposed to be useless on its own. It seems I underestimated you."

"Took you long enough." I leaned in closer. "Now." I pushed the door open, and before he could move, zapped him with second level magic. Walker fell, without a sound, even as I snapped the cuffs around his wrists.

"You're making a mistake," he whispered.

"No," I said softly. "For once, I'm not." I pushed Walker after me, a knife pressed to his throat with my free hand. "If you have any more hidden weapons, I'll hand you over to Enzar with your throat cut."

"No," said Walker. "Central's security has certainly upped their game. But forgive me if I request some means to defend myself. I am no magic-wielder, and entering a dangerous area unarmed is against Alliance policy."

He actually went there. "So is committing genocide." Blood streamed from his neck as my hand shook.

Noises from upstairs. Shouts, and weapons clashing. We were already being attacked.

"If I die," said Walker, "you lose your only way out."

"I'm quite good at improvising."

But I knew the bastard was still keeping his secrets. Under pressure like this, he'd have no choice but to reveal everything, either to me, or to the enemy. I pushed open the last door, and stopped short, Walker held in front of me like a shield. As I'd expected, the fight had moved to the entrance hall. Someone had pushed up a boundary in front of the door, and a row of armed guards faced down whatever was on the other side. Not just guards, but some of the offworlders who'd been downstairs. But on the left-hand wall, the screen showed the carnage. Cethraxian monsters storming the cities across the Multiverse, hideous shapes crawling out of nowhere in places on Earth, Valeria, Alvienne. And on Klathica, the sim-controlled army dominated the city. Tens of thousands of people. Their lives were at stake, held in the magebloods' hands. If they found out Nell wasn't really Ada, what would they do to their hostages? I couldn't defend everyone. I couldn't be in ten places at once.

"Markos," I said, as the centaur cantered past, armed with two spears.

"What are you doing?" The centaur stared at Walker.

"Taking our *hostage* to Enzar."

"Good," said Markos. "We can handle things here."

A blast shook the building.

"Or perhaps not," said the centaur.

But my eyes were fixed on the screen. On the view of the sky above London, pierced by lightning. Panic, chaos and confusion. And above all, magic, raging free like it had no right to on this world. As lightning flared up again, the building shook again.

"Kay!" Amanda ran towards me, a gun in her hands. She focused on Walker. "What are you doing with him?"

"Enzar want him. Or they'll attack us…"

"They just did," said Amanda.

"Dammit." I dragged Walker towards the stairs.

"We're still standing," said Amanda. "The shelters weren't the only thing Elizabeth built. This place is a lightning rod."

"What do you mean?"

"I mean, a magical blast just hit London, and Central *absorbed the damage.*"

A shifting movement from Walker drew my attention back to him. "That scheming woman…" he muttered.

"Just saved four million lives," said Amanda, without even blinking.

"Damn," I said, because there wasn't much else *to* say. "Come on." I pushed him in the direction of the stairs.

"Kay… she left a tunnel underneath Central, too," said Amanda. "Linking this place to West Office, and the Passage on the outskirts—the one near the Academy. We can do a full evacuation. If we need to."

I nodded. Not mentioning that there was no safe place in the Multiverse anymore. "Where's your sister?"

"She went through the doorway port," said Amanda. "She and Iriel had an idea. They're trying to counter that signal Klathica sent."

"She's not fighting here?"

"She decided her talents were best served in Valeria. They're the next in line to Klathica, and all their communications are pouring into Neo Greyle. She and the tech team are sending a counter-message to Klathica directed at everyone not under the kimaros's influence. To tell them it's not over. The Alliance isn't giving up."

"Damn right it isn't," I said.

"Pathetic," said Walker. "What good will words do?"

"You should know the answer to that already," I said. "Your whole life is built on lies and empty promises. You've nothing left now." I nodded to Amanda. "I'm taking him to Enzar. Even if they've gone back on their word, it might give me the chance to sneak up on them."

She glanced at Walker, mouth pulled tight in an expression that made her look like her sister. "Don't let him escape."

"I won't." I rattled the cuffs for emphasis. "I don't know if you heard, but the thing controlling the Klathicans is a source with no limit. I'm going to try and stop it, but if I can't, the only way is to cut them off. Can you tell your sister?"

"And give up on everyone else? Danica would never do it."

"Better than what happened on Thairon," I said quietly, with a meaningful shake of Walker's cuffs. The faintest gasp escaped him as the magic-shock hit. "She'll know I didn't make the choice lightly."

Words flashed across the screen, the picture changing so Klathica's main street dominated. Except it didn't look like it had before. A line cut down the middle from sky to grey pavement, with three reflections like a gigantic mirror. They'd opened their doorway port there. On one side was a giant metal walled room, bigger even than Central's entrance hall. And it was packed with monsters. Before I could focus on it, the doorway shifted, and my eyes were drawn to the street of Klathica. The crowd parted to let a single figure through, towards the doorway. The person walked from one world to the other, past the blank-faced Klathicans. *Ada.* A fist clenched over my heart. *No. it's not really her.*

None of the monsters were attacking Nell, but it must mean whoever had given them orders had told them not to attack her. *Yet.* They didn't know she was an impostor.

"What *is* that?" Amanda stared at the hall of monsters, who'd mobilised into tight lines with a discipline they never could have achieved on their own.

"Cethrax," I said.

"The transition point," added Walker. "The fools."

"Cethrax is the transition point?" Amanda gasped.

Crash. The building trembled, and the row of guards at the door was driven back as a rumble louder than thunder boomed overhead.

"They're breaking in!" someone shouted.

Amanda swore and ran over to join them. "Not on my watch."

"Where's everyone else?" I called after Amanda.

"Attacking them from behind!" she shouted back.

Guards ran left and right, wielding weapons of all kinds. Not just Earth, but Valerian guards using hover-tech, and winged Alvienne soldiers. They must have come through the doorway port.

The elevators opened, and a herd of *centaurs* poured out, led by Markos. I jolted to my senses when it hit me I'd get trampled if I didn't move out the way. I dragged Walker after me, who openly stared.

"Yeah, we're working with Aglaia." I gave him a shake. "You didn't manage to totally destroy our offworld relations."

A blast of magic knocked me off my feet. The cuffs clattered to the ground, and Walker looked down at me with the same disdainful expression I'd seen a thousand times before.

"Disappointing, Kay," he said. The tips of his fingers glowed blue. What was it, some kind of enhancement?

"No you fucking don't." I was on my feet in a second, but he'd already dropped to the ground, fingers tracing symbols. He had auros embedded in his hands. With the adamantine around his cage, he hadn't been able to use it before... or had he been saving it until this moment?

The building shook again. I tackled Walker and sent us both flying—but suddenly, the floor wasn't there anymore. We fell into empty air.

I landed on top of Walker and instantly had him pinned to the ground. Metal floor, and walls, all smothered in the dark blue colour of auros. The Passages. Eerily silent, apart from the chill wind beating the walls. A wind that shouldn't be here, because all the doors were supposed to be sealed, the worlds behind them abandoned. But one wasn't. Not completely.

Door Sixty-Five.

17

KAY

I stared at the door. Ada had used it before, countless times. She'd told me. I thought I sensed her magic-trace lingering around the cold metal door, which was ridiculous. *She's not here.*

"That's our way in," said Walker, who stood beside one of the neighbouring doors—one I hadn't even looked at last time. "I can take you directly into Enzar's territory via a transition point even the magebloods don't know about."

"A likely story." I dragged him to his feet, acutely aware he wasn't wearing cuffs this time. But I was the one with the built-in amplifier. I turned invisible, shoving him in the spine. "Go on."

The doorway he'd opened had closed, and the path back to Central was blocked by the ruins of the crashed Klathican drone. I didn't have time for this. Central was under attack, and the magebloods wanted Walker. But here was a path into Enzar.

"What the devil?" He stared at the space where I'd vanished.

"Central's new tech," I said. "You're not the only one with

tricks. And I'm not saying I won't hand you over to the enemy, given the chance."

He pushed the door, just slightly. It slid open, to a metal-plated tunnel. There were no windows, and the tight space made the hairs stand up on the back of my neck. I was here, alone, with the man whose presence had been stamped on my whole life.

He was no threat to me anymore, alive or dead.

I shoved him roughly, making him stumble a few steps. "If we're attacked, I'm not responsible for your safety."

We turned one last corner, and reached a hexagonal-shaped room. Each side was set with a door except the one we'd come through and the one opposite, which led to another tunnel.

"First door on the left," said Walker. "At least it used to be, twenty years ago."

"That's reassuring." I pushed him towards the door. While he was paused, I got out my gun. Still invisible. He tensed as the barrel clicked.

"That's not necessary, Kay. I'm not going to hurt you."

"Huh." I shoved him again. "Get on with it."

Walker extended a hand, and lightly sketched a series of glyphs on a raised section of the door. He pressed the palms of his hands to the door, which lit up, gleaming blue then transparent.

And on the other side, stooped under the low ceiling, were two chalder voxes.

Walker cursed, stepping back, but the door was already sliding open.

"Give me a weapon," he hissed.

"Let me take care of this." As long as I had the element of surprise, I could take them.

Dagger in hand, I crept up on the voxes. Behind me, Walker lurked out of sight, but the idiot creatures hadn't even turned around. I'd stabbed one of them in the neck before its partner even noticed.

The second vox twisted around, its third arm snatching at empty air. I ducked, using the hover boots to launch myself into the air and aim for its head—but it was stuck under the lowered ceiling, blocking me from reaching its weak point.

I shot the tiniest measure of magic at the ceiling. The spark bounced off the metal plating and hit the floor. Spotting it, the vox ducked, clumsy hands snatching, and it was simple to aim my dagger for the back of its neck.

I jumped clear of the falling monster, switched off the invisibility and beckoned Walker to follow me—only he wasn't there anymore.

"Get back here," I snarled, sprinting into the main room to find him in the act of palm-scanning another door. I grabbed the scruff of his neck and threw him over my shoulder.

Walker cursed, sprawled on the ground. "Did you think I'd follow you into hell without weapons?"

"No." I yanked him to his feet again. "But I thought you'd have the common sense to stay put. What's down that way?"

"A safe house."

"Which world?"

When he didn't answer, I pressed the gun to his temple again.

"You've outstayed your usefulness, Walker. Which world does that lead to?"

"Cethrax," he snarled. "Like all the safe houses."

Crash.

I spun around, gripping the back of Walker's jacket. The sound came from the tunnel where I'd killed the voxes… and half a dozen goblins ran towards us.

Walker jerked his head towards the other newly opened door. "Are you prepared to revise your decision?"

"If it *is* safe, I'm not drawing the goblins that way." I aimed my gun. Three went down instantly. I cut the throat of a third, kicking a dagger spinning out of another's hand. My own weapon glided through the air, severing its spine. The surviving dreyvern ran down the tunnel he'd come out of. Past the vox, towards a wall of shimmering light.

"What the devil is that?" Walker stared at the patch of light, which seemed to have grown in the past few seconds.

"Doorway," I said. "The kimaros."

The mist swirled through the corridor, engulfing the two dead chalder voxes. Fuck. The damn thing was heading right for us.

"How do I shut this door?" I demanded of Walker, who just stared, frozen in terror. "For god's sake—"

Red smoke surrounded us, masking the other doors, and Walker's hands gripped my shoulders. I swore and twisted myself free in a heartbeat.

"I'm saving your life, Kay!"

"Like *hell* you are." But the voice of common sense screamed louder. The other door. He was trying to drag me out of range. Though the outline of the second door was faint, Walker stumbled towards it. Keeping my gun trained on him, I pulled him back as the smoke surrounded us. Eyes gleamed from within.

Not *the* kimaros, but a smaller one was dangerous enough on its own. I had to shield my face with my arms as sparks shot at both of us. I fired my gun, the bullet sparking off the walls and exploding in a second shower of light. But a cloud of swirling smoke told me there was more than one, and if the other corridor really did leave to a safe point, like hell was I letting those monsters near it. I shoved the door closed from the side.

"Fine. It's time for Plan B." That kimaros had left Enzar's

trace all over the walls. I took the world-key from my pocket, one eye on Walker, who'd staggered to his feet.

And held my dagger. Bastard had taken it out of my pocket.

I sketched the last symbol, letting the tracker's signal guide my hand along the same glyphs Walker had drawn on the door. But my other hand was searching out the trigger on the gun. Good job I'd learned to shoot with my left hand, too.

Walker wasn't looking at me. He staggered to the door I'd shoved closed and pressed the edge of the blade to the hinge.

"I'm sealing it closed," he said. "Believe it or not, I wouldn't let that creature escape into the last safe haven in the Multiverse."

"What, you want a medal? Take your pick. We go that way, or use my shortcut. I picked up Enzar's trace."

"Amplifier," said Walker. "You could have done so much for the Alliance, had you been willing."

"You could have, too, had you not been a total bastard."

I let the door slide open, a patch of nothingness opening in the wall. I stood back, just in case, but the magic signal pulsing through the door was recognisable even though I'd never been there before.

Because it felt like Ada.

Enzar.

The burnt-red ground, the reddish-purple-tinged sky— and scattered pieces of metal on the ground.

"You found it?" said Walker. "You realise Enzar is the size of Earth's moon?"

"There'll be a source nearby," I said, now certain. Not that I'd be able to sense another signal, because Enzar's masked everything. Like the magic came alive in my veins, beating in time with my heart.

"Come on." I made sure Walker was behind me, positioning myself so I'd be able to strike back if he tried anything. He might have one of my weapons, but he was no magic-wielder, and the air was alive with magic.

We stood at the crest of a hill. Blackened pieces of metal were scattered all around, and in one direction, the horizon cut off in a black line. In the other, I made out the distant shape of some kind of construction. A building? No…

"Stay put," I said to Walker, activating the scanner again. This time, magic burned so intensely, my hands shook, and I was glad I'd kept the gloves on.

Nothing. Walker had already stepped back through the doorway, and I followed, cursing under my breath. Enzar itself was like a giant source—that had to be why I hadn't been taken immediately to wherever Ada had ended up. I tried the doorway again, three times, before we hit civilisation. It might have been the outskirts of a city once. Stone houses all around us, but they all looked empty. Some were in pieces, but the majority were surprisingly intact. Again, there didn't seem to be a source around. But we were close to the black-lined horizon, and there was something awfully familiar about it.

"Damn." I retreated back into the room again.

"It's dead," said Walker. "The whole world's dead. Most of their population must have left to join the magebloods or gone into hiding on the outlying worlds."

"Oh? What makes you so sure? Because it sure didn't feel dead to me."

"Maybe you magic-wielders are different, but it's plain to see it isn't a habitable world any longer. And that means the nexus is gone."

"What?" I stared at him, unable to help it. "I thought the nexus—if it even exists—is the core of magic on a particular world."

"It's a core *source*," said Walker. "What you felt, I would guess, is just the echo, the aftereffect. Sources are living, or as close as magic gets."

"You really think it's gone?"

But if the source wasn't there, Ada might be walking into a trap. *Shit.*

"This, I believe, was once their capital, if I remember my father's accounts correctly."

"You *what?*" I looked out at the ruined buildings, the scattered pieces of… adamantine. But dull and lifeless. Even the antimagic had been drained from this place. "It can't be gone. The magebloods would have nothing to draw on."

"The magebloods are no longer here," said Walker. "There are a half-dozen outlying worlds with magic. None compared with Enzar, but without the core source, it will fall into shadow and break into the void." He gave me a sharp look. "Unless you expected us to find another source. You know what monsters the Royals were, don't you? That girl was one."

Damn. "If you mean Ada, I'm not telling you a thing about her, so give it up."

"She came out here alone, didn't she?"

"Shut up," I said, through clenched teeth. "It's irrelevant to you. And so's this place."

"I think it's relevant," said Walker. "If the source is missing, it means one thing. Humanity has fallen. The living sources reign supreme."

"If you mean the kimaros, it isn't here, is it?"

"Thairon's nexus is on the magebloods' side, and it may be the only thing keeping Enzar alive."

I twisted to face him. "What?"

"Living sources feed on magic," said Walker. "That is the true nature of the Balance. Living sources absorb magic until it overpowers them and they are no more. Echoes of their power remain and leak into other worlds, and the cycle begins again. It was never meant to be contained inside a person."

"You're shitting me. What you did to me was no accident. You wanted to give the Alliance an army to send against Enzar, or Thairon, right? Or was a lie, too?"

"It was the best I could do with what I had," said Walker. "Thairon was never meant to betray us. Almost all of our weapons were there, before the Enzarians destroyed them. The Royal scum who started the war."

"Wait, now you're saying the *Royals* were on Thairon?"

"It was the Royals who created the kimaros," snarled Walker. "Through enslaving one of Cethrax's beasts and infecting it with magic. They meant to use it against the magebloods, only to become enslaved by the very monster they created. Now their weapon controls the magebloods, too. Two centuries-old enemies united against the Alliance." Walker's hand clenched around my wrist, sending a visceral jolt through my skin. "You're going to kill it, Kay Walker. You're going to kill the nexus, or die trying. And I'll be there to watch."

"You're fucking deluded." I wrenched my hand away, ignoring the tremors. The magicproof sleeve had blocked most of the shock. "There's no way to kill that thing. It's unkillable—that's why you shut it on Thairon before, right?"

"Yes, but you showed me I was mistaken," said Walker. " You channelled its power, didn't you? How do you think the war started? Humans playing at being gods. But the nexus was never meant to be contained. That's why I could never risk leaving doors to Enzar open. It'd always try to escape, to conquer more worlds. And now it can—unless someone destroys it first."

Ada and I did. Before. They might have all the worlds' sources on their side, but not the amplifier. Not me. They didn't know what I was. Neither did my father, in the end.

Magic pulsed through my veins and burned in my blood. Enzar fuelled it. Just being here made me feel like live wires ran underneath my skin. Was it the same for Ada?

Stop it, Kay. I shook off the feeling, but it persisted. Magic ruled here, even though the world was dying.

My eyes focused on my father's face, dead eyes alight with triumph, and something recoiled inside me. *I don't want to be that. Not an instrument of destruction. Not even now.*

Not in the way *he* wanted me to be.

Magic sparked from my palm, born of a world where the Balance didn't exist, where it ruled. I smiled, letting the charge build until the world pulsed red around me, and my father's eyes widened, their black glassy surface reflecting my own crazed smile.

"This is how it ends for you, Walker. You didn't think I'd let you get away with destroying Thairon?"

"You're making a mistake, Kay." The panic in his expression was unmistakeable, and something inside me delighted in it. *It's been too fucking long...*

The charge built. I let a small amount of it flow through my hand, striking him down. He writhed on the ground, and a dark creature inside whispered, *Do it again. Make him suffer as he did to you.*

God only knew I'd imagined it enough times. Enough that in reality, he looked pathetic lying there. I wanted him to fight back. I kicked him, hard. "Get up and fight me, Walker."

The magic built in pitch until every cell in my body hummed with it, in synchronisation. In his eyes, I saw myself, standing in a blaze of magic. Bright enough to draw any magic-wielders here—any living sources that recognised one of their own.

I let the charge die down.

"No," I said. "I think I'll leave you here."

I took the world-key in my shaking hand. The bastard

had had a point. I *could* sneak into the heart of their operation and find a way to destroy it. But I had no clue where Ada was. I couldn't stop them alone.

I raised my hand to the earpiece and tapped it twice, waiting for the answering signal that it was safe to talk. Nothing. I could only assume it was too dangerous where she was. I didn't let myself consider the alternative.

The sky split open, a blast of magic knocking me back. I swore, pushing the world-key into my sleeve and going for my dagger instead. The world divided, a cloud of red smoke heralding the arrival of two black-clad figures. I froze, cursing myself for not switching on the invisibility. But they weren't looking at me. They were looking at my father.

"I knew you'd come crawling back, Walker," one of them said softly, and fired magic directly at him.

Walker didn't try to run. Didn't have time. The magic hit him in a crackle of thunder, his body momentarily suspended in the air. Then he fell, crumpling into the dust.

I couldn't move. Every inch of me felt numb, bruised with shock. Some instinct had turned me invisible again, but the magical aftershock rippling through the air knocked the effect off almost immediately. I had about five seconds to come up with an alibi before the two people who'd killed Walker blew me sky-high, too. Unless there was enough magic here for me to counter their adamantine armour.

"Who the hell are you?" I asked them.

"My name is Dox Nelson," said the man on the right. *So that's it.* He was my grandfather's former partner at Kimaro-Tech, and Lawrence Walker's enemy. His companion, however, was a woman with violet eyes and tanned skin over wires. A mageblood with cyberware. Her eyes were blank, glassy.

"You're his. You're from the Alliance." She raised a hand. A shock ripped through my body, the world burst apart in violet light, and for about the hundredth time in my life, I thought I died. Seconds melded together as the magic burned inside me, reacting with the amplifier in my blood. Pain pulsed through every inch of me, inside and out. I gasped, certain each breath would be my last. Then all was dark.

18

ADA

I took a moment to assess my options. I had no auros, nor a world-key. But there *was* a way out. This was the palace Nell had escaped. To the transition point, through an underground tunnel.

The palace ruins gave way to more wreckage that stretched to either side of the horizon, littered with broken buildings and crumbled stone. Nothing remained behind but the void. I checked my hover boots were still working. I could cover more ground, but without knowing where I was going, I'd only given Enzar more chances to strike back at the Alliance the longer I stayed here.

Footsteps, scrambling noises. I stopped dead as several figures emerged from behind the cracked remains of pillars. All wore sand-coloured armour that covered their entire bodies, but which looked lightweight as guard gear. Even their faces were masked, which made it impossible to tell whose side they were on. I'd thought the magebloods were gone. And the nonmages, too.

I pressed my heel into the accelerator of my hover boot,

rising a few inches off the ground. I had my weapons, but I couldn't take out all of them at once.

"Who are you?" one asked.

They didn't know me by sight. I weighed my chances. "I'm here from the Alliance." The speaker was clearly Enzarian by their accent, but they spoke *Klathican.*

"It's too late," said the speaker. His visor rose, and I stifled a gasp. Pale eyes. Not mageblood. These were nonmages—not Royals. They had no magic, so they weren't affected by the kimaros's control. They must have been hiding here all along.

The rebels.

I pointed shakily at the void. "Who did that?"

"The Royals."

So it was true. "You're not mageblood," I said to them.

"Half-blooded, most of us," said the first speaker. "We lived underground, aiding in offworld operations... but it's over now. All of it."

They're not with the magebloods. But though I'd found the rebels, I'd got here too late.

"You were the ones who helped..." I let myself drop back to the ground, on a level with the nonmages, and stared at them.

"Royal," one of them said. "It's you..."

"Adamantine?"

Oh. My eyes were on full display. "I'm not here to hurt you."

"You gave yourself up to them. We watched. What are you doing here?"

"That... was a decoy." Nell. "What happened to her?"

"The magebloods took her. They've taken our transition point. They have a magic-creature—but you already know, Adamantine." He stepped towards me. "Isn't that why you're here?"

"I came to find you. So… they're operating from *that* transition point? The place linked up with the palace?" Nell. Maybe they knew her. "I've been there before, but not since I was a baby. Is it really… gone?"

One of the nonmages tapped something on the side of their helmet.

"Just got an update," said a female voice. "Klathica is still under attack, but the Alliance seems to be fighting back."

Of course they were. A rush of pride shot through me. Central was still standing.

"Please," I said. "I need to get through the tunnels. If there's nothing left here, I want to help you bring them down. I can fight them." *I can drain the magic right out of a source. Maybe even theirs…*

The nonmage man beckoned me to follow, and the other nonmages moved to one part of the ruins, where stone steps were hidden amongst the wreckage.

"Nobody ever comes here," one of the nonmages explained. "Nobody has used the tunnel aside from us in years. This part of Enzar is uninhabitable."

"Because of the void. Is there no way to close it?"

"No," said the female nonmage, "but Enzar is far from the only world to fall to the void. All we wished to do was help those escape who asked for no part in the war, but even they have fled this world. Enzar itself is no more, as are a dozen other worlds formerly part of the Enzarian Empire. We stayed to save those who were left behind."

"Did you know they're on Cethrax?"

"We did." Deep sadness filled her expression. "We held them off for a time, but it wasn't enough. Their magic… it's limitless."

"I know," I whispered. "They have the kimaros, a living source, linking up every world. I might be able to destroy it —or at least break its hold over their army, but I'll need to get there without them knowing where I am. That's why I want to use the tunnels."

"I see," said the nonmage. "Cethrax is the boundary between the dead worlds and the allied worlds. If this continues, it will fall into the void, dragging all the other worlds down with it. This world has already fallen."

It's true. For all the magic burning in my veins, all would fall into the void soon. The Balance didn't exist here. But on Earth, it did. And I had to save it.

"I know," I said again, my voice cracking. "I just—I just wanted to see it. But I... I have a new homeworld now. Earth. I'm here to fight for them."

"It would be our honour to help you, Adamantine."

"Just Ada," I said. "I—I never got to thank you for saving my life all those years ago. But is it true? The Royals *and* the magebloods are enslaved? Including... the ones from the palace?"

"There were a handful of survivors," said the leading nonmage. "According to rumour, anyway. But there's nothing left of them. They'll have been assimilated into the magebloods' army by now. Few of their fighters serve them of their own will."

The kimaros. But whatever had happened to the Royals, what they did to me and the other kids was inexcusable. If they lived, I wouldn't spare them, not in the end.

"Just one more thing," I said, before I followed them into the narrow tunnel opening. "I... I wanted to ask for a cease-fire on behalf of the Alliance. That isn't possible now, is it?"

"No. They won't listen to reason. Few of them remain in control of their own will, and the ones that do, including the Alliance traitor..."

"Who?"

"The one called Nelson, who sold the magebloods weapons and enabled them to enslave their army."

The guy who'd betrayed Lawrence Walker? Holy shit. I shook my head, not willing to think any more. Any hopes of a ceasefire were futile. All I had to do was take as many of them down with me as possible, before they took out the Alliance and the Multiverse along with it.

"Is—is there really nobody left here?" I took one last glance at the palace, at the burned out pieces of adamantine littering the path to the gaping void. Knowing this would be the last time I ever saw my birthplace.

"Nothing," said the nonmage. "Come. We planned to seal the tunnels after we got everyone out."

"I have hover-tech. I can move fast." I didn't like the idea of going into total darkness in this place, but magic lit up the air even underground. "Could you tell me the quickest route?"

He gave me a series of instructions as we descended the staircase. I fervently hoped the rebels would make it out.

"Others are closer to their territory," he said. "Spying, and looking for a weak point."

"The kimaros," I said. "It has control over their army, but it doesn't *want* to. It was trapped under their army's control, and then turned on its masters, only to end up enslaved again." Could it be persuaded to let go? I doubted so, but the alternative was doing the impossible and finding a way to contain it. What the magebloods had done to hold the creature couldn't be permanent. A creature like that, made of magic and hate, would devour them, and every world along with them.

I dropped into the tunnel, kicking the accelerator. The walls were smooth, like the earth had been hollowed out. Man-made, I assumed.

"Then maybe you can stop it, Ada."

Maybe I could. Or maybe I'd become the weapon myself. There hadn't been a source here, at all. The rebels had nothing left, and yet they were still fighting the magebloods. And so would I. There'd be no more hiding.

"Thanks," I said. "I mean it. Hopefully I'll see you soon."

The tunnel's darkness brightened a little as lamps lit up along the walls. Claustrophobia threatened to close over my head as I moved further, step by step, then hit the heel of the hover boot and picked up speed. Wind rustled in my hair as I flew down corridor after corridor. It'd take days to cover this much ground without the boots. I tried to shut off the image of Nell running down these tunnels, alone and desperate. *That won't happen again. You'll never see this place again. They're dead.* The Royals had deserved their fate. Whether my former family survived or not, they'd be empty shells, enslaved by the creature they'd helped dominate in the first place. I had no pity left for them. I couldn't afford to.

It took a minute to reach the first checkpoint, a ramshackle little underground house. Nobody was inside. I moved ahead, counting turnings, heart beating in my ears, magic sparking in my veins, building again. Like a sense reawakened, immersing me, flowing through my every particle. Like a clamp had lifted from my lungs, letting me breathe again. The live current sent trails of sparks behind me. I'd left the void behind, but I must be approaching a source. Or maybe it remained in the very atmosphere, an echo of the magic which had once held the world captive.

I reached a door set in the darkness, of a metal now familiar. Blue, gleaming auros. So it was true. This way must lead to the transition point—and Cethrax.

My dagger gleamed in the near-dark. One side adamantine, one side lustre. Antimagic and amplifier. I clenched my fist around the handle and used the other hand to open the door.

The blood rushed to my head as a giant hand lifted me into the air. A chalder vox held me high, so my head scraped the ceiling. I tried to wriggle free but it held me firmly, so I kicked out with the hover boots, the acceleration knocking its head back. The chalder vox bellowed with rage, but now I was free, I launched myself over its head and stabbed downwards with the dagger.

Five more vox-kind waited ahead, in the entryway to a circular room. Cethrax must have taken the rebels' base. *Damn.* I hoped the ones back on Enzar would escape. The circular room was wide, filled with computer monitors and other machinery. Maybe a communications base.

One of the vox-kind lunged at me, colliding with a second as it grabbed at me through the doorway. I clicked on the sciras boost and kicked the boots into gear, flying at the voxes like a bullet. My dagger swiped, knocking one of them down, but the moment my eyes locked on the door at the back of the room, I nearly stopped dead in my tracks.

The room on the other side, more like a hall, was full of vox-kind. Hundreds. The stench of the swampland filled the place, through two doors open on either side of the hall. Cethrax. I supposed this world being the transition point to Enzar made sense, considering it was the world where doorways opened most frequently, and the Alliance rarely came calling. Maybe it even accounted for my constantly seeking out monsters to fight even as a kid. But none of that mattered now.

The twin metal doors at the back of the hall opened, revealing a haze of red smoke. The doorway port. So this was how they were attacking the Alliance.

A hand grabbed my foot, and I remembered the surviving chalder voxes. I steadied myself on the ceiling, just out of reach of the biggest vox. I couldn't kill all of the ones in the hall, not without alerting the magebloods to my presence. The army must be waiting for orders, because they stood in lines, grunting and occasionally kicking one another. So, acting of their own will, then. At least for now. The walls on either side gleamed blue. Auros. This whole tunnel was a gateway to the rest of the Multiverse.

The attacking vox-kind reached for me, hands grasping, and I dived at it, sinking the double-sided blade into the back of its neck. Three left. These must be the security guards. I risked dropping to ground level to see if anyone else waited on the other side of the door, and caught sight of two bodies thrown carelessly into a corner behind one of the voxes I'd knocked down. Rebels. The chalder voxes had crushed their skulls.

Rage ignited and I flew at another of the vox-kind. Black shadow-like blood sprayed as I stabbed each of them in the weak point. Maybe it didn't matter if the magebloods caught me. If I could take as many of them down with me as possible, it'd be worth it.

Wait, Ada. I kicked at a chalder-vox's grasping hands and brought the knife down, sinking it to the hilt in the back of its head. My back pressed to the cold wall as the voxes closest to the door shifted, a couple glancing over their shoulders. But others moved forward, and I caught a glimpse of the wall on the left. It was made of auros, and there wasn't just a door to Cethrax there. Another door revealed the view of a city from above. A second, beside it, revealed a jungle. This was the doorway port, opening into a dozen worlds at once.

I was too late. The army was leaving, to take down the Alliance.

Desperately, I flew into the entryway to the hall, my dagger stabbing one monster at a time. Two fell into one another. Renewed fury filled my veins. *Stay away from my homeworld. Stay away from Earth.*

I can drain the magic from any source.

The whole room was made of auros. I stilled, a new revelation occurring to me. Then I flew high, out of the reach of the remaining monsters, reached out my free hand and pulled the magic into me.

For a second, nothing happened. I flew high enough to brush the towering ceiling, also blue with auros, and pressed my free hand to it. I might not be on Enzar any longer, but the magic still burned through my veins. I was a living source, and nobody would ever destroy the world I loved again.

Magic poured into me from the auros coating the walls and floor, my skin buzzing all over. Second level. It was working. I pulled harder, gritting my teeth against the buzzing sensation as the magic surged from the walls, into me.

Something cracked, and I zipped out the way as a piece of dead auros dropped from the wall. Then another.

I kept tugging at the magic. Another cracking sound came from the ceiling as the blue tint blackened. On my left, the scene of a cityscape abruptly vanished behind the door, replaced by swampland. The monsters stopped, blinking stupidly, as their destination vanished.

Magic filled my bones until I was certain I couldn't hold any more without breaking—yet it kept coming. Another doorway switched off, the scene of a jungle vanishing. Then another. My teeth rattled in my skull as though I clung to the side of a moving train, and the magic kept on flooding me. *I'm adamantine. I'm unbreakable. I can kill any source, even this one.*

The entire wall on the left turned from blue to black, the doorways replaced by ordinary doors leading out into the swamp. That side of the army halted, while the other became confused as door after door winked out. A crash sounded from the room behind as pieces of the auros-coated ceiling collapsed.

The auros was the only source of light in the hall, aside

from the smoke, and every second darkened a corner of the room until I became acutely aware that I was glowing—my eyes were glowing—and nobody would ever doubt what I was.

Maybe I didn't want them to.

One final tug, and magic flooded the room. Lights burst behind my eyes, and if not for the hover boots, I'd have fallen over. As it was, I hung there, suspended in the air, blinking rapidly to clear my vision. The red smoke was still there, but the monsters had stopped as the doors closed.

Someone else had entered the room, opening a door to let natural light spill into the darkness.

There was no hiding. There never had been. I held my breath as three figures clad in jet-black gleaming armour stepped forwards, out of the smoke.

The Cethraxians had edged to the outskirts of the room… those who'd survived. The corpses of dreyverns littered the ground. The magic had broken right through their armour.

I did that.

I hadn't stopped the whole army, but I'd slowed them, and cut off their destinations. The three humans looked oddly small compared to the vox-kind, and their adamantine masks made their identities unclear. Until the masks came down, revealing violet eyes.

The breath froze in my lungs.

"Who are you?" one of them asked in fluent Klathican.

"She's an Alliance spy."

"Your eyes are fake," said one of them. "You wear a mask, a bloodrock mask, like the false one."

My heart beat too fast. "No. I'm not a spy." *The false one. Not Nell. Please.* "I'm here to talk to the leaders of the magebloods."

And destroy their source. If I got close to it. Maybe I could pull off the act. But my eyes gave the game away no matter what. There was no use pretending to be anyone other than who I was.

"We have already rejected the Alliance's proposal," said the mageblood on the right. "Give us one reason why we should not kill you."

Ice flowed down my spine, and magic rose like a cloak around me. *They have Nell.*

The wild magic remaining from the auros sparked off the walls, buzzing around me in an electric storm.

"Give me one reason why I shouldn't kill *you.*"

I flung my dagger at his eyes.

Magic repelled me, sudden and sharp, and a cracking noise sounded as the hover boots cut out. I fell, my back slamming into the metal floor, and a hand clamped down on my wrist. All traces of magic vanished, as abruptly as a blindfold thrown over my eyes. I bit down on a gasp at the shock at having my magic torn away by their touch, like being plunged into an icy sea. God, it *hurt.* He was as strong as a Stoneskin.

I still have the sciras switched on.

I yanked my hand free, gritting my teeth as pain lanced through my wrist, but the other two closed in. They had me cornered. The only way out was back the way I came—or into the void. The ceiling had collapsed in the room behind me, and I was less than certain it even led into Enzar anymore. It didn't matter, because there was no way home from there. There never had been.

Before I could move, the red smoke shifted, and a pair of gigantic pit-like eyes stared back, from the other side of the door.

Oh. Hell.

"If you don't want us to feed you to the kimaros," said the —Stoneskin? Mageblood?—"tell us who you are."

"I'm the one who's going to kill you." I breathed in and

out, my heart beating fast. I'd only heard a cracking noise from one hover boot, and as long as they weren't touching me, I *did* have an unlimited store of magical energy. Didn't change the fact that the only way out of here was either through the swamp with the monsters or through the void with the kimaros. But if they touched me, my magic would go out and I'd be at their mercy.

I hit the heel of my boot, quick as a flash, and shot up into the air. I flew in an arc towards the doorway, towards the pitted eyes in the smoke. I'd dominated the kimaros before. It would remember me.

Right now, that was all I had going for me.

Destroy the source. Get to Nell. Those two thoughts collided as I braked, on the edge of the pit which rotated between the Cethraxian swamp, and other worlds too quick to recognise.

Oh god. The room wasn't the real doorway port.

Cethrax lay on the other side of the cliff-like mirage of the void, and rather than monsters, the swampland was covered with machinery, huge war machines. Tanks, missiles, other weapons. Figures moved amongst them—black-clad, human-shaped. Magebloods with Stoneskin armour.

So they really had moved their war base over to Cethrax. And from here, they could reach any world in the Multiverse.

Below me, the kimaros waited in a pit, suspended between the rotating doorways. Like the void, but alive, not dead. Was there a way to end the invasion without draining the magic right out of the allied worlds?

Over the electric hum of magic, raised voices shouted in Klathican, too quick for me to make out the words. So the army didn't even speak Enzarian. Like their weapons, like the beast they'd harnessed to the void, they'd taken their language from an Alliance world. Or it'd been freely given to them. Their hi-tech black suits even looked like the uniforms worn by Alliance personnel and police on worlds like Klathica and Valeria. For a brief, bizarre moment, the doorway rotated again and I glimpsed a city superimposed over the endless swampland. The world Cethrax might have been, had it not fallen to the likes of these people. Or Robert Walker. The desolate wasteland, burned out by magic and war, was *his* legacy.

Thinking about Kay was a mistake. I faltered, even as the magebloods moved to grab me again. Those pitiless eyes gleaming in the abyss held my gaze.

You don't want to be here any more than I do, I thought at the kimaros, willing it to hear. *You're stronger than they are. Break free.*

The beast gave no reaction, but the shouts grew louder. Others had seen me, and I flew awkwardly high over the abyss, aware that if the second hover boot broke, I was royally screwed. I propelled myself across the abyss, above the magebloods, and their metal contraptions. *Sources.* There were sources here, buzzing with power, harnessing energy from the kimaros itself.

A shock went right through my bones, and I fell, head over heels. This time there was no magic to catch me. My eyes squeezed shut, my hands grabbing for the magic slipping away by the second. Every part of me cried out in pain.

Magic shock.

Antimagic shock.

A deafening cracking right behind my ear. Somehow it registered the earpiece had broken into pieces. Kay's face flashed before my eyes as I braced myself for the impact.

It never came. Softness cushioned me, but my eyes wouldn't open. Spasms rocked my body. My hand twitched, clutching the dagger by sheer reflex. Second level antimagic shock. But the suspiciously soft landing...

Gasping, fighting the spasms, I forced my eyes open a

fraction. Wires snaked beneath me. Thin wire. A net. They'd caught me in an antimagic net. Beneath, the restless form of the kimaros swirled and reformed in the abyss. They'd put a net over the void, to keep it encased. The wires were thinly meshed over the kimaros, hidden in the smoke. I thrashed, fighting a scream—but if they removed the net, I'd fall into the abyss, or into their army.

Shouts jumbled together in my ears. I gritted my teeth, made myself sit upright, but the net sent me sliding down again.

"Tell us," said the magebloods, from above, "who you are. Or die."

"I'm Adamantine," I said, wildly. "The last Royal. I'm your nexus!"

A long pause. My heart thudded. One slip, and even I wouldn't survive that fall, and that's if the net couldn't go higher than second level. If it could, I'd be fried from the inside out like any magic-wielder.

"Nexus?" asked the mageblood.

I hadn't wanted to go there. There was the chance they wouldn't believe me. But now my options had run out, there was nothing to do but see if they were as desperate to end the war as the StoneKing had said. "I'm here to negotiate on behalf of the Enzarians whose lives are being destroyed by the war. My family implanted the nexus of Enzar's power inside me in order to bring an end to the conflict. If you destroy me, you destroy your own magic, too."

I had no idea if it was true, even if I *had* been the nexus. But I knew magebloods didn't have an internal magic source. They were dependent on the magic in the atmosphere of the world they fought on—that was how the Royals had gained the upper hand, because sources could potentially be limitless whether they were used internally or externally. The magebloods were borrowing power from the kimaros. But it didn't look like they were under its influence. Maybe their high tech suits stopped it.

Please don't let this be a mistake.

"Adamantine?" The mageblood who'd first caught me leaned over the pit. "The Alliance deceived us? You aren't theirs?"

Yes. I'm theirs. But you don't have to know that.

"I never was," I said. "I'm Enzar's. Yours, if you want me to be. Just end the war, and you'll get to keep your empire. If you destroy the Alliance, you'll knock out the Balance across the Multiverse, including here. High-magic worlds will end up like Enzar, swallowed into the abyss. You'll create a disaster on a scale even you can't defend yourselves against, and for what? You have all the power you need."

I fell silent, breathing heavily. My skin itched from the magic-shock, and my whole body continued shaking. But my words were steady.

"You kill me, you kill yourselves. Spare my life and I'll help you rebuild your empire. I'm Adamantine, unbreakable, because if you try to break me, you'll break yourselves too."

I scanned the crowd gathering around the abyss. Hundreds of them. The magebloods were easy to pick out, with their chipped purple eyes. But there were other Enzarians, too, in the same uniform, but without the signs of magic. One pair of them approached, and my heart dropped when I saw their eyes. White as diamonds.

The Royals.

The breath stuck in my chest.

Don't look at them. Don't speak. I had to play my role, use it to destroy their weapons, and then—what? How many of them really wanted to fight? None of them wore curious expressions, and more than a few moved in time with one another, like Cethrax's army had. The reddish tint covering my vision became more distinct. The kimaros wasn't contained by the abyss. Thin tendrils extended out, fanning across the doorway port to the people on the other side. Touching all of them.

I tried to stand, again, but the net was too slippery. I settled for kneeling. Like I was about to give myself up.

"She is ours," said a voice. One of the Royals. She spoke Klathican, but her voice was oddly flat, free of any emotion.

"I'm not yours." I risked a look at her. Fair hair, almost shaved away. Royal eyes. Otherwise, they might all have been identical. I'd never know if any of them were my birth parents.

"You are Royal. You have the eyes."

"So it is true?" asked the leading mageblood. "She is one of you?"

"She is," said the Royal, in that dead, robotic voice.

"I told you we should keep them alive," said another mageblood, with a chilling undertone to his voice. Magic cloaked him, and he bared his teeth in a smile when he saw me watching. "They might be all but useless now the kimaros has broken their minds, but I'll bet our little intruder will tell the truth swiftly if her family is threatened."

If I hadn't been lying in a net over a bottomless pit, I'd have spat in his face.

"Tell us, girl," said a female mageblood. "Your family seem to have no recollection about the procedure which granted you extraordinary gifts. You claim to be a *nexus?*"

Shit. So they didn't know what the Royals had done. Nell had told me that, after the Stoneskins had taken me. They had never known where the Royals' power had come from. Even now, when they had Royals in captivity. They hadn't given away their secrets, even though they must have been tortured. A sick feeling rose in my throat.

"I'll tell you all about me," I said, "if you tell me what you plan to do with the other Royals, and if any others are still alive."

What are you doing, Ada? The voice in my head sounded like Nell, but the sight of the Royals being controlled by the magebloods' kimaros woke a desperation in my heart. Maybe I'd hated them from the start, but they'd kept my secret. They'd never given away the source of their—our—power. Whether they'd truly known I was alive or not, I didn't know. Maybe their minds were gone, and I'd never know. But I couldn't give myself up to the magebloods without some leverage.

"You are in no position to be bargaining," said the second mageblood who'd spoken to me. "The last Royal. You've led us on quite a dance. Your people's operation is to be admired. You might have lived in any city, on any of the Alliance worlds. Hidden amongst the commoners. Royalty." He laughed. The hairs on my neck stood on end as I noted how close behind the two Royals he stood. Like an executioner. Had he been the one to interrogate them?

"Why?" I asked, my voice rising. "Why imprison and torture them when you wanted them dead? You've tried to bring down their empire for years. Generations."

"You do know your history." His violet eyes gleamed. "They had certain information we needed."

"You're all one big, happy family, aren't you?" I snarled. "Like it wasn't enough to sack Enzar. You had to take everyone else under your control as well. First the Royals, then the StoneKing—what the hell was with him, by the way? He came after me and got himself killed."

"The disgraced Stoneskin caused us a lot of trouble, but his ability was valuable."

The tracker. "What? You already have a doorway port."

"The Stoneskin carried the traces of the Alliance world he

came from. Through him, we found our way to Klathica, where our source now rules."

I gaped at him. They'd used the *StoneKing* to get to Klathica? Then it wasn't Walker's fault, after all.

"Adamantine, I'm certain you will prove just as useful to us as he was."

"I'm not going to do anything for you if you threaten my family."

I hadn't considered I'd have to pretend to care about the blank-eyed people whose minds had been broken by the kimaros they'd created themselves. Despite everything, a painful curiosity stirred. How long had they been like that? Had they ever remembered me, or was I just another name on the death records? As if they'd even have death records anymore.

The mageblood opened his mouth to speak, and a sudden metallic whirring filled the air, like the feedback from a microphone turned to full volume.

"The accursed ones," snarled one of the magebloods. "Shut that off!" He seemed to be shouting at the magebloods gathered near one of the huge mechanical structures.

"We can't," someone shouted back. "The Alliance—they took our communication centre!"

Another voice overrode all others, loud enough to make the ground shake and the antimagic net tremble.

"You cannot win this fight. Give in."

Holy hell. That wasn't the magebloods. It sounded like—

"What's that?" I demanded, but no one listened. Everyone shouted at each other. But above all were of screeches and whirs from whatever machinery—or microphone—the Alliance were using.

"Give in," said a female voice. Ms Weston? "Your war will be the end of you. We've cut off your communication systems. Klathica is ours again."

"And if you don't give me my sister back, we'll make you sorry."

My mouth fell open. That was *Jeth's* voice.

"Enough!" shouted the leading mageblood. "You—take her. Teach her some manners."

The net shifted, depositing me on the edge of the cliff, on Cethrax's side. Rough hands grabbed me, hauling me to my feet. I fought against them, scrambling to better grip my dagger, but stopped when I saw their prisoner. The brief flash of triumph died out. A Royal had grabbed me, and two more approached. Between them, hands and feet chained, was Nell.

19

KAY

My father was dead. I was a prisoner.

Those two thoughts connected. I opened my eyes.

I was tied to a chair, by the look of things. Or a piece of rock in the shape of a chair, anyway. Black adamantine. And so were the chains on my wrists and ankles. The pressure, and the sudden absence of magic, made my head spin too much to focus on anything.

I can't move. I can't get out. I was in a room with metal walls, ceiling and floor. Cethrax, judging by the blade-like trees outside the single window on my right. Red sky above swampland.

The magebloods' base. A prisoner. Locked in a cage again.

I fought against the chains. My wrists were bleeding within minutes, and I couldn't break the chains without magic. I gritted my teeth and tugged harder, but my wrists would break under the pressure and I still wouldn't come close to getting through the adamantine. No magic-wielder could escape this trap. Not without a source. But I *had* one—in my pocket. If I could reach my stunner—

A grating noise behind me. I looked over my shoulder as a metal door slid open. Dox Nelson and the mageblood woman came in.

"You didn't kill him," Nelson remarked.

"I told you," said the mageblood woman. "He's enhanced somehow. And he's from the Alliance. He can give us information." Her voice was a monotone. Just like those Klathicans caught under the kimaros's spell. Did that mean she wasn't acting of her own will? Whether she was or not, she'd nearly killed me. And her buddy had turned on KimaroTech and sold Alliance secrets to the enemy. A plan—desperate, as usual—came together in my head.

"I can hear you," I said, furious with myself for landing in this mess. "Who are you? You're with Enzar, right?"

"We are the ones asking questions," said Nelson, pulling out what looked like an Alliance stunner. Sweat beaded on my forehead as he approached. So they planned to torture me. Well, they had the wrong guy. Nothing would work on me.

"I wouldn't struggle." Nelson eyed my bloody wrists. "We'll make the last minutes of your life a living hell."

"I don't doubt you will." I forced an ironic smile. "But you're mistaken if you think I'll talk."

The two looked at one another. "Tell us who you are, and you won't have to find out."

"My name's Kay. I'm Lawrence Walker's son. My mission was to be a secret. He didn't want me to tell you, even under duress."

For a heartbeat, I thought that was it for me. The mageblood woman turned to Nelson. "Lawrence had a son?"

"Yes, he did." Nelson paused, holding the stunner. "Have you got proof?"

"My Alliance ID, yeah," I said, "for what it's worth. You

shouldn't have killed him. He was here to apologise for being a dick to you all those years ago."

From what my father had told me, of course, Nelson had been the betrayer. But there were always at least two versions of a story. And I was willing to bet if I aligned with Nelson's, I'd have a chance to talk my way out of here.

Now I needed to keep up the lie. Not like I hadn't had the practise.

"You killed him," I said, "but he regretted defying his father. His last words to me were: *find the nexus. Destroy it.* That's what I have to do. Because if I don't, your own source will destroy you before you can fight the Alliance. You'll destroy yourselves. The kimaros is too strong to be contained."

"You lie," said Nelson, the tightness in his voice giving away that he, at least, was somewhat in control of his actions. "The source is what has given us the edge in the fight. The Alliance is nothing."

The stunner brushed the back of my neck, and I took my chance. Before the magic could shock me, I pulled on it, sharp and harsh, willing the amplifier in my blood to do the work. Here, it was a thousand times stronger. And the blood dripping down my hands formed a barrier between me and the handcuffs. Here, close to Enzar, magic had no limits. The cuffs were like the ones the Alliance used, and if you applied enough magic, they'd break.

"What the—?" He tried to pull away as the magic level rose higher, sparking through my palms, and the cuffs broke in fragments. I launched myself off the chair, hover boots activated, and sent Nelson crashing into the far wall.

Then I turned on the mageblood, throwing the remains of the chair. The adamantine did no damage, but blocked the sparks of magic from hitting me as the mageblood attempted an attack. I tapped into the Chameleon, and disappeared.

Go. I could kill them, but that would draw attention, and I needed to move *fast.* I felt the source now, the power pounding against my skin. The kimaros must be close, just outside this building. I shot out into a corridor that ended in a door open onto the swampland. A red glow opposite told me where the source was.

But I can't destroy it alone.

I flew outside, still invisible, and faced the doorway port. The kimaros *was* the portal, open over an abyss. Flashes of other worlds passed by as the doorways rotated. Even if I'd been visible, no one looked up. Crowds milled about around the abyss, but I didn't dare strike, not when I couldn't tell whether the kimaros could sense me or not. I didn't know who was acting of their own volition and who wasn't. They all had reinforced armour. Like the Stoneskins.

A gleaming machine on the right hand side of the void drew my eye. The tracker I'd tapped into buzzed. That had to be one of their sources. They were using a number of them to hold the kimaros in place. Not antimagic. I activated the hover boots and glided up to it. *Damn.* I stared at the contraption a moment. This was a bomb—a giant one, not unlike Klathica's models. They had the kimaros captive by threatening to blow it into pieces. And if I touched it...

I wasn't adamantine, not unbreakable. But I had my dagger. I had an amplifier.

And everything had a weak point.

I stabbed the adamantine blade into a corner of the contraption. As I did, the doorway flickered. *So that's how it is.* The source held parts of the doorway open. The creature was as much a slave as most of their army. Who even held the power here? Who had enslaved whom first? It didn't matter. I drove the point of the blade into the machine's gleaming battery core, and tugged on the magic, pulling it through the lustre side of the point.

Heads turned in my direction. *Crap.* I withdrew the blade, leaving a trail of magic leaking out. As I hovered above the crowd, I saw their attention was fixed on the abyss... and on someone at the edge.

A group of Enzarians, with gleaming white eyes.

Ada. They'd caught her.

~

ADA

Nell—still identical to me—held her head high, but the tremble in her limbs told me they'd shocked her with magic. More than once. Fury buzzed in my veins. I readied myself to attack—and her gaze locked with mine. She shook her head, a faint gesture that told me not to move. It also said, *you shouldn't have come.*

I wouldn't be anywhere else, I thought back, desperately. *Not now.*

Hands clamped mine behind my back. I was still weak from the magic-shock, and though I fought, I couldn't free myself.

Two Royals laid their hands on Nell's back, pushing her to walk forwards. Closer to the pit.

"Cooperate with us," said the mageblood, to me, "or the false one dies."

Come on! I desperately clutched for the magic I knew was there. But those bastards blocked it.

I'm adamantine. Unbreakable. They're nothing. I have adamantine inside me, and I can't be broken.

Magic buzzed underneath my skin. The mageblood

holding me hissed, the tiniest crack appearing in his armoured hand.

"Let her go," I said, "or I'll kill you. All of you."

"You can't do that, Adamantine," said the mageblood. "Not even you. But we'll use your power. Do it," he said, to the Royals. Their eyes gleamed white but startlingly empty, and fear shot down my spine.

They're not human. Not anymore. The kimaros's tendrils wrapped around them, wrapped around everything here. Magic had a mind of its own, and these people were merely the voice.

Nell's eyes said, *it's all right.*

I'll kill them, I thought back. *I'll save us.*

Magic burst through, seeping through my skin in a flood that broke the mageblood's hold on me. I screamed as my skin burned with the pain like I'd thrown myself into the fire. But the net didn't hold me any longer. Magic was mine.

The mageblood fell back, yelling in pain. His armour split all over to reveal broken skin and wires, a black liquid spilling in place of blood. He was part cyber. Either he couldn't feel himself dying, or the kimaros's influence was too strong, and he'd been dead the whole time.

The charge built higher. The second mageblood fell. I grabbed for Nell's chains and shot magic into them, too, breaking them into fragments. My knife was in my hand, my last weapon, and I swiped...

The Royal drew a blade, too, stabbing at my heart.

I jumped, sparks flying out, and the knife missed me by inches. I landed on my feet as the Royal swiped again. For an instant, a different kind of pain hit my heart. *They want me dead. They're following the magebloods.* Our daggers crashed into one another, and the jarring sensation reminded me I wasn't just fighting with adamantine, but with reinforced lustre on the other side of the blade. *It's not them. They're dead.*

The Royals were just puppets, no longer in control of their will. I was faster with a blade, my skill easily matching theirs, but not against more than one.

Nell turned on the other, mouth stretched in a snarl. She grabbed a knife from one of them and turned it on its owner, but she didn't have magic, and the magebloods all wore reinforced armour. I fought the best I could, but every step drove us closer to the edge.

My knife struck out, drawing on the ever-present magic. The charge built higher. The blade cut into the Royal's arm, drawing blood, and he cried out as the magic broke through his armour. Of course, it wasn't as strong as mageblood armour. They were prisoners, too.

"Kill them!" roared the first mageblood, the one who'd laughed at me. He gestured at the thick haze of magic in the air.

The ground shook. Tendrils of red smoke reached from below, dragging me along with them, and it was all I could do to keep hold of my blade. My feet stumbled over the edge, magic cloaked my vision, and I kept falling.

The kimaros's tendrils gripped my legs.

"Nell!" I screamed, hanging onto the thing like it was the last thread connecting me to the world. My feet remained suspended, but I wasn't falling, more floating. *The hover boot.* One of them still worked, but it was beyond me to tell how long that would last.

My grip on the handle of my dagger was sweaty, yet the twin sides melded together. One rang with magic. The other repelled it.

My dagger had two sides. Lustre and adamantine. One enhanced the other. Both reacted to the kimaros—because it was a living source. If it was feeding into all the machinery *and* mind-controlling the entire mageblood army and half Klathica's major city, there *had* to be a limit. When I'd closed the door, I'd knocked out some of its power. One source couldn't stretch as far as the magebloods were pushing it. The eyes in the pit looked at me, savage, desperate.

I pulled magic towards me, this time not fighting it but letting it flood every particle of my skin. *I'm unbreakable.* This was my homeworld. For whatever purpose, this was what I'd been designed to do.

You'll obey me, I thought at the kimaros, *because we're one and the same.* Nexuses, in a way. But magic wasn't made to be gathered in one place. It wasn't meant to be controlled.

My vision clouded red as the magic climbed. I didn't need to be able to see, not when I could feel the magic, pulsing through me. My hand shook on the dagger. The charge built under my skin, but I didn't release it. Not yet.

Rough hands grabbed me and let go just as quickly, the owner crumpling to the ground. I blinked again, squinting through the magic haze. I was on the cliff's edge. I hadn't fallen because the abyss was *gone.* The doorway port had closed, leaving only the swamp. A circle of dead magebloods surrounded me. They must have tried to touch me when I'd been channelling the power. It burned in my blood, sparks dancing across my hands. When I stepped forward, the air itself appeared to be charged. I couldn't see the kimaros anymore.

The magic was mine to control.

But the magebloods remaining, pointing daggers at me, wore *frightened* expressions. They weren't under the kimaros's control anymore. The dazedness of their eyes, the way they looked to one another for confirmation... The kimaros had lost power, enough to relinquish control over some of them.

I hadn't imagined it. Somehow, while I'd been channelling all that power, someone had *closed* one of the doors. Not just the one I'd closed myself back on the transition point.

Behind the magebloods was nothing but swampland. My heart beat faster. I glanced down at the pendant around my neck, but there was no power in it anymore.

Magic flared up again, and I staggered back as the air turned purple-red. The static buzz under my skin released itself in a flare that lit up the sky. The kimaros was now a writhing shape in the sky, thunderbolts raining down on magebloods and others alike. It had escaped the pit. *Did I somehow free it?*

A scream drew my attention to the fleeing crowd. Near the pit, Nell fought the remaining Royal.

I swore, pushing the hover boot to its limits across the abyss. I caught a brief glimpse of the machine. Power was leaking out of it in spirals, joining with the kimaros in the sky and reforming into thundercloud-shapes. The power was uncontrolled, dangerous, and at this rate...

I touched down on the opposite side, but hands grabbed me, dragging me away from Nell. Two armoured soldiers, their thick adamantine-enhanced hands apparently unaffected by the power shivering under my skin.

"How dare you," one said. "How dare you take away our power? What did you do?"

"I didn't do a thing," I snarled. "But I will, if you don't let me go."

"Not before you see everyone you love suffer."

My heart dropped. Nell and the Royal had been pushed right up to the cliff's edge. Beyond, the magebloods had put up a barricade of black stone, probably adamantine, and I couldn't see anyone but the fighters on the cliff's edge.

But a group of white-clad figures had joined in the fighting. The magebloods hadn't opened the doorway, but someone else. The void showed... Enzar. The palace, the dead spot where the void replaced what had once been a magic source. The other Enzarians, the rebels—they'd caught up. Shots fired, thin laser-like beams breaking through armour. Daggers swiped, bright with magic. *Sources.* The enemy wasn't the only side with Alliance level technology.

I'm not alone.

A smoky tendril wrapped around my throat. *The kimaros.* The magebloods let go of me, pushing me into the kimaros's smoky embrace once again. It dragged me above the ground, above the magebloods, above everything.

"Let me go!"

There was only so much I could stand, and if the full extent of the kimaros's power hit me at once, even I wouldn't survive it.

The kimaros, however, seemed more intent on striking down the magebloods. They'd pushed it so far past the realms of stability, stretched it into a doorway and used pieces of it to power the source, all the backlash had crashed together and now everyone was in danger of getting hit. Except not all of us had the same level of protection as the soldiers did.

I hit the hover boot's accelerator, swinging my dagger to sever a tendril of smoke. I could both block and amplify its power. It was out of control magic, and the only way I could see to stop it was to drive it over to Enzar, into the void. But how could I control the uncontrollable, without hurting the others?

Nell.

I swiped again, magic flooding me, heightening my senses. My vision blurred, and suddenly I wasn't Ada anymore. I was the kimaros, swirling above the ground, just like I'd been Xanet... but this time, I didn't feel a healing pulse, but the fading heartbeat of a dying world. The battle below had closed, and bodies littered the edge of the cliff next to the void. Many wore sandy-coloured armour, stained crimson with blood, their eyes sightlessly reflecting the blazing sky. Amongst them, the Royals, white-eyed, the light dying out. My vision swam, focusing on one of the bodies…

My own face looked back at me, blank-eyed, changing. The familiarity punched me in the chest.

Nell.

I tried to scream, sob, I didn't know, and couldn't, but the kimaros's presence left as I slammed back into my own body. My knees hit the ground, tremors racking my body.

No.

I lurched to my feet and ran, through the bodies, to Nell. A mageblood man stood over her, surrounded by the bodies of the others who'd stepped in to defend me. The charge built behind my skin, again, and I welcomed it with open arms.

Chillingly blank eyes met mine. All of the magebloods on the battlefield wore identical expressions. Still under the beast's thrall. Or were they? The kimaros fired lightning-sharp blades of magic down amongst the enemy. Insanity flickered behind the mageblood's eyes, more blue than purple. The bright blue of technology, and *wires* behind his eyes. Alliance tech.

I raised my hand and sent a bolt of magic at the mageblood. The enemy crumpled. I turned to the next, to the army hiding behind their adamantine barrier.

"You cowardly bastards," I whispered. "Come out and fight me."

And the *kimaros* responded. The tendrils wrapped around me not as a prison but as armour. I pointed with one hand, and a bolt of lightning seared a hole in their defensive adamantine wall.

I turned to the mageblood cowering behind it, took an unsteady step towards them. "You're next," I whispered, my voice ragged. "You murdering scum."

The charge built, the world flashing to black then white

as I struck them down with third level magic. A ripple hit the ground, and their machinery collapsed in a collection of crashes as it tore apart piece by piece. I felt every second, and thrilled in it. I could decimate their army. It would be easy. So easy.

"Ada. The Balance."

Nell's voice rang in my head. She'd warned me enough times. If I kept going, the entire Multiverse would be wiped out. The void would spread into Cethrax, and from there, into the Passages. To the rest of the Alliance.

The kimaros was still partly inside me, like it was in every magic-wielder here. I could draw on as much power as I needed… but at what cost? The kimaros was dying. I'd felt it. It'd been in the void for too long, and now the void was pulling it back in.

Beside my feet, bodies littered the ground, these clad in black adamantine. Dead.

"Stop, Adamantine, or we'll shoot you where you stand," said a voice. It took me a minute to pinpoint it—the speaker was inside one of the remaining giant tank-like shapes. The charred remains of several others surrounded it.

The kimaros writhed above, delighting in the chaos.

"That won't harm her," said a dark-armoured mageblood from the tank. This must be their last defence.

"I told you," I gasped. "I'm the nexus. My power is far beyond yours."

No lie was too outrageous. Not now Nell was gone. I could unleash all the power into the void itself and still not come close to emptying my heart of the pain building inside me. Nothing else mattered but her.

Nothing but the Alliance. The world I loved, and the people who'd become my family. I looked at the magebloods, and quelled the raging storm inside me.

"If you don't stop the war," I said, speaking in Klathican,

"I'll kill all of you. I'm adamantine." The word rang out in the silence. "I was made to be unbreakable. I *am* unbreakable. If I activate my power, you all will die, and I will live. So I suggest you listen to me."

Silence.

"I want you to make peace and stop this war." My voice was rough, and I had no idea who could even hear me, but I didn't care. "I'll give you one warning. I can wipe you out of the Multiverse, but I'm going to give you the chance to beg for your lives."

Again… nothing but silence.

"Say something," I croaked, wanting a face to punch, a person to strike down for murdering Nell. But I'd already done that, and it brought me no joy. My entire body was trembling.

Just let it end. Someone come and end it. But I was the only person left. And I wasn't sure if even *I* was in control of my own will anymore.

So I spoke, into the emptiness. "My parents made me into a weapon before I had any choice in the matter. I was saved by a person who I owe the Multiverse, and you bastards slaughtered her. I'm out of patience. I'm offering to spare you in exchange for the lives of everyone in these worlds. End the fighting."

"That would make a pretty argument," said another voice. Female. A mageblood woman approached from behind the tank, alongside an adamantine-uniform-clad man. Her voice sounded oddly familiar. But I didn't have any curiosity left in me.

Not when I saw who they had trapped between them, hands chained and streaming blood.

Kay. I didn't dare look him in the eyes, not even as tears burned through the numbness. I'd killed so many… and I wouldn't watch another person I loved die in front of me.

"You two know each other?" said the man. "I thought so. This is another of the Alliance's little experiments. He was responsible for destroying our other source. He claims to be here on Walker's orders, to destroy the nexus."

He said what? It had to be a lie. A ruse. Kay was better at improvising than I was.

"She's the nexus?" asked the female mageblood holding Kay's other arm. "I thought the Royals would pull a trick like that. Hiding their source in a person. How ingenious." Her tone was flat, and it chilled me that I couldn't tell if the kimaros controlled her or not.

Maybe that was the price of spending so long close to a magic source. It claimed you, body and soul, until whatever humanity remained had burned out of you.

And speaking of burning out…

The magic was gone. I couldn't feel it anymore. I'd channelled too much. Rather than burning me up inside, the kimaros had withdrawn itself from me entirely.

The magebloods climbed down from the tank. There were more of them than I'd expected, all armoured and blank-faced with cyberware built into their armour. I stumbled back, hit the heel of the hover boot… and nothing happened.

That source was dead, too.

Hands grabbed my shoulders. I struggled, and horrible pain forced a gasp from my lungs. They were Stoneskin, enhanced, and I'd depleted all my energy already. Suffocation pressed down on me as their freakishly strong hands pushed on my shoulders.

Don't fight, Ada, a sensible voice told me. If I did, I'd die. They'd get hold of my source and it'd be game over for everyone.

"There is an easy way to find out," said the man to the people in the tank. "You magebloods know the technique.

Extracting a source from a person seems to be your special-ty." There was distaste in his expression, and it struck me equally hard that this man *wasn't* under the kimaros's control. The cyberware visible on his armour was… familiar.

Klathican.

But if the kimaros didn't affect him… was he not a magic-wielder?

"Do it quickly." The man gave Kay a shake. My heart dropped. He didn't meet my eyes. *He must be thinking of a plan.* That was what Kay did. Even when things seemed hopeless… he'd think of something. If I used magic now, there was no way I'd risk him getting caught in the fallout. He'd been lucky to escape it already.

"The source is under her skin," said the guy holding Kay. "Cut it out."

I found my voice. "Like hell. What will killing me achieve? You clearly don't care about destroying yourselves, seeing as you tried to blow me up already. Try it again and you might not be so lucky."

"The Alliance has already pushed us to the brink, and they closed our doorways. She wiped out half our army and the other half was under the kimaros's control. They're useless now, empty shells." He gestured up at the kimaros's form, which had turned semi-transparent. "It's being sucked into the void. Can't you see that? The Balance is self-sustaining. We've lost everything already." He laughed, entirely humour-less. "You've lost the fight, so take what you can. Kill the girl, take her source. Then maybe we can salvage something before the Alliance cut us out of the Multiverse for good."

The Alliance are winning the war. Suddenly, death didn't seem to matter. This place was as good as dead anyway. I'd already killed most of them. But we were cut off from the Alliance, with no way back, no way to avoid being sucked into the void along with them.

Unless we drew enough magic here to make a way back.

There was only one person here who wasn't magicproof. Only one person who could amplify a source. I looked at Kay, mouthed two words. *Kill me.* His eyes widened, uncomprehending. I willed him to understand. They thought he was here on his father's orders. They thought I was an unending magic source. There could be only one outcome.

I let my arms fall to my sides. "You're right. I don't have anything else to lose. I never wanted this power. You already killed Nell." My voice cracked on the last word, unintentionally giving my plea more credibility. "You took everything from me. Take my magic, too, and try not to destroy everything this time."

"Then I'll be the one to do it," said Kay.

20

KAY

"Then I'll be the one to do it," I said.

My heart beat fast. But my voice was steady. They wanted one thing: a solution to their problem. *Kill me,* Ada had said. I could keep up the act if she did.

"I have a weapon that can drain the power right out of her without letting her use it on you." Maybe I could have come up with a better lie. But I couldn't stop my gaze straying to Nell's body. And Ada, trembling all over, surrounded by fallen magebloods. "I know what the Royals did, and I can undo it."

"If I die, it all ends." Ada looked them in the eyes with determination. She knew what they believed. She'd really convinced them she was the nexus. "There aren't two sides to the war anymore. There's only magic."

She put an odd emphasis on the words *two sides.* Her eyes slightly wide, and fixed on the dagger in my right hand. The double-sided weapon. Amplifier and antimagic in one.

But they didn't know that. Their antimagic was too strong, and they couldn't sense the presence of another source. *God. You're a freaking genius, Ada.*

"We do not ally with the Alliance," said the mageblood woman.

"You worked with my grandfather. I can make my father's wrongs right."

You better believe it.

"Whatever your aim, it's too late," he said. "The girl is good as dead. I don't suppose either of you knew this world was once home to magic-wielders?"

"I guessed," I said. "I also guessed the aftermath destroyed most life on this planet. Like your doorway will, if it isn't closed."

"This world was once the centre of the Multiverse, if you can believe it, Kay," said Nelson. "All doorways led here. Pity Cethrax's native species didn't care for sharing their space. Rather like the Royals and the worlds they conquered."

"What's your point?" I kept my expression blank. Another possibility had occurred to me. *Cethrax was linked with other worlds.*

There *was* a way out of here.

"My point is that as long as people like the girl exist, others will fight to the death to claim her."

"If *you* kill her, she'll take you all with her," I said, without hesitation. "You know what she's capable of. You've seen it. I'm stronger. I can stop her. I know how to drain the magic right out of a source before she can unleash it on you." I directed the words at Nelson. I'd got the measure of him pretty quickly. He was no magic-wielder, the only person here entirely in control of his own will. Non-magic-wielders were treated as a joke back on Klathica, and I'd bet Walker had made him empty promises, same as everyone else.

"You underestimated the Alliance," I said. "Luckily, they trusted me with their knowledge. I can use it to stop the war and take care of your enemy."

"Walker was always one for smooth-talking," said Nelson, through gritted teeth. "You're little more than a child."

I blocked his strike, but not before magic shot through me like a whip. The blow almost took me off my feet, and the ground swayed unsteadily as pain flared through every nerve.

He moved closer to me, his face a mask of hate. "You're just like him." His cold hand found mine, which I jerked away, cursing the spasms shaking my body.

His metal hand latched around my wrist. *Dammit.* The magicproof adamantine blocked my magic immediately, and my shaking hand went for a weapon—but not fast enough. His hand clenched. Pain exploded in my wrist and I wrenched my arm away, stumbling back over the ground.

"What the *fuck—?*"

Two of the magebloods were behind me before I could spin around. I stuck one of them, but I was too slow to block the rain of punches. I kept ground for half a second before they knocked me down. A dull agony spread across my shoulder.

Stabbed. You've been stabbed. A fuzzy sense in my head blocked out everything else. I drew on magic, and the magebloods pushed back, so hard the force pinned me to the ground. I didn't have Ada's ability to pull the magic out of them, and once they had their paws on me again, my power was cut off. Blind panic shot through me as one of them snatched the dagger I'd half pulled from my sleeve. They went for my other sleeve, and I clenched my teeth as the movement jarred my shattered wrist.

"What is this?" asked Nelson, holding up the sciras-chameleon.

Shit.

"So you did have a source."

A mageblood took it from him, and the air sparked as it

crumbled to pieces. He'd drained the magic right out of it. And they were removing my other weapons from my pockets, too. I kicked desperately at nothing, pain shooting up my foot as it connected with Stoneskin armour. Real alarm rose as they held the world-key.

The only way back.

The mageblood dropped the source. Dead. I had nothing left.

A boot connected with my injured shoulder, and pain blacked out the world.

My vision cleared under the red haze, though the pain remained as though part of a different world. Maybe this was what death on a high level world felt like. My face was pressed to the ground, something sharp digging into me. The world-key. My hand closed over it, though I knew it was dead.

I also knew I was bleeding. A lot. But they hadn't hit anything vital. Otherwise I wouldn't be able to stand as Nelson dragged me to my feet. He shook me, and I gritted my teeth against the explosion of pain in my wrist. There were fewer magebloods than I'd expected, and no offworlders aside from Nelson. Had the others fled when the kimaros's control had dropped? Or been slaughtered like the Royals?

Another shake. "You won't die. Not yet. We need you alive."

My wrist was a torrent of agony. My shoulder felt like I'd been kicked, not stabbed, but the amount of blood soaking into my shirt meant I was in serious danger of passing out again.

"The hell... was that for?"

"So you can't run," said Nelson, coldly. "In case you lie, and her power does kill all of us along with her… you won't be spared. You'll share your grandfather's fate."

Screw that. "My fate is mine." I swayed as he let go of my wrist. Magic was there, thick and urgent, but I couldn't draw on enough of it to wipe these bastards out.

And they'd killed all my sources. Their antimagic blocked everything…

I could only amplify the magic that was already here.

"Don't I at least get my dagger? It's adamantine." No, it was also lustre—and the last hope for both of us. From outward appearance, the magebloods couldn't tell one source from another.

"You wish to use your own weapon?" The mageblood in the metal tank spoke this time, and it was barely a question. He was even more expressionless than Walker had been, and I knew that was down to the magic. The kimaros. Had these people ever been human, even before the savage magic had driven them to madness and infected their minds?

I shrugged my non-injured shoulder. "Either works."

Nelson looked from me to the magebloods and back again. But he had no magic of his own. The magebloods might be adamantine down to the bone, but they didn't know how to drain the antimagic from a source because they were incapable of seeing it as magic in itself.

I stumbled forward before anyone could object, my hand closing around the dagger. They'd broken the blade in two, probably when they'd knocked it on the ground. But the lustre side was still intact. And so was the world-key, still held in my other hand.

Two magebloods dragged Ada into view. Our eyes met before I could look away, and I heard her gasp as she saw me bleeding.

Her eyes said, *save yourself first. Please.*

I couldn't do that.

The first man I'd killed in simulation had looked at me with glassy eyes as he accepted his fate.

I'm sorry.

Visions exploded before my eyes, of every life I'd taken. Every death I'd caused. But I'd always, through everything, remained under my own power. I had magic, but it was up to me to decide what to do with it. It was neither a blessing or curse, but a weapon I'd been handed.

Like the world-key in my hand, drained of all power. Only one person could get us out of here.

Magic sparked from my palm. I looked her in the eyes. And raised the dagger.

21

ADA

He moved without hesitation. Eyes focused, intent, he lowered the dagger with deliberate slowness, the point brushing below my ribcage. Each detail of him hit me—the bruises on his face, the blood staining one arm. His expression was blank. Was he carrying a source? Thanks to the magic sparking in the air, there was no way to tell.

But then, neither could anyone else. They were living adamantine, and they'd dug their own graves. They couldn't sense *any* source.

I'd tell any lie to the whole Multiverse if it meant I got to see you again.

The blade nicked the skin just under my ribs, but I faked a shocked gasp, eyes widening at the bright blood dripping down the dagger. The magic swirling free.

But magic wasn't bleeding from me. It was amplified. That was *lustre.* He'd used the double-sided dagger, and pierced me with the part that amplified my magic, not dampening it.

And clenched in his dagger hand—the blue glint of the

world-key. In a rush of understanding, I got his plan. His life was in my hands, and mine in his. As long as we were connected, I could unleash the magic, and he wouldn't get hit. And we could both get out alive.

I pushed back on the magic, sending it through the dagger, into the world-key. The lustre came to life under the touch, though blood trickled down my front.

The man who'd held Kay lunged forward, face twisting, figuring he'd been duped. Kay shifted out the way, his jaw clenched. Blood dripped from one hand. They'd stabbed him.

He didn't move. Kept amplifying my magic. The charge climbed ever-higher through the dagger that linked us, through him. The world-key glowed, bright.

A second dagger flew through the air, burying itself in my ribs.

It was a moment before the first dull pain kicked in. Like a bruise, not a fatal wound. I coughed, and tasted blood.

And still, magic bled out of me, swirling in clouds. The world swam. *No.* I grabbed at the magic, but it slipped through my fingers. I dropped to my knees, Kay's dagger falling to his side.

Nell's face flashed before my eyes, frozen in death. A dozen others, and the countless thousands of nameless faces who'd given their lives, who'd lost everything, in the name of this war.

Keep breathing, Ada.

It hurt, God, it hurt, but as long as agony pierced my chest, as long as my heart kept beating, I was alive, I'd stay alive. My eyes flickered open a fraction.

Kay looked down at me. Only I read the pain in his eyes as he held onto my hand, pressing the cold metal to my skin. The world-key.

The level rose, higher and higher. White lightning crackled around me, power I'd never dare, never be able to unleash anywhere but here. But Kay was holding onto me, and I was adamantine. I was unbreakable. And so was he. As long as he kept amplifying my power, the magebloods couldn't do a thing as they were paralysed by their own shaking, sparking weapons, the kimaros's power pulled into me. Mine.

I unleashed the magic in a wave that swept the ground, swept through the doorway, through everything. The last line of their defences crumbled, their machines breaking in the wake of the kimaros's power, pulled through me, fed back into the void again.

They fell. Every mageblood, illuminated in stark white. Their eyes glazed over and they dropped to the ground.

The world blurred. I coughed again, my breath sticking, my hands shaking. Kay was holding me. But everything was fading, too fast, and I couldn't speak, couldn't say my final words.

Blackness.

~

KAY

No. I held Ada tight, reached for the magic crackling in the air, and sent a last burst of energy into the world-key. It burned the skin of my palm, but I held tight.

Close the doorway. It was breaking apart already. The kimaros had been stretched across the void, and the monstrous form of the creature was already gone. Ada's power, amplified, drained the remainder of the magic closing the rift between Enzar and Cethrax. But she didn't see her homeworld fade away. Her eyes were closed. The blade had missed her vitals, though far too much blood soaked her shirt.

And there was only one thing to do. I had to believe it would work. This world had once been linked to another, one the humans had escaped to after the monsters drove them from here. The trace remained in the atmosphere, and I lightly sketched the symbols in the dirt with the edge of the world-key. My own blood and Ada's mingled in the mud.

Find the source world. The world-key burned fiercely as I sent wave after wave of power into it, joining with the magic radiating from Ada's skin. Into me. I opened my palm.

The world divided in two, the dagger falling from my hand. Blood dripped, trailing magic after it.

We fell through the doorway to Vey-Xanetha, as the magic drained from me, as the power crackling around us faded away entirely.

Please. My chest hurt like I was the one who'd been stabbed. My aching shoulder reminded me I had. Magic bled from me, swirling in clouds. I held onto the lustre blade tight, willing all the magic to flow into me.

Blackness crowded my vision. *No.*

The blackness tugged at me, exhaustion setting in, draining the last of the life from my limbs. I clenched my teeth. No. I'd be there for her last breath. I owed her that.

I owed her more than that.

The world faded, the colour dulling, the sky darkening. I couldn't see the magic anymore.

I could do no more to save her.

Ada's still form wavered before my eyes. Blood dripped down my hand where the lustre had cut it. Her breaths were faint, shallow. So were mine.

"Adamantine," I whispered, as the vines pierced my arm, too, healing the stab wound.

She coughed, her spine arching. The vines withdrew from

her skin. She shuddered all over, gasping, taking one shallow breath after another. She coughed again. Her eyes opened a fraction.

"Kay," she gasped out. "Dammit, I told you to save yourself."

Alive.

She was alive.

"Ada."

Words crashed into one another in my head, all inadequate. The world around us disappeared, in a rush of light-headed relief. I all but collapsed over her, bowing my head to whisper in her ear.

"You're the one who saved me."

22

ADA: SIX WEEKS LATER

The door slid open, and the cold light of the Passages spilled out onto the swampland. Turning to give the Enzarians behind me an encouraging smile, I stepped over the threshold.

"This is the Passages," I said. "Cynthia will take you to the transition point from here."

At my side, Cynthia nodded to me. Maybe she'd never entirely forgive me for what I'd done, but she'd always wanted to help people through the Passages. Thanks to the Alliance, she had that chance.

The refugees moved into the Passage, leaving a trail of mud and swamp water. This was the last group to leave Cethrax. We'd had to use the old transition point as a shelter for anyone we could rescue from the remains of the other worlds of the Enzarian Empire. Enzar itself had already half-collapsed into the void, but now the magebloods were dead, it was less of a hazard to traverse the far reaches of the old Empire in search of survivors. The other Enzarians had been more than happy to piece together a map of places likely to have escaped the large-scale destruction, and with the help of the world-keys, teams of Alliance members from across the Multiverse had pitched in. It was hard-going, especially the debates over whereabouts to relocate the Enzarians left behind. Klathica was top of the list. I had a feeling Izen was trying to regain his standing in the Alliance.

I caught Kay's eye, at the back of the group, checking for trouble. The monsters avoided this part of the swampland, the part scorched black by the magic I'd unleashed. Probably for the best that they did.

"This way." Cynthia directed the rest of the refugees down the corridor. But I hung back until they'd gone, and it was just Kay, me, and the open door. Door Sixty-Five. He pushed it closed, and nodded to me without having to speak.

Grief choked me, cold and sharp, as Nell's face flashed before my eyes, wearing the distant expression she always did when she spoke of our homeworld. I took in a steadying breath and pressed my hands to the door. Enzar might be dead, collapsing into the void, but we'd saved everyone we could. I pulled on the magic thrumming through the metal surface, feeling the life drain out of the auros as Kay's hand rested against mine, amplifying it. I staggered back as the door's blue sheen faded to grey-black.

"It's done," I whispered. I'd always known my homeworld wouldn't survive. It didn't make it hurt any less.

"You did everything you could." Kay's hand was cool against my face as he cupped my chin.

"I know."

The buzz of magic faded. It had never been quite the same, after what I did to the magebloods. I couldn't use it for long. If not for Kay's amplifier, I'd never have been able to close the remaining handful of doors onto Enzar once we'd rescued the remaining survivors. The council had asked my opinion first, as if I didn't know the dangers of keeping unmapped doors open. The surge of magic on Cethrax had knocked all their doorways out of sync and things weren't back to normal yet, but there wasn't really a default normal in that place. At least the swamp monsters wouldn't be able to get at the survivors.

"Ada…" Kay hesitated. "Are you sure you want to speak at the council meeting tomorrow?"

"I have to." My voice cracked. I'd kept out of the limelight the best I could. The first week had been the worst, when we'd been stuck sheltering at Central while news reporters from various worlds flooded the place, most of them getting the facts disastrously wrong. I'd lasted through one press conference then shut down, refusing to speak to them any longer. They wanted clear-cut answers. I didn't have any, only the blood of countless Enzarians on my hands.

At least the journalists didn't know Alber and I were living with the Knight family in a new shelter, set up after that first awful week following the war's end. Jeth had been stuck with the choice of whether to stay on Earth with me and Alber, or help the Alliance clean up the aftermath. Alber and I had insisted we didn't need looking after. I didn't think any of us were fooled even for a second, but the Alliance needed Jeth's tech skills now more than ever. It had been six weeks since we'd lost Nell. Life should have resumed a new 'normal' by now.

There were some good parts. Ms Weston was well on the way to taking leadership of Earth's council. She'd only recently returned from a cross-world trip visiting every Alliance branch she could reach. She wasn't well-liked, but she was respected, and everyone could tell that she was sincere. After what Walker had done, Earth needed no less for leadership.

As for me, I'd turned down a dozen roles offered to me by well-meaning higher-up Alliance members. It seemed like a joke for the Alliance to even consider letting me speak for my homeworld, since I'd single-handedly obliterated hundreds of Enzarians.

Sure, nobody outright blamed me for the way things had turned out, no more than they would any other soldier who'd taken lives on the battlefield. I'd even told Cynthia. The guilt would eat at me from the inside for the rest of my life if I didn't tell the others from my homeworld I'd killed the last of the magebloods. The press didn't see it that way. I'd even had to correct more than one person who thought I was *from* Earth, not Enzar. Not the Enemy. I'd gone from dangerous magic-wielder offworlder to war hero overnight, because I'd helped kill off half an army.

It kind of sucked. A lot.

"You don't have to," Kay repeated. "Ms Weston would let you sit this one out, if you asked her. She'd understand."

"Yeah, but..." *Nell would have wanted you to.* No, Nell would have... I didn't even know. Old Nell wouldn't have. New Nell, who'd changed as much I had in the past few months? I hadn't a clue. *Before* and *now* were split like the double sides of that blade. But I didn't want to be seen as an object. A symbol. The girl who'd ended the war.

As if it was that simple.

"I fought a war, I can make a speech to the council about my homeworld." My voice shook. Given the choice, I reckoned most people would rather fight a battle than deal with the aftermath. There wasn't a world unscathed by the war, even the outlying ones. Magic had exploded across the void, and even on Earth, it had left permanent marks. The war had ended the instant the kimaros had been wiped out, the Klathicans had returned to their senses, and Cethrax's army had exhausted itself. But we remained, it was up to us to decide what we did with what we had left.

"I know you *can* do it," said Kay. "But do you *want* to?"

My eyes burned again. I'd thought I was done crying. I'd

been through every stage of grief under the sun, worked through it all with Kay and my brothers. I could speak for her and the others. It'd go a way towards making up for everything she'd given me.

"Yeah." I reached out to squeeze his hand. "I want to."

"Come on," he said. "Let's get out of here. We might be able to sneak into Valeria before someone comes looking for us."

I smiled at that. "Ms Weston will flay us alive."

"I think she'll make an exception."

Exceptions were the rule these days. Now the survivors had been rescued, we could all rebuild our lives. The remaining Enzarians wanted nothing more than a safe place, away from the worlds burned to ruins. The Alliance could give them that.

If only it hadn't come at so high a price.

KAY

"You're going back to Central?" Simon's voice was a static buzz on the other end of my communicator, suggesting he was somewhere busy. Maybe Valeria.

"I have to report to my boss before she chews my ear off. Have you filed yours yet?"

Simon had been promoted to Ambassador a couple of weeks ago. Mostly we went where we were needed. There wasn't an inch of space in the Multiverse without some problem to solve. And I lived for solvable problems.

I looked up at the blade-like shape of Central. It was a miracle it had escaped any damage. The car park hadn't been so lucky. While Ada and I had fought the magebloods, Central had fought a battle of its own.

"Yeah, once I'd dealt with the rats."

"They made *you* deal with it?" I said. Our most recent expedition through the lower levels of the Passages had resulted in an encounter with Cethrax's infamous swamp rats.

"Could have been worse," he said, with an attempt at casualness. I let it slide. He wasn't wrong that swamp rats were hardly the worst Cethrax had to offer. "Anyway, you'll never guess who showed up here at Central in New York."

"Who?"

"Sonja from the Academy. You know it was her griffin that escaped last time?"

"Seriously?"

"Yeah. I'm gonna ask her out."

"Just don't send her a dead rat."

"As if."

I rolled my eyes, crossing the car park to Central, and paused when I spotted the memorial on the front, with the names of everyone who'd sacrificed their lives here, in every war. Including her.

"Kay? You still there?"

I exhaled. "Yeah. Just saw they put up a memorial at Central. Guess I didn't expect them to listen." Simon didn't know all the details of my mother's death. Only the official statement. Ms Weston and Amanda had dug into the history of all the deaths the Alliance had covered up. Even the Walker family.

I'd declined to look at the files. Yet. Nobody aside from a handful of us at Central even knew my grandfather's connection with the war, and the last thing I wanted was to drag up ancient history when Earth was in enough of a state of shock already.

I found my gaze travelling down the list of the dead. *His* name wasn't on the list. There was no mourning for traitors. I still didn't know how I felt about the way things had ended. Sure, I hadn't killed him, but it felt like I did. The official statement was that he'd died in the fighting. No more details than that. Nobody cared how he'd died, only that he was gone.

At the bottom of the list was the name *Nell Fletcher.*

I'd been able to do that much for Ada, at least.

"Of course the Alliance listened to you," said Simon. "You're—"

"Don't." The last thing I needed was to hear the word *hero.*

"I was going to say 'a bloody pain,'" said Simon. "And a moron who made me trek through the swamp yesterday. I have Cethrax's stink all over my uniform."

"Tragic."

I dragged my eyes away from the memorial. Central looked the same, but the Alliance had changed, not least on Klathica. KimaroTech, for one, was in disgrace. Klathica blamed them for the simulators malfunctioning, and now Walker's funding had disappeared, they had significantly less clout. A smaller branch of KimaroTech had reformed around Alliance-trusted individuals who'd never even been near a simulator. Oddly enough, they weren't keen on the idea of anyone exposing their history selling weapons to Enzar, and I made sure to give them a very good idea of my opinions on magic-based human upgrades, helped in no small part by the constant reminders that the kimaros had controlled half the population through those very same enhancements. Suddenly, upgrading wasn't so popular anymore. Not to mention nobody wanted a repeat of the doorways opening and tearing the world in two.

Maybe I'd never know if everyone who'd worked with Walker was dead or jailed. But in the end, he'd been the one behind the experiment, not them, and KimaroTech didn't need to know it had worked. One human amplifier was enough for the Multiverse.

"All right, I'm going in. Talk later." I hung up the phone and used my key card to get into Central.

It had become an ongoing joke that Central seemed to suffer *less* damage with each battle. Carl was back on duty, though he'd had enough of his new cybernetic arm setting off the metal detectors. He waved me in, and I headed for the first floor.

Will she be here? Ada had given her speech to the council today. I wished I could have been with her, but I'd been on clean-up duty on the lower floor of the Passages and Central still had a shortage of guards. Monster attacks weren't as common as they used to be. The Cethraxians who'd survived the war had scattered, and spent their time wandering aimlessly around, looking for their missing Undergod. It wasn't any use expecting to be able to explain to the Vox what the kimaros had really been. One of them. The beast was gone, sucked into the void along with Ada's homeworld. Free from the magic which had enslaved it. The best that could have happened, really, after what the magebloods had done. At least, Ada had said so.

But there were too many periods of empty silence where she'd just zone out, and nothing I said broke through to her. I wasn't equipped to handle someone else's grief on top of my own. More guilt than grief, really—guilt at the relief of finally being free of Walker's presence, when the cost had been so high. The war with Enzar had ended, but part of me still expected Walker to come back. And with Ada, I'd done the same as he had—obliterated an army, and won a war at the expense of others' lives. If I could have taken the burden from her and shouldered it all myself, I would have.

"Kay, I'm glad to see you've decided to show your face here today," said Ms Weston, as I opened her office door.

"Yeah, Simon and I finished the last job. Cethrax seems pretty quiet, really."

"About that," said Ms Weston. "The Vox wishes to extend his apologies to the Alliance."

I raised an eyebrow. "Seriously?"

"It seems he feels the Alliance has its merits after all."

"You aren't thinking of offering him membership."

"Maybe in a few decades."

I blinked, then realised she'd actually made a joke. Maybe the end really was here.

"Okay. I've just been scouting the lower levels of the Passage. Doesn't look like there's trouble."

"I've no doubt it'll find you wherever you end up." Ms Weston paused. "Ada's here, by the way. I asked her to come and check in with me after she spoke to the council. She's in the office."

"What did they say to her?"

"Ask her yourself."

I left my boss's office, hoping Ada was okay. I'd thought the council would leave Ada alone now she'd helped the last of the Enzarians assimilate into an Alliance world. She'd already said she didn't want a leadership role in the Alliance's relations with Enzar.

"You're back, human," said Markos, tail swishing. "I thought the swamp had eaten you."

"It tried," I said. "You look official."

"Isn't it snazzy?" He showed off the embossed badge on his coat. Markos himself was now head liaison with offworlders. If anyone could convince people who hated one another to suck it up and work peacefully, it was the centaur. "I've already got the novices working on a project involving research into worlds that, according to the Alliance, no longer exist," said Markos. "Someone has the enthralling task of backtracking through several hundred years' worth of files for records of worlds lost to history. Enzar was a special case, of course, because of the reasons it was cut off, but the Alliance's history has gaping holes in it."

"Yeah, I don't doubt that." I edged past the centaur into the office. "Did you scare Ada off?"

"He tried," said a familiar voice.

"I'll let you get on with it, humans." The centaur moved out of the way of the door.

"Kay." Ada crossed the office to me. "I'm sorry." She buried her head in my neck. "I should have called."

"You don't have to apologise."

She drew back, eyes brimming.

"What did the council say to you?"

She took in a shuddering breath. "It's okay. They've agreed to offer all the surviving Enzarians Alliance member- ship and protection, whichever world they're living on. Some of them are applying to be Ambassadors already."

"Really? That's good news."

"Of course it is." She wiped her eyes. "I'm being stupid. I… I tried to use magic again. The level's higher now, it should have worked. But it didn't."

"After you closed the doorway?"

"Yeah. Like I said. It's been acting up ever since, and I… I always wanted to use it to help people. Only there's no one left to help from Enzar. Guess I overreacted a little."

"It's not stupid. You think anyone cares if you can use magic or not? You think *I* care?"

"Says the invisible man."

"Please don't start calling me that. Life would be a damn sight simpler without it."

"I know. I'm sorry. I got caught up in thinking about Enzar again. It's stupid, but when I used magic there… it was like nothing else. I just feel like I left a part of *me* behind. The magic."

I knew what she meant. I'd felt the power myself, when I'd amplified her magic, that wild uncontrolled chaos inside and out. But that was magic itself. Not me. Not her.

"You didn't," I said. "You're here. All of you."

Her face relaxed, but she sighed. "Nell would tell me to pull myself together. She wanted me to be strong."

"No," I said softly. "She wanted you to be human. You wouldn't be human if you couldn't feel. There's more than one way to be strong."

Maybe I was a hypocrite, because I still hadn't opened the files Ms Weston had unearthed from the back of the archives about my mother's past achievements, somewhere my father obviously hadn't looked. A large part of me still flinched at the thought of laying the past out for the world to see. The survival mechanisms I'd developed as a kid worked a little too well, because I'd never let myself think about her. In the end, maybe she'd saved me from Walker after all. The world needed to know what Elizabeth had done for the Alliance more than they needed another reminder of Walker's crimes. And maybe I needed it, too.

I had a feeling Ada suspected, because she nodded. "Yeah. I know. Just it's hard to think about—about Nell without thinking about how shitty it is that she's dead. And I'm scared people will forget her. If it wasn't for her, we'd never have been able to save anyone from Enzar."

I drew her close to me, and she rested her head against my chest.

"They won't forget," I said quietly. "We'll make sure of it."

She titled her head to give me a faint smile. "Yeah. Of course we will."

∾

ADA

Time didn't heal wounds, not this kind. There were days when I just didn't feel like leaving my room at the shelter. There was no waking up from this with the world reset to the way it was before. But life always went on for someone, somewhere, leaving everything behind. Though the memory remained.

Sometimes Alber and I shut out the world and played video games all day. We were amongst the oldest at the shelter, though Al was applying to university. I'd encouraged him. With Jeth working odd hours at Valeria's Alliance, someone had to. If not for Kay, I didn't think either of us could have held it together the first two weeks, with the media hounding us. The new shelter was hidden on London's outskirts, which made it a pain to commute to Central, but I didn't mind. The further away from our old haunts, the better.

Some days I walked around London alone. Pretended I was a tourist, that I didn't have a home. But *home* was a relative term. Nell was a home, and her absence had ripped open a hole like the void. But day by day, through the nightmares and guilt, therapy sessions and long hours watching the clock, reality had shifted. *The new normal,* Kay had said, and though we all battled our own demons, there were flashes of hope. For everyone who'd died, a dozen others had been saved. We'd finally done what Nell had always wanted. Saved everyone we could. Seen families reunited when they'd given up hope. Brought safety to those who thought they'd never live another day.

There were moments when the grief rose, thick and

choking, to pull me under, but there were good times, too. Dawn always came after night.

And one day, I woke from a sleep blessedly free of terrors, to a sky unusually bright for a January morning. The sunbeams through the curtain beckoned me outside. Kay's eyes were closed, one arm around me, undisturbed by the sunlight.

I slid off the bed, careful not to disturb him. Nobody objected to Kay coming to the shelter when he wasn't on Ambassador duty. The war's aftermath had buried all enmity. People were too consumed with their own grief to worry about petty differences. The Alliance had saved all our hides enough times now, even the oldest generation who'd hidden from Central for decades accepted their help now. Grudgingly.

I found myself in the back yard, where I'd set up a dart board. None of the kids were about, so I figured I could get away with some knife-throwing practise.

"Yo," said Alber, perching on the wall. "You're back to your old tricks?"

"No magic," I reminded him. But I still scored a bulls-eye. I did a mock-victory dance.

"Nice," said Alber. "I just got an email. Conditional offer from Bristol."

I twisted to stare at him. "Seriously? That's awesome, Al."

"Conditional," he said. "Means I have to actually get the grades. I bombed last term's mock exams."

I tutted, sounding so much like Nell I had to bite the inside of my cheek to keep from crying.

"Well, you're actually gonna have to study. In case you've forgotten, I failed half my exams. I won't be any help."

"Lucky the Alliance doesn't care about grades," said Alber. "They can be my backup plan."

"Don't say that to Ms Weston if you get an internship

interview." I paused. "Hey, guess you'll be moving out this summer, then, if you want."

"Guess so." He glanced back at the house. "I don't mind this place, but it'd be nice not to have a curfew. A *curfew*, really. I'm eighteen in a few months."

"How do you think I feel?" I rolled my eyes.

"I think you should move in with Kay," said Alber.

I nearly dropped the knife.

"Oh, don't pull that innocent face on me. I can hear you two through the walls, you know. It won't break my heart if you move out."

"Good," I said, though I glanced back at the house all the same. "I don't know, he hasn't asked. I was thinking of running lessons for the magic-wielder kids here. Help them stay out of trouble."

"You're gonna teach the kids?"

"Yeah. I guess so. Supervised, at first, because I'm a terrible influence." I swallowed down a sob. I figured he knew I was changing the subject, but I really hadn't had the mental space to think about the future when surviving the present was painful enough. After the two weeks of hell, Kay had given me space to figure things out. It wasn't fair to place the burden of my grief on him, or anyone else, but I couldn't put my life on hold forever.

Alber squinted at me. "You're keeping the lenses in?"

I nodded. "I was kinda tempted to take them out in front of that media mob. Maybe the bright glare from my real eyes would have broken their cameras."

"Those dickheads?" Alber shook his head. "Don't let 'em get to you."

I shrugged, tugging at my newly short hair, pale gold now I'd let the dye wash out. I kind of liked it that way. I didn't look like the pictures in the newspapers and all over the internet. I looked like a stranger.

"I'm okay with keeping the eyes hidden. And the name, too."

Nell was the only person who could say *Adamantine* as a name. It wouldn't sound right coming from anyone else. Except Kay. He'd accept whatever name I chose. Ada. Adamantine. Royal or Alliance Ambassador. Names didn't matter.

My hands shook as I steadied the dagger again, and took aim.

A faint noise behind me. I paused, and sure enough, fingers brushed mine, over the dagger.

"Slightly to the left," said Kay's voice.

"You know I heard you coming. Admit it." I threw the dagger, hitting the board dead-centre. "Want to see if I can do it invisible?"

"Show-offs," said Alber. "I heard you as well," he added to Kay.

"Huh." Kay retrieved the dagger and handed it to me.

"You're lying," I said. "He scared the shit out of you last night when he climbed through the downstairs window. Admit it."

Alber stuck his tongue out at me.

"You okay?" Kay had noticed I hadn't taken the second knife back.

I shrugged. "Yeah. What did you want to do today, anyway?"

"No idea. I'm off-duty. Wanna go for a walk?"

"Sure." I went back into the house to put the daggers somewhere the little kids couldn't get hold of them.

"I need to call Jeth at some point," I said, shutting the cupboard door in my room. "He's worried about me."

"I can do one better," said Kay, from my doorway. "We can go pay a visit to Valeria later."

I nodded, but something inside me tensed. I hadn't dared

go offworld since that day. Not because magic scared me, but I'd rather be on a world with no magic at all than feel the emptiness from the void again.

"I'll be back soon, Al," I said over my shoulder.

"Sure thing, Ada," he said.

My hand slid into Kay's, and neither of us spoke as we walked alongside the river. Past tourist-crowded boats, past a world apart from the images in my head. It wasn't an uncomfortable silence: it just was. I watched the boats, the tourist traffic, and the occasional appearance from a serpent-like head that plainly *didn't* belong to anything from Earth.

Kay paused as the serpent's head broke the surface of the waves again. "I hear they're turning that thing into a tourist attraction now."

"Are they?" I watched the scaly beast disappear again. "Doesn't it scare people off?"

"Nah, they like it. The Alliance have caved into the inevitable. Earth's never gonna be completely magic-free now."

No. Things would never entirely go back to normal. I'd never forget the others we'd lost. And I knew Kay wouldn't either. You couldn't erase the past. And there were never any guarantees. But right now, the present was enough.

"Are you going to stay at the shelter?" asked Kay.

Oh. Had he overheard me and Alber? It wasn't like I'd ruled out getting my own place, but the old habit of watching out for my family and the shelter first remained. Even though I couldn't take Nell's place. I wasn't her. Whatever happened, Earth was home, far more than Enzar had ever been, but I'd never meant to settle for one world.

Even now, it stirred in my blood. Not magic, but the call to somewhere else.

I shrugged. "I don't know. Al needs me, but he just got into university today so he might be moving out in a few months. I'm thinking I might teach the kids with magic how to use it and not get hurt."

"Good plan," he said. "I was looking into doing something similar at the Academy, if I can. But now we're done clearing up Enzar, I'm being asked on other missions. Further afield."

I turned to him, my chest tightening unexpectedly. It wasn't as though I'd asked him to stay on Earth. I knew he'd always wanted to move away, and he'd only stuck around for my sake.

"And did you say yes?"

"I said I'll think about it."

"You want to leave Earth. I—I get it. I don't blame you." He barely had any ties here, not like I did. But though the past few weeks hadn't been easy, one of the few parts that made my heart lift was watching Kay's barriers come down. Mostly when we were alone together, and I knew he didn't like the media attention any more than I did. The shadow of his father hadn't entirely disappeared, but I knew he was trying. For me.

He shook his head slightly. "No. Earth's not so bad these days." The corner of his mouth tilted up. "Suppose you wanted a more permanent residence on Earth... my new place has all the benefits of the old one. Plus a river view. There *may* be an apartment in Valeria with my name on it soon, too. Perks of being an Ambassador."

My heart flipped over. "You're asking if I want to join you."

"Do I need to spell it out?"

"Maybe." I smiled. "You had me worried for a second there. But it's a good thing. I want you to be happy. You've always wanted to see the Multiverse, so..."

"Yeah," said Kay quietly. "I always did. But there's something I want more than that." He wound his hand into mine.

I rested my head against his shoulder. "You might regret

bringing me along for the ride. There's not a world in the Multiverse I don't want to see."

"I should warn them in advance."

"Hey," I objected, swatting at him. Predictably, he anticipated it, and I nearly pitched forward into the river—he reached out to grab my arm, but I'd already steadied myself on the bank. "One of these days I'll catch you off guard."

"I can hardly wait." And his lips were on mine. I let my mind blank out the world, blank out everything but the present, this sensation, and him. Always him.

Our path brought us back to where we'd come from. To the place where it had all started, where we'd collided and I'd been dragged into his world, where we'd nearly died, where Earth had nearly fallen for the first, not the last time. And there'd be others. All eyes were open to the Multiverse now.

My own eyes were on the door sliding open, revealing corridors lit with a familiar blue. And the buzz of static awakening under my skin. As if it had always been there, always waiting for me to come back.

I looked out into the Passages, at the doors to worlds beyond counting, turned to Kay, and smiled.

ABOUT THE AUTHOR

Emma is the New York Times and USA Today Bestselling author of the Changeling Chronicles urban fantasy series.

Emma spent her childhood creating imaginary worlds to compensate for a disappointingly average reality, so it was probably inevitable that she ended up writing fantasy novels. When she's not immersed in her own fictional universes, Emma can be found with her head in a book or wandering around the world in search of adventure.

Find out more about Emma's books at
www.emmaladams.com.